For Bibi.
For helping me stay motivated,
especially with this book.
Our sexy Santa has come to life because of you!
Ho Ho Ho!

CONTENT WARNING

Subbing for Santa is a standalone MF contemporary romance that has a HEA. This story is linked with Sarah JD's other stories, but does not have to be read in any order.

Please note: This story contains dark themes and subjects that maybe triggering to some readers, including, but not limited to: Detailed violence, killing, dub-con, explicit sex scenes, different kinks, Dominant and submissive themes, and a backstory relating to crimes against children.

THIS BOOK IS FOR READERS 18+ ONLY

You have been invited to play a game.
The name of the game is,
Subbing for Santa.

The rules are simple.
If Santa issues an order,
the submissive must obey.
If not, the submissive will be punished.

To accept the role as submissive in this game,
please collect the package from your mailbox.

By taking the package, you acknowledge your
role as the submissive and agree to the rules
which will commence from
12:01am tomorrow, December eighteenth,
and conclude at
11:59pm on Christmas Eve.

So what will it be my little elf?
Will you play with me?

Chapter One

The Game

Agatha

Holy shit. What is this? Who is this from? Is this some kind of joke? The insatiable part of me hopes that this isn't a joke, the dominance alone setting my blood on fire under my skin. I can't deny how excited it makes me, but I have no idea who this invitation is from. No idea who I'll be subbing for.

What if it's a serial killer?

I'm not sure a serial killer would give this sort of warning, but you never know. There are a lot of fucked up people out there in the world. It could be part of their sick plan.

Still, I clutch onto the red and white card and read over the information again, hoping I missed something. That another clue will magically appear about who it is that slipped this under my door.

I have no idea how long it was lying on my floor. I paid the front entrance no attention when I got up earlier this morning and went through my daily routine of yoga and meditation before eating breakfast. I even made it through lunch without paying my front door any notice. It was by chance, when I was ordering a Christmas gift for myself online, that I went to the entrance to rummage through my purse for my credit card. And there it was, lying face up with my name written in black ink.

Agatha Fiera.

This person obviously knows me to have used my name, so I must know him or her. I just need to figure out who exactly it is.

Opening the front door to my Hamptons lake house rental, I poke my head out. My eyes travel up the gravel driveway that disappears around a bend, surrounded by thick Australian bushland. I never heard a car pull in, so whoever delivered it must have been on foot. There's no stamp on the envelope either, so it wasn't delivered by a postie.

Glancing in the other direction, my eyes fall to the jetty, jutting out from the bank into Redfield Lake. The little tinny at the end of the jetty is still tied up. Nothing looks disturbed down there either.

A slither of fear travels up my spine, and I step back inside, slamming and locking the door before moving back into the living area.

It's so quiet and peaceful here. There are neighbouring houses, but they are divided by thick scrub, giving the sense of isolation. It's why I chose to hide away here. I was too exposed in Fox Pines. Too many old clients or party acquaintances that could potentially throw me to the wolves. I figured 'out of sight, out of mind' was the best option after the scandal at Vixen's Lodge hit the news. If my name ever came up, hopefully I'd be harder to find.

I'm lucky that one of my good friends is a cop. He was also an attendee at the Vixen's Lodge Sex Parties, so in a way, he has more to lose than me. Just his attendance would destroy his career, but he never indulged the way most of the attendees did, and I'm ashamed I was also one of those people. The indulgence was called Kitten, and I often forgot how young she was because we became close and are still friends to this day. But in the eyes of the law, Kitten was a minor, so what we did, even if it was as simple as turning a blind eye, is considered a crime against a minor.

Even though I moved here to lie low, I've done a shitty job at maintaining my cover. Maybe I can blame my loneliness for human interaction, or maybe I can blame the depraved hunger burning inside me. Either way, I lasted a week here by the lake before I got antsy and decided to hold my own exclusive sex parties. As stupid and reckless as that is, it's what's helped keep me from drowning in a pool of emptiness.

I've considered that maybe I've got an addiction issue with how much I hunger for sex. Although, maybe it really is just loneliness. I never seem to let people get close to me. I'm so terrified they will break down my walls, discover my truths, and run screaming in the other direction.

Rejection is hard. So is disappointment. The best way to avoid them is to not expect anything from anyone. Don't wish for a relationship when it's only just sex, and in return, my heart can avoid getting hurt.

Do I wish I could have more with someone?

Hell yes! Every. Fucking. Day!

But, I learnt a long time ago that you can't trust anyone completely, so I'm better off keeping a distance. My secrets will remain locked tight that way.

Shaking myself out of my head, I do a walkthrough of my rental, glancing out the windows to double check that there are no lurkers nearby, but all is quiet. I'm more likely to come across a koala or wombat before running into another person out here.

Back in my living room, I fall back onto the couch and stare at the red and white card. Christmas is only a week away. A time of year I hate because of the loneliness. Maybe this game with a stranger is exactly what I need to keep my mind and body occupied this Christmas. Which is why I find myself putting the card on the coffee table and making my way out my front door to see what's in my mailbox.

As I step out into the hot setting sun, I glance around, checking to see if anyone is nearby. I'm completely aware that this invitation could be a trap. Either to lead me to my death, or to somehow expose me and lead me to jail. I should care more, yet as the stones crunch under my slides loudly in the silence, I realise I don't care. Maybe owning up to what I did at Vixen's Lodge is a better option at this point. After all, what sort of life am I living by hiding away? If I must be alone, I think I'd rather do it in jail, or six feet under.

With my mood flat, I walk slowly up the driveway, rounding the bend to see the old beat-up milk tin mailbox up on the side of the road which in no way matches the pretty beach style Hamptons house that sits by the water.

Reaching the road, I look both ways, noting the other mailboxes in each direction. If it weren't for them sitting beside each driveway, I'd never know there were other people out here. There are, though. Especially this week, as Christmas nears and the Aussie summer gets warmer, the houses hiding amongst the bushland of Redfield Lake are coming to life.

Sighing, I turn to the mailbox, remembering the instructions on the invitation. If I take the package inside the mailbox, it means I'm accepting the terms of being Santa's submissive.

The thought makes me smirk. I could be playing sub for a big burly white bearded accountant for all I know, yet here I am, still willing to play.

Why?

Because I'm lonely and not particularly picky at this point.

And pathetic, but I'll worry about that part later.

Opening up the large mailbox, I spot a shoebox sized package inside, and without another thought, I pull it out and walk briskly back to the house.

Closing myself inside, I move to the air-conditioning remote and turn the cooling on before I place the package on the dining table and stare at it. For like an hour.

Part of me is eager to see what's inside, but the other part of me is seriously questioning my judgement right now. So I sit, and wait, watching the box like something is going to explode from it at any moment. Meanwhile, the bright rays of the day's sun turn the sky pink as night draws nearer.

Wrapped in green and gold paper, the package sits like an elephant in the room, and after staring at it for way too long, I realise I'm being stupid. I've already accepted the package, so I may as well look inside and feed my curiosity.

On top of the package is a white tag which reads:

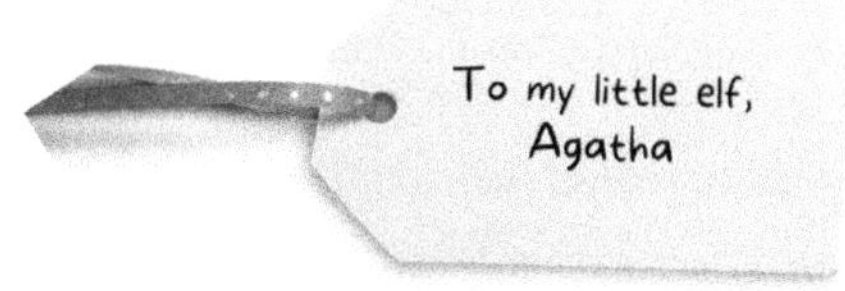

My heart races at seeing my name again, and Jesus, I just know the suspense of not knowing who the hell is behind this game is going to drive me crazy.

Sucking in a deep breath, I start tearing at the paper before lifting the lid off the box.

Wrapped in red tissue paper is another note, a lacy set of red and silver lingerie, a mobile phone, and a black remote controlled egg vibrator.

Heat prickles over my skin as anticipation creeps in and I pick up the new note.

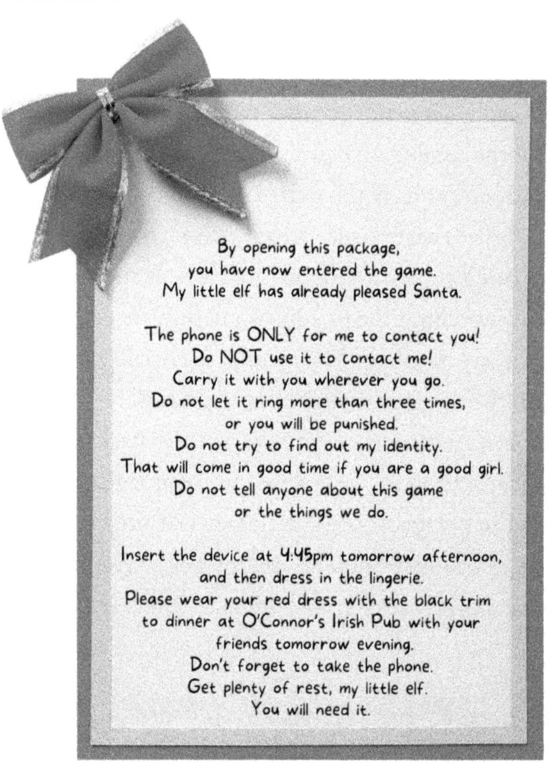

By opening this package,
you have now entered the game.
My little elf has already pleased Santa.

The phone is ONLY for me to contact you!
Do NOT use it to contact me!
Carry it with you wherever you go.
Do not let it ring more than three times,
or you will be punished.
Do not try to find out my identity.
That will come in good time if you are a good girl.
Do not tell anyone about this game
or the things we do.

Insert the device at 4:45pm tomorrow afternoon,
and then dress in the lingerie.
Please wear your red dress with the black trim
to dinner at O'Connor's Irish Pub with your
friends tomorrow evening.
Don't forget to take the phone.
Get plenty of rest, my little elf.
You will need it.

What the?

How does he know I'm going out for dinner with friends tomorrow night?

Is it one of them?

No. Shane and Ben are in love with each other. They have no interest in having me join them. They only go to the sex parties to have time together, since they are still in the closet and haven't come out to their friends and family.

And my red dress? How does he know about that?

What the hell is going on?

Since I've already taken the package, I've entered the game, but shit, now I'm not sure if it's such a good idea. Am I safe? What the hell have I agreed to?

Shit, shit, shit.

With shaky hands, I pick up the phone and unlock it easily since it doesn't have a passcode on it. A quick check shows me there's only one number saved. Santa.

Without thinking, I hit call, and it rings once before connecting and a deep male voice booms through the line.

"You were told not to contact me! Can't you read?!"

I flinch back at his harsh assessment, the insult hitting hard.

"W-what? Y-yes, but how do you know about dinner with my friends? And my red dress? And my name, for that matter?"

"You were warned!" He hisses before hanging up.

A moment later, the entire house goes dark.

Santa

I'm both furious, and turned on by my little elf's disobedience. She knew the rules, but she let her emotions get the better of her. Little does she know, she just made the game more exciting.

I watched her stew over what to do when she finally noticed the invitation.

My little elf was so torn between her need and her brain. I was almost certain she was going to refuse my invitation after a while, but then, she gave into her carnal need and left her house to get the package.

Because I'm a risk taker, I stood only meters from her driveway in the thick scrub, watching as she wandered from her house, up to the road to her mailbox. She didn't even know I was there. Didn't even know how fucking close I was.

I could have snatched her up and given into my desires right then and there. But no. I need to play this game with her. I need to see if she has what it takes.

Chapter Two

Punishments

Agatha

Blood rushes in my ears as my heart nearly leaps out of my throat. The little lake house is plunged into darkness, with only the hint of the pink sunset filtering through the gum trees to give a touch of light.

I strain my ears, trying to hear past the rush of my blood to listen for a sign of a storm rolling in, or wind that could have knocked out a power line. But all is still. All is calm.

On shaky legs, I move to the large glass wall that looks out over the lake, only to find the yellow glow of lights from the other houses across the lake. I ease the door open and step out onto the decked balcony, moving to the railing to glance to the east and west of my rental, only to see the same yellow glow coming from houses further up the bank.

Part of me is screaming, RED FLAG! The power went out when Santa, or whoever the hell I called on the phone, reminded me that I'd been warned about calling him. My gut twists with fear, and I try not to acknowledge that the man on the other end of the phone is highly likely responsible for sending me into darkness.

Who am I playing with here? A psychopath trying to scare me?

Fuck.

If it is, then it's working, because I am scared. I hate the dark, especially when it's forced on me. Something I don't want to even think about as memories of a childhood I've tried to forget start beating at the corners of my mind.

Using the torch on my phone, I move back inside, locking the glass door behind me, before slipping my shoes back on that I kicked off by the front door earlier. Then I nervously crack open the front door, peering out into the dark bushland surrounding the house.

I need to get to the meter box, but since this isn't my house, I'm not certain where it is. Typically, they are on the outside of garages here in Australia, so I make that my destination, and move slowly out into the humid night.

Walking with quiet feet down the stony path, my eyes dart everywhere as my heart thrashes in my chest and my ears pick up nothing but loud crickets and some sort of weird bird call. All these noises weren't there before when the sun was still up, and are now freaking me out, so I hurry along to the side of the garage where I find the meter box.

Shit! There's a fucking padlock on it.

What the fuck?

Fear freezes me in place for a moment before my brain kicks in, and I remember I've just done what all the stupid girls in the movies do, and I went outside where the fucking predator could be lurking.

Could I get any dumber? Seriously!

Turning, I run like a bat out of hell back to the porch, flying through the door where I slam and lock it. Pressing my back to the cool wood of the door, my chest heaves with panic. I stand like that for a minute before my brain finally kicks in, forcing my feet forward to check that every window and door is locked around the house, with the flashlight on my phone lighting the way.

Once I'm sure I'm safely locked in, I get the candles I use for my clients and light them, placing them throughout the house, filling the area with a gentle, warm glow. By the time I sit my arse back on the couch, my heart is beating wildly, more from anger now than fear.

I glare at the phone this Santa creep left for me, wanting to call it and tell him to fuck right off.

I don't though, because I don't want to torment him into breaking in and slitting my throat.

Instead, I pick up my personal phone and call the one person who knows some of my secrets.

"Hello."

"Hey, Shane. It's Aggie."

"Hey, Aggie. It's a bit hot tonight, hey?"

"Yeah, it sure is." I nod, even though Shane can't see as I glance around at the candles flickering around me.

"What's up? You sound worried."

Worried is an understatement. I don't really know where to start or what to say. The rules of the game stated that I wasn't to speak of the game to anyone.

"Uh... Have you heard anything about the list?"

Shane stays quiet for a few beats before answering. "No. Not the original list."

"Right. Ok. So, it was destroyed right? All traces of it gone?"

Shane clears his throat. "What's this about?"

I want to tell him to just answer my fucking question, but I don't. Shane hasn't done anything wrong. He's a good friend, and I'm just freaking out.

"Oh, nothing. It just plays on my mind. That's all. And with Master Hill being murdered last week, I guess I'm just a little on edge."

Master Hill, AKA Terence Hill, was the owner of Vixen's Lodge. He was a Timber Valley solicitor by day, and the Master of his own exclusive anonymous sex club by night. He and his wife operated the sex club from their mansion, Vixen's Lodge, for over five years in the town of Fox Pines until things turned south with their prized possession. A seventeen-year-old girl with a sex addiction.

She nearly died when they went off the rails and kidnapped her, but she fought for her life, and now, Vixen's Lodge is a pile of ash. Victoria Hill's burnt remains were buried last month, and her husband, the master, survived long enough to be slaughtered by what sounds like a professional assassin of sorts, in the Melbourne Burns Clinic while under police guard just last week.

It's only natural that I'm freaking out of late. The original list of anonymous guests has my name on it, which automatically links me to the crimes against the underage girl. Officer Shane Kent—my good friend—used some of his not so legal connections to remove my name, as well as some others off the encrypted list, therefore severing our connection to the crimes. The only problem is I'm extremely paranoid that the original list will somehow resurface, and then I'll be arrested.

"Shit, yeah," Shane says quietly through the phone. "I totally get it. I've been checking on things in the department. Nothing about the original has come up. I had to outsource to find the list in the first place and have our names wiped off, but that was with a trustworthy ally."

My shoulders slump both with relief that I can't be linked to the Vixen's Lodge scandal, and disappointment that I'm no closer to figuring out who this psycho is that I've agreed to play a fucking Dom and sub game with.

"Thanks Shane. Sorry for calling."

"It's ok, Aggie. You can call anytime. You know that." I can hear the warm smile in Shane's voice. "Are we still on for dinner at O'Connor's tomorrow night?"

I should cancel, since this Santa creep knows all about that. Yet I don't. I'm not sure if it's because I need the brief time I can get with my friends, or if it's because I'm curious about subbing for Santa.

But hell, we all know that curiosity killed the cat.

"Yep. I'll see you tomorrow night." I agree and then we say our goodbyes before I end the call, feeling the loneliness of my life seep in and wrap itself around my heart.

I hate this time of year. A time for families and friends to come together, yet here I am all alone.

I don't know where my mum and sister ended up after I left them over ten years ago. Are they even still alive? Did their lives turn out better after what I did? Or worse?

I often wonder where they are, or how they are spending their Christmas' this time of year. I wonder if they have traditions now. New people to share the holiday with.

I guess I'll never know, and perhaps having a normal Christmas like everyone else out there in the world is something I'll never know either.

The thought isn't new to me, and like so many times before, my emotions kick in. A tear pops free, searing my cheek as it travels down, and I give in to the heartache clawing at me, and allow myself to sink into the darkness surrounding me. I let go of the barriers I usually keep in place to not think about my past, and for the first time in a long time, I let the memories slam back in with so much force that a scream rips from my lungs.

Sleep only comes hours later, after I've spiralled into such an exhaustion of internal pain that I can no longer stay awake.

Santa

My little elf is scared. She's surrounded herself with the flicker of candles as she tries to mentally accept what's happening.

Perhaps she thinks I'm a psychopath. Maybe she's right to think that. Maybe not. But she should be scared. I need her to be scared. I need to see how she handles the fear. How she copes.

I'm not prepared for her tears though, or the heartbreaking scream that rips from her lungs.

Fury washes through me as I try to piece together what the hell is going on. That scream wasn't from fear. It held too much pain.

My little elf is hurting.

I have to fight really fucking hard not to go to her. Of course, if I did, she'd probably kick me in the nuts. She doesn't know who I am. I'm nothing but a stranger to her, even though she's anything but to me.

So here I sit, watching my little elf battle emotions I'm not privy to until she finally cries herself to sleep.

What is going on in that head of yours, little elf?

Chapter Three

Vibing with Friends

Agatha

In the light of a new day, I drag myself out of last night's pity party and focus on my daily routine. I try hard to ignore the fact that the power is still out, instead embracing the cold shower and setting myself up on the deck overlooking the lake for my morning yoga and meditation.

I try hard to focus, forcing my empowering mantras past my lips as I work for calm and peace.

"Every day, I get stronger. Everything I need is within me. I love myself. I believe in myself. I support myself."

I meditate for longer than usual today, needing more time to centre myself and remain in a good place to help me get through the rest of the day.

After I finally feel like myself again, I move inside and eat some fruit before deciding to re-check the meter box, only to find it's still locked.

And it remains that way the other six times I check throughout the day.

The urge to stand this fucker up and do the complete opposite of what he asked plays on my mind. I can cancel my dinner plans with my friends. I can stay home and not put that lingerie on, or insert the toy, however, I can't bring myself to do that.

Maybe it's my loneliness, or maybe it's utter idiocy, but I can't bring myself to cancel my plans because then, whatever this is with the stranger will be over before it's really begun. And yes, I know that sounds like the dumbest reason ever, but the thought of drowning in my loneliness is terrifying.

I'll admit, just thinking about playing this game with a man I don't know sends a thrill of excitement through me. I've never considered myself an adrenaline junkie, but shit, I must be a junkie of some sort to be going along with this so willingly.

I also know if I cancel and end this game with this so-called Santa, I'll end up dwelling over my curiosity, and wondering what would have happened if I had followed the command. I'll end up pulling my hair out with frustration over who on earth this man is, and how the hell he knows me. The identity of this man would forever tease me.

I know if I go through with it, I'll find out if this man's intentions are decent or not. I'll learn if this is really just a Dom and sub game, or if he means me harm.

See where my head is at? He could be planning to kill me, yet I'm willing to take the gamble that his only interest is in pleasuring me.

A sensible person would call the police.

Apparently, the non sensible part of my brain needs to know if this man is just a Dom asserting his authority. Which is fucking scary because it means he was here last night, turning off my power, right outside my house. And he probably watched me run out to the meter box in the dark.

Deep down I know I should be bolting for safety, yet here I am, staying put, wondering who this man could be.

With no power, I had to use my phone for background music for my 2pm client. Not that he cared. He was only interested in the tantric therapy I offer. The candles still created the right atmosphere, and everything else I needed didn't require power. I was just thankful the house hadn't turned into a sauna since today's sun was hidden behind the clouds for an overcast day.

I take another cold shower before getting ready for dinner with Shane and Ben. I make sure I'm clean-shaven and smelling fresh, and at 4:45pm, just like instructed in the note, I insert the egg-shaped device. Lube wasn't even required, despite being annoyed at this guy for taking my electricity away. Just the mere anticipation of what's to come has me aching with need. Hence, no lube being required. I'm already dripping.

The idea of slipping the egg vibrator inside me is all sorts of hot. I love sex toys. I have a drawer full of them. They help take the ache away, and do a bloody terrific job at that, but they are no substitute for a warm body. The toys can't look at me lustfully. They can't grin sexily and give me dirty talk that makes my knees quiver. They may be able to hit the spots that send me soaring easily enough, but when I come down from my high, I'm always left feeling empty.

When used with a partner, sex toys can be thrilling. Just another way to be vulnerable and reach new heights. The fact that Santa is entering the game so strongly has me aching between my legs.

Fuck, I hope I'm not talking him up in my head too much and he turns out to be a lazy lay. I think I'm the one he should be scared of if that's the case.

I love sex. I had to learn to love it after I ran away when I was seventeen, needing to use it to help get me food, shelter and transport across the country. I can't really complain. Even though some of the men were slobs, they treated me well, making sure to teach me what they liked, while showing me how it can feel good for me, too.

I've never had sex against my will, but there were times I almost said no. They were situations I didn't really know how to get out of, so perhaps a few times it was a little against my will, but ultimately, I said yes. Sometimes I wonder if I had said no more often when I was younger, if my life would have turned out differently, or if I was destined to be on this path of a lonely, yet sex consumed life.

Ultimately, I used what I had to in order to survive. And it worked.

Am I proud of some of the things I've done? Hell no. There's a lot of shame carried on my shoulders, but I'm here and alive, and for that I remind myself daily that I'm thankful.

I know I'm doing nothing more than existing right now, but maybe, with time, and as the Timber Valley region forgets about the sex club scandal, I'll be able to really live.

A girl can only dream.

I stare at my brown eyes in the mirror as I slip the red and silver bra on, wondering if the person I see in the reflection is the same person other people see.

Do they see my golden blonde hair, or is it ashier in colour to them? Are my eyes a nice brown, or a boring brown? Have my twenty-eight years given me deeper smile lines than I see, making me look older? And are my C cups sagging yet?

It blows my mind that the lingerie fits me perfectly. Has this guy been snooping around my underwear drying on the line outside? How does he know I'm a size 10?

So many questions rampage through my head, which is one of the many reasons why I'm going through with this. I need to get the answers to my questions straight from the source.

Once the lingerie is in place, I slip on my red dress with the black trim, and step into my Top End heels before making sure I have the phone tucked safely in my handbag. I give myself a once over in the mirror, running my hand over my styled waves one last time, and then nod.

Yep. I'm ready for Santa.

The Irish Pub is in the main street of Redfield and is a popular meet up place for dinner, drinks and a night of dancing. Shane and Ben are already there when I arrive, sitting across from each other like they are nothing but good mates.

It's sad that they can't be themselves in public and show the world just how much they care about each other, but my presence will help to keep their secret hidden, just the way it's been for the last four years.

I slide into the booth next to Shane, and their brows shoot up at the red number I'm wearing.

"Looking fine, Aggie. I hope you didn't dress up just for us," Ben remarks with a smirk and I grin back, shaking my head.

"Just trying to get into the Christmas spirit." I lie, and they nod, none the wiser.

We place our order for drinks and food, and our conversation is light as my eyes take in my surroundings and the people filling it.

It looks like the regulars are here. Nothing out of the ordinary, so I quickly forget all about Santa and his twisted game as I relax with my friends.

I'm halfway through my chicken parma when a dull vibrating sensation reminds me that I have a sex toy inserted inside me. I nearly choke on the food I'm trying to swallow, as I realise exactly what Santa's intentions are.

Don't get me wrong. I understood that he was going to tease me with the device inside me, but I kinda thought it would be later, when I'm dancing or something. Not trying to eat dinner.

As I cough a little, Shane and Ben glance at me in concern, offering me a glass of water and a pat on my back.

"You ok, Aggie?" Ben asks, and I nod, sipping on the water.

"Food went down the wrong wayyy." My voice squeaks as the toy speeds up, the vibrations more obvious to only me, making it hard to speak.

Shane chuckles. "You sure?"

I nod, too scared to speak as the toy builds pleasure deep in my core.

The guys go back to discussions of cricket, while I grip my napkin in one hand, and the edge of the table in the other. I can feel heat rising over my body and my cheeks light up as the vibrations grow bigger and faster and a whimper escapes me.

"Aggie? You sure you're ok?" Shane asks from next to me, and I have to work really fucking hard not to grab his hand and put it between my legs.

Shit.

That would be like assaulting him. Especially since I know he bats for his team, not the one I'm on.

"Sorry, I think I ate something off." I manage to say without sounding like a needy whore. I shift in the seat, ready to flee, when the phone on the table lights up with a text. Picking it up quickly, I open the message, and almost wish I hadn't.

Santa

Stay at the table and maintain your poker face.

Holy shit. This guy is crazy. Stay here and pretend like I'm not seconds away from a 'When Harry Met Sally' moment? I want to argue, but I can't because the egg speeds up, so I pretend I'm listening to Shane and Ben, nodding and smiling at whatever the hell they are talking about.

Another message lights up my phone, gaining my attention, and I rush to open it again.

Santa

Finish eating your dinner.

My eyes widen before darting around the pub. Can he see me? Is he here?

I search for anyone paying me attention, or looking suss, but I can't find anyone looking at me. There are so many people here as well. It could be anyone.

The vibrations inside me increase, so I start eating quickly as ordered, and as a reward, the intensity eases off to a low vibration.

My shoulders drop as I relax and set to work on finishing my plate of food. Once my plate is empty, I take a drink of water, and once again, the damn vibrations increase, causing me to nearly spill the drink.

That's it, I can't take it anymore.

"Excuse me." I mutter before fleeing from the table, the phone gripped tight in my hand as I beeline for the toilets. I barely make it halfway across the restaurant when my phone rings. I nearly drop the damn thing, but manage to right myself quickly to answer it.

"Where are you going?" the deep gravelly voice asks.

Oh yeah. This crazy guy is definitely here somewhere watching me. There's no doubt in my mind about that now.

"Bathroom."

"Nope, turn around and walk out the front doors. Stay on the phone with me."

"But..."

The egg speeds up unbearably, and another whimper escapes, nearly bending my body in half in the most embarrassing way before I change directions and dash for the door.

The moment I step out into the cooler night air, the vibrations ease off.

"See, little elf. It's not so hard to just obey me." His raspy voice almost sounds amused through the phone. "It really is in your best interest, Moxie."

My feet skid to a stop as my eyes widen at what he just called me.

Only *certain* people know *that* name. It's my club name. My sex club name. And only someone from Vixen's Lodge, or the parties I've held lately, would know I use *that* name.

"What?!" I shriek loudly. "How do you know that name?"

"I know a lot about you." The vibrations increase. "Now, go to your car and get in the passenger seat."

"But..." I pant and he growls.

"If you want the electricity back on when you get home, go to your car, Agatha."

Shit. His voice! While sexy, is demandingly scary. Even if I wanted to disobey him with all my heart, I don't think I could.

I do as he orders and dash to the car, getting in the passenger side.

"Put me on speaker." He demands, and I hit the loud speaker icon on my phone before placing the phone on the dashboard inside my car.

"I'm going to step up to the side of your car and watch you through the window. Do not turn your head and look at me, or you will receive a bigger punishment than losing electricity."

Holy shit.

He really is here.

"Ok." I nod, my heart thrashing in my chest as moisture pools between my legs.

"Eyes cast forward and down, little elf." His voice is so sensual as he speaks softly, and I do as he says, finally letting myself feel the sensations building inside me.

In my peripheral, I see the shadow of a man standing outside my door. I'm tempted to turn and look at him, but I'm also extremely compelled to do exactly as he says.

Since my car is parked under a streetlamp, it illuminates my car and where I sit, giving him a perfect view.

"Pull your dress up, little elf. Bunch it around your waist."

I release a moan as I move, doing as he asks, excited that he's finally near.

"Panties off." He demands and I obey, nothing but his puppet.

"Atta girl." He rumbles and fuck me, that is so hot.

Atta girl. I'll do anything he wants if he keeps saying that to me.

"Spread your legs for me. Nice and wide."

I do as he asks, shuffling my arse forward a little while I move the seat back and part my legs, opening myself. The vibrations start to increase again, and I moan, palming my tits over the top of my dress.

This feels amazing.

"You're a squirter, aren't you, little elf?"

Shit!

How does he know that?

He must be from the sex parties. It's the only way he can know.

"Y-yes." I stutter, trying to think, but my body's rising heat shoots fog to my brain.

"Make sure you spray for me. I'll arrange for your car to be detailed after Christmas."

Fuck. His voice. His words. They are too much combined with the toy inside me working at my core.

"Here we go then. It's time."

His words are followed by an extreme increase in the toy's intensity, and I cry out, no longer able to control myself. I buck under the onslaught, pleasure heating me deep in my core as my focus turns to reaching my climax. My hips rise off the seat, gyrating before my muscles start to tighten around the egg. And then I explode, clear fluid spraying from between my legs in a forceful rush.

My panting is loud in the small cabin of my car, and I feel utterly spent until I hear his voice again.

"Clean up the spray on your seat with your panties and leave them on the bonnet of your car when you get out. You can return to your friends and finish your night out."

"W-what?" I stutter again. Did I hear him right?

"You heard me, Agatha." He growls with a dominating tone.

Shit. I did hear him right, but I kind of hoped I heard him wrong.

"You want me to go back in without panties?"

"Yes."

"Um..." I bite my lip as my cheeks flush. "Ok."

"Good girl."

The call disconnects then, and it takes a moment to push past my shock and remember to search for him. I look out the window as well as the mirrors, not seeing anyone nearby.

What the hell?

Disappointment seeps in as I come to terms with the fact that I never got to see his face or touch him. I may have only just come a minute ago, but I'm yearning for more. This guy has me twisted in knots. I'm utterly intrigued.

Shaking my head, I use my panties to clean up my mess before tugging my dress back down in place. Getting out of my car on shaky legs, I look up and down the street in search of my Santa, but still come up empty. He knew what he was doing. He must have already scoped out my car. He must have been watching me from either inside O'Connor's, or outside through the windows. He planned this tonight, and the fact that it's so unorthodox makes me desperate for more.

Sighing, I lock up my car and leave my balled-up panties on the bonnet as he requested.

This is certainly a first for me.

Santa

Fuuuck! Her panties smell like heaven. I've never been so fucking hard in my life. Watching her through the windows of O'Connor's as she tried to pretend I wasn't teasing her from the inside out nearly had me storming in there and throwing her over my shoulder.

Why has this woman gotten under my skin so damn much?

To look at, she has an aura of innocence about her. Her face is sweet, and she presents herself with such a relaxed class that you automatically know you are beneath her.

But I know her confidence is for show. Hell, I think she even pretends to fool herself by doing all of that yoga and meditation shit.

And the affirmations.

Damn. Why does she think she needs them?

She doesn't see what I see, but by the time I'm done with her, she will see her worth. I'll make sure of it.

I was wearing a cap when I approached her car, hoping it would help shade my face in case the little minx tried to peek.

I'm glad she didn't, although that probably had more to do with the pleasure building inside her. She likely couldn't think straight.

It was something else to see between her legs, so close for once. Her cunt was glistening. Her hips writhed and gyrated, and the way they fucked the air had me salivating.

Then she sprayed.

Fuck, I love that about her. She's not shy about it. She gives in to how her body responds to her sexcapades. I can't wait to taste it. My mouth longs to drown in everything she has to give me.

When she was done, I eased back into the shadows and slipped into my car. She didn't even see me there as she walked past a few minutes later after cleaning herself up and leaving her panties on the bonnet like I instructed.

Now, I'm back in the car, freeing my dick as I inhale her scent and feel the dampness from her spray. I groan loud inside the cabin of my Mercedes, wrapping my hand around my dick and giving it a squeeze.

This is going to be the quickest wank I've had in my life. I just know it. But fuck, who cares? The lead up has had me on edge all fucking night, so I take the panties and wrap them around my cock and then start fucking them.

"Fuck. Yes, Aggie." I pant, dropping my head back to the seat as I shut my eyes and let all the visuals she gave me tonight swarm in.

I pump and pump, relishing the damp fabric of the panties as images of Aggie palming her tits, fucking the air, screaming out in ecstasy, and spraying her seat engulf me.

A deep rumble escapes me before I hold my breath and then release it as I explode, my intense pleasure shooting streams of cum into the fabric to combine with Aggie's scent.

Fuck yes. So far, tonight has been perfect.

I hope my little elf is prepared though, because the night isn't over yet.

Chapter Four

Big Brother is Watching

Agatha

O'Connor's is loud and bright when I go back inside. People's eyes fall to me as I walk through the space, and I feel like they know I'm not wearing any panties, even though it's impossible for them to know.

It must be the red dress. It's hard not to be drawn to it, which means drawn to me, so I own that shit with my head held high like I didn't just spray my car interior a few minutes ago.

"You ok?" Ben asks as I slip back into the booth.

I nod. "Yeah sorry."

"What's going on?" Shane frowns, always in cop mode, being way too perceptive.

"You don't want to know." I grin, knowing he'll wish he didn't know if I tell him.

"Actually, I do. Something is going on with you." Shane frowns, his dark brows meeting in the middle.

Ben nods. "He's right. Spill."

Sighing, I weigh up my options. The rules of the game state that I'm not to tell anyone about the game, but it doesn't mean I can't blur the lines a little.

"So I have this thing going with a guy. He kinda issues challenges for me. Sexual challenges."

Ben's eyes light up with interest, and Shane simply smirks, shaking his head.

"You're right. I'm not sure I want to know."

"I want to know." Ben's smile spreads wide. "What are the challenges?" He wags his brows, and Shane chuckles next to me.

"Well, tonight, for example, I have a sex toy inside me that he has control of."

Ben laughs and Shane nearly spits out the mouthful of beer he just drank.

"You're kidding?" Ben laughs louder, his eyes darting to his secret lover across the table as he tries to wipe up his drink.

"Not kidding." I grin, relaxing back in the seat.

"So before, when you said you were having tummy issues, you were..." Shane cringes at me, his eyes wide this time.

"Trying not to come." I nod. "Yes."

"This is brilliant." Ben chuckles and Shane shakes his head.

"Of course you would think that."

"Hell, yeah I do. We are gonna play that game." Ben beams and Shane's eyes widen in panic.

"There's no fucking way I'm walking around with a toy inside me that *you* have control over."

"Chicken?" Ben teases and I can't help but laugh as I address Ben.

"Why don't you pass the power over to Shane? You wear the toy inside you and let him have the control."

Ben's smile drops from his face. "Not in public." He points a stern finger at Shane, who just sits back in the seat, crossing his arms over his chest wearing a shit-eating grin.

“Fine.” Shane shrugs. “At the next party.”

Shane and Ben stare at each other silently for a few beats, like they’re having a conversation with their eyes or something, and then Ben nods.

"Deal."

I feel lighter after admitting I have a vibrator inside me. I didn’t tell them the truth, so I didn’t break the rules, but it’s nice to share a little of the excitement between me and Santa with my friends.

As the night progresses, the dinner patrons leave and the place fills with people who want extra drinks to celebrate Christmas. An old Irish pub never used to be my idea of a fun night out, but I’ve had to adapt now that I moved myself away from Fox Pines.

I leave early, not interested in dancing, my mind desperate to indulge in the memory of Santa watching me come earlier.

I only drank one glass of wine tonight, so driving back to my rental is no problem. The night is clear and balmy as I pull up to the house and see the porch light on, and I can’t hold back my grin, knowing Santa was true to his word. He’s turned my power back on, which means I can use the air conditioner.

Back inside my house, I turn some lights on, loving the sense of calm the illumination brings, and I head to my bedroom, taking my dress off as I go.

The egg-shaped device is still inside me, and I consider taking it out but realise Santa hasn’t instructed me to do so. It could be an oversight on his end, or a test to see how well I follow instructions, so I leave it in and take a shower.

The hot water on my skin is a welcome relief compared to the cold showers I had to take earlier today, but given today’s heat,

I'm only able to bear it for a few minutes before needing to add more cold to the stream.

As I wash my hair, my thoughts fall to the shadowed figure in my peripheral beside my car earlier. He was right there, watching through the window.

From what I could make out, he didn't seem like he was overweight. He wasn't jacking off as far as I could tell, his body standing still as he watched me come undone. One might think this whole thing is a little too twisted, but fuck, it turned me on knowing he was right there.

As I soap over my tits, the familiar sensation of the toy inside me starts up again, and I bite my lower lip as I grin. It's like he knew I was thinking about him, bringing the toy to life so I can enjoy the pleasure in the privacy of my shower where no one can see.

Leaning back against the tiles, water cascades over my body as my hips slowly gyrate in time with the pulsing inside me. I release a loud moan, revelling in the way it bounces off the tiled walls, surrounding me like a blanket of arousal, fuelling me on.

My hands press flat against the tiles as I writhe, not needing to touch myself while the toy is doing all the work.

"Yes." I pant, enjoying the new pulsing action of the toy as it increases in speed. I arch my back as the pleasure builds, my head tipping back against the tiles, and I give in to the sensations building inside me.

I come fast and hard, my cries loud as I let down my walls and let it consume me. The toy doesn't stop, and I consider tugging it free, but I can't make myself end the pleasure and let it quickly do its thing again. Greedily, I add my fingers to work over my clit as I seek more from this moment, and it doesn't take long before a scream rips from me and a stream of clear fluid bursts from between my legs.

The toy stops then, and my heaving pants are loud in the small space as I try to catch my breath. For a moment I enjoy the blissful feeling of the high I just reached, but with every high, comes a crash, and as my lonely existence creeps in again, so too does the realisation that I'm still alone right now. Santa may be playing with me, but he's not here with me.

Feeling the burn of tears, I step under the spray, letting the water cascade over my face as I let myself cry just a little. I'm not normally so pathetic in my loneliness. It's because of stupid Christmas. I'm sure it must be fun for those who have families to celebrate with. I just have to suck it up and deal with the next week and a bit, and then I can focus on New Year's events that are more suited to my lifestyle.

When I eventually get out of the shower, I dry myself off and hang the towel over the rail before the loud ring of the phone startles me. I slap my hand over my heart in an attempt to stop it from leaping through my ribcage, but then I realise the incoming call is from the phone Santa gave me.

I leap forward, remembering the rules. I can't let it ring more than three times.

"Hello." My voice is breathy as my heart races.

"Did you enjoy your shower?"

His deep voice is so incredibly soothing, working like a drug to calm my turmoil. That is until I comprehend what he just asked.

Did you enjoy your shower?

How does he know I was in the shower?

I look around the small space frantically, my eyes landing on the mirror as a frown pulls my brows down. Leaning forward, I press my long fingernail to the mirror to see if it's really a mirror, or if it's somehow double sided.

Can he see me? Are there cameras in here?

"Yes." I mutter, realising I haven't answered him. "It was nice to have hot water again." My eyes stay fixed on my reflection as I speak, confusion keeping my frown in place.

"Are you pissed off at me, little elf?"

Why would he think that? My tone wasn't snappy or anything, so my only conclusion is that he must be able to see me, or he's psychic. I'm going to go with the former.

"That depends. If I say I am, will I get punished for it?"

"No, of course not." He grunts. "I'll only punish you if you lie. Or break the rules. Have you broken the rules, little elf?"

My brows shoot up at his question. Have I? I think back to O'Connor's, and the story I told Shane and Ben. I hadn't said I was subbing for Santa, so I feel like I'm safe.

"No, Santa. I haven't broken the rules."

"Good. Then why are you pissed off at me? Tell me why you're frowning."

Shit.

He can see me.

How the fuck can he see me? Surely, he's just making assumptions. Maybe he's good at reading people through their tone and stuff. That's a thing, right?

To test the theory, I stick my middle finger up, flipping myself off in the mirror.

He chuckles.

"That would be a yes, then. You are definitely angry."

I leap back from the mirror in shock, still not ready to accept that he can see me.

"Yes, I'm pissed off." I snap as my eyes dart around the bathroom, looking for cameras.

"Why?"

"Because you know personal things about me, and I don't know anything about you."

"I guess that must be frustrating." He sighs. "Fine, besides my identity. What would you like to know?"

"How about where you are right now?" I snap, glaring into the mirror again.

"I'm at my home. Sitting on my couch."

Evasive as shit.

"Are you far from me?" I ask, glaring at my own naked reflection in the mirror.

"Further than I'd like."

Ugh. He's impossible. Yet sexy. How is his voice so sexy?

"Have we met before?" I ask.

"No."

My brows shoot up. How would he know to call me Moxie if we haven't met at a sex party?

"Then how do you know me?" My voice is high pitched as my panic builds.

"I can't tell you that, little elf. Not yet. It will ruin the game."

I huff and poke out my tongue before deciding to just ask him what I really want to know.

"Can you see me right now?"

"Yes."

My eyes widen and I look around the bathroom again, still not finding any cameras.

"What am I doing right now?"

He chuckles. "Looking for cameras."

I frown again and roll my eyes. "That's an obvious answer."

"Don't roll your eyes at me, little elf."

My eyes widen again, and I quickly leave the bathroom, going into the bedroom and start searching for hidden cameras in there. Is this what it's like to be on Big Brother?

"Now you're in your bedroom, standing by the door, looking at the light switch."

I spin around and cover my naked chest with my arm.

He chuckles again. "It's too late. I've already seen it all. I even saw you masturbate in bed yesterday morning before you got up and counted all that cash your party friends handed you the night before."

I freeze.

What. The. Fuck.

"What did you just say?" I almost whisper, and he chuckles.

"You heard me. I know about your little parties. Maybe one time you'll invite me."

Those parties are a secret. Only members know about them. So, either this guy is already a member, or he's been watching me for a while and knows exactly what goes on in this house. I fear it's the latter since he said we haven't met before.

Shit.

He insinuated that he'd like to be invited, so it's more likely that this guy has been watching me ever since I moved in.

I don't know how I feel about that. Violated, but the fucked-up part of me is also intrigued.

I swear I'm going to be found dead one day because of my intrigue.

"Y-you would come?" I ask, losing my bravado.

"Multiple times, I'm sure."

I grin, my worry lightening a little at his playful tone. "You know what I mean. You would turn up to the party?"

"Yes. When is your next one? Before or after Christmas?"

"Before. Next Monday night."

"If I'm free, I'll join you. That is, if you're a good girl between now and then."

Slowly, my lips spread wider until my teeth show as I fail at holding back my smile. I don't know who this guy is, but the way he makes my heart race has me here for it. Putty in his hands.

"Deal."

"Be a good little elf and lie on the bed for me."

I hesitate for a moment, wondering where he can see me from, but then I figure it doesn't really matter, so I lay on my bed.

"Now, spread those long legs for me. Nice and wide."

My heart rate picks up, my chest rising and falling heavily as I do as he asks.

"Now, slip your fingers inside and pull out the device."

Slowly, I slide my hand between my legs, spreading them wider as my fingers grip the tag on the device and I ease it free.

"Atta girl."

Fuck. Why is that so hot?

"Remember your aftercare. Keep clean. Hydrated, and get plenty of rest. The next part of our game will arrive in the morning."

Santa

She cried again. In the time that I've been watching her, I've never seen her cry this much. Before it was maybe once a week, but now it's every day. A couple of times a day.

Am I doing that to her? Is she scared of her Santa?

She should be!

I don't feel like it's my doing, though. But then, what the fuck do I know about women and the way they think?

It's been fun confusing her, but I hope it's not what's distressing her so much.

Watching her in the shower is a pleasure on its own, but add to it an internal sex toy, and then some self-pleasure, and you've got the hottest fucking scene ever. It's almost hypnotising to watch the water roll down her body, over her nipples and in between her legs. Add to it her moans of pleasure, or her fingers that know exactly how to play with her needy little clit, and it's nothing but pure erotica.

I had my hand wrapped around my dick the entire time as I watched her in the shower, and when I came, I came hard, shooting my load into her panties again.

One of the best things to do with my little elf is talking to her. I love how annoyed she gets with me at times. I love hearing her sensual voice, and how it sometimes sounds breathy.

Fuck, I can't wait to be in the same room as her. To touch her.

I love how she got annoyed with me when I spoke with her on the phone. The eye rolling and flipping me the middle finger to see if I could really see her set my blood boiling. In the best way. Straight to my dick.

I wasn't sure how she would react after finding out I've been watching from inside her home. She had to wonder that perhaps I'd been watching from outside like a fucking peeping tom, but watching from inside is some serious stalker shit. She could have ended what we have going right then and there. But she didn't. She huffed and showed her frustration and disbelief, but when I gave her an order, she still obeyed. Which means she's still mine, even if she doesn't realise it.

Chapter Five

Cam

Agatha

It's around 12pm the next day when I hear something outside my front door. Santa had told me a package would be arriving, so naturally, I've been eagerly waiting.

With my heart racing in anticipation, I dash to the door, swinging it open wide, hoping to catch whoever delivered it, but as usual, there is no sign of anyone. Just a small package wrapped in red and gold foil paper with a gold bow on top.

Since Christmas isn't something I tend to celebrate, I never get presents. I know this is all part of the game, but with each package I feel like it's Christmas morning and someone who cares is giving me a gift.

It's stupid. I know.

Hurrying back inside, I unwrap the gift to find a leather choker with a large stone of some sort embedded in the strap. Then I take out the note.

My brows reach my hairline as I read over the note again, before I pick up the choker and take a closer look.

Fucking hell. The stone is actually a mini camera. He wants me to wear this so he can watch what I do with my client today. The idea of it is confusing, because I was sure he had cameras everywhere, even though I'm yet to find one. Why would I need to wear this if he has cameras installed?

I've spent the better part of my morning searching my entire rental for hidden cameras and have come up empty. I figured they would be big enough to spot if I were looking for them, yet I've found nothing.

This would be the time where having a close friend of the female gender would come in handy. Someone to bounce concerns off. Someone to tell me, *'Agatha, there are red flags everywhere about this guy. Cut and run now.'*

Hell, I don't even listen to the rational self-talk in my head.

Instead, I secure the choker around my neck and continue cleaning and setting up for today's client.

At 2pm, Meagan arrives, and I lead her to the spare room I have set up for my tantric clients. We sit on the oversized cushions on the floor for a few minutes, going over what we did last time, anything she especially liked, or didn't like, and go over the importance of getting ourselves centred first.

I don't leave the room for her to undress. We do that in front of each other, ensuring there's comfort and trust between us. And yes, I feel guilty that she doesn't know she's being watched right now by a man I don't know, but it's too late to back out, so I pretend the heavy choker isn't squeezing my neck and carry on.

The light in the room is low, candles are lit, the music is serene and soft. We each stand on a mat facing each other and go through some basic stretches, and then some yoga positions, switching on our breathing.

We move to the cushion pile on the floor then, Meagan laying back, getting into position.

Using oil, I lather it over her naked body, keeping my movements slow and sensual, my voice just above a whisper as I direct her to focus on her breathing and slow it down.

To help her relax and get centred, I start my massage on her arms and legs before moving to her breasts and abdomen. This is where the magic starts to happen. Sexual energy stirs. And to help it along, I run my hands over her belly, applying sensual pressure, then run them back up to her breasts to work over her nipples. After doing this a few times, I hear her breathing deepen, so I move the massage lower.

Some women are able to reach their pleasure from a tantric breast massage alone, but Meagan is booked in for a yoni massage, which means the ultimate focus needs to be on her clit and g-spot.

She keeps her breathing slow and deep, falling into the meditative state as I stimulate her body. I circle her clit, nice and slow, before changing technique to push and pull on it, increasing and releasing pressure. Soft moans float up into the room as Meagan starts to build more pleasure within her, and I shift my technique to tug at her clit between two fingers and then roll it to apply pressure.

I use a little tapping technique but don't do a lot of this because she doesn't seem to respond as well as some do. When her hips start to lift, seeking more, I slide two fingers inside her, easily finding the swell of her g-spot, and curl my digits, grazing them over the spot, while returning attention to her clit, using my thumb this time.

The entire process lasts just over forty minutes, and the orgasm she reaches is long, drawn out, and incredibly intense.

When it's over, Meagan stays laying down for a few minutes, catching her breath and letting her body ease out of its meditative state. It really is a full mind and body experience, and I'm yet to have an unhappy customer.

I used to get turned on by my sessions in the beginning, but now the tantra massage I offer is nothing but a way for me to earn money, and my clients aren't interested in me joining in on the fun. They are there for release. Stress relief. Therapy. Much like a regular relaxation massage, just with a focus on tantra.

As soon as Meagan leaves, Santa's phone rings, and I hurry to answer it in time.

"What do you call what you just did?"

Jesus. Will I ever get used to the deep rasp of his voice?

"Tantra massage." I clear my throat. "Specifically, a yoni massage."

"Yoni massage?" he asks, sounding curious.

"Yes. It's where the focus is on the woman's sex."

I pad through the little house and flop down on my couch, feeling exhausted from needing to be focused for so long.

"Why all the other stuff before that?" Santa asks. "The stretching and the upper body massage."

"Tantra is about energy. Building the pleasure for a full body experience." I try to explain, and he hums for a moment.

"Does it work the same for men?"

"Kind of." I grin. "A goal with men is to learn how to achieve orgasm without ejaculating."

"Why the fuck would anyone want to do that?" He scoffs and I giggle, loving how casual he is with me right now. Like two friends talking.

"Well, for one, a man can struggle with achieving an erection again for a decent period of time after ejaculating. By learning how to orgasm without ejaculation, it offers the possibility of multiple orgasms."

"Shit. Ok, then." He truly sounds amazed.

I grin, biting my lower lip. This is a new side of Santa.

"Did you enjoy watching, Santa?" I ask, hoping he won't be annoyed with me asking questions while he's not acting so dominant.

"Yes. But I think I enjoy watching you come more." He states. "Go to your laptop, little elf. Turn on your webcam."

My brows shoot up.

"You want me to go on cam? Can't you already see me?" My voice raises in pitch at my confusion, but the low rumble of a growl that comes through the line tells me Santa is getting annoyed.

"Little elf, when Santa gives you an order, you'd best not question it and instead do what you're told."

I roll my eyes.

"I saw that." He growls, and hell, I think I like annoying him.

Sighing, I drag myself up off my couch and move to the study nook where I have my laptop and cam set up. If I'm having a slow tantric week, I do some camming to make up the rest of the money I need. I don't particularly like it, but again, I use what I have and know to help me get by.

While I get set up, I let curiosity get the better of me, and risk asking another question.

"Santa, have we cammed before?"

"No." He grumbles. "And the next question you ask will result in a punishment."

FML!

I huff, still stumped as to how this guy even found me. I get that he has cameras set up, which is obviously how he knows my sex club name, but how on earth did he find me? And how did he get cameras in here in the first place? Is he an old tenant?

"I've just sent you a link to your email. Open it and let me see you, little elf."

With everything he says, I have more and more questions, but unless I can be guaranteed that my punishment is going to be a good spanking, and not cutting my power again, I decide to remain quiet.

I open the link, and a few clicks later my cam is live. Santa disconnects our phone call, and his voice comes through the speakers next to my laptop instead.

"Pleasure yourself for me, my little elf."

My brows shoot up at his command before a frown settles over my face.

I can't see him. He hasn't turned his camera on.

When will I get to see my Santa?

I focus on what he said, slipping out of my robe and getting comfy in the chair.

"Can you see me properly?" I ask, and he answers quickly.

"Yes."

I slide my hands to my breasts first, rolling both nipples at the same time, letting the stimulation grow and shoot straight to my core.

"Santa?" I ask, adding some extra sweetness to my tone.

"Yes, little elf?"

"Can I see you on camera, too?"

"What have I told you about trying to find out my identity?" He growls, but I don't let it bother me as I run my hand down my front to start circling my nub.

"I don't want to see your face." I pant. "I want to see your cock. Will you show me?"

"Hmmm. I do like the way you say 'cock'."

I grin, liking how he likes the way I say it.

"Please show me your cock, Santa," I say sweetly, and a low groan comes through the speaker.

"How can I refuse that? Give me a minute, little elf."

Holy shit! Really?

I have to school my features not to look overly excited about him agreeing to this. It may not be his face, but it's a start.

I hear some shuffling, the sound of a door closing, some more shuffling, and then the screen flickers as his camera switches on.

The cam is positioned low so I can only see his bare chest and abs, and thank you baby Jesus, what a beautiful work of art it is. Sculpted to perfection, his pecs look strong and defined, his nipples totally biteable, and his six-pack is taut and teasing, leading to the top of a V that disappears below the screen.

"Shit, Santa. You're mouth-watering."

He chuckles. "I'd prefer to be pussy-watering."

I giggle in response. "Oh, don't worry. You are."

It's no lie. I'm ridiculously wet. I hadn't expected him to be in such good shape. From what I can see, he is totally lickable, and I wasn't lying about my mouth watering. Or my pussy.

"I can't see your cock, Santa." I whine and he chuckles, stepping back until the V appears and then vanishes from my sight because I now have tunnel vision for his long, hard, thick straining cock.

"Oh wow. You have a nice cock, Santa."

He growls low in response as his hand comes into view, wrapping around the object of my desire. There's a tattoo on his hand, but I can't make it out, so I focus on my building pleasure as I watch him squeeze and pump his dick, bringing it closer to the screen.

"Fuck, Aggie. I can't wait to taste you."

Excitement rushes through me at his words. Part of me was wondering if I'd ever get to see him, but there is hope yet. Hope that one day soon his head will be buried between my legs.

The thought sends a rush of pleasure to my core, and I cry out as my fingers speed up their assault on my needy clit. I know I'm not far, and I want to see him cum, so I use his words as his dick pistons in his tight grip.

"I can't wait to taste you, too."

"Fuck." He hisses, and it does the trick.

As the first stream of white jiz shoots from his dick, I soar high in a clenching orgasm that, as usual, jets my own stream from my pulsing pussy.

Both of our panting breaths fill the room, and while I like that I can hear him, and see part of him, I still yearn to touch him.

I feel so touch starved. And not in the sex touch way. I mean in the caring caress of a lover as they worship every inch of my body. The feel of their arms as they hold me close, not wanting to have any space between us. The press of their warm lips against my temple as they cherish me.

I've only had that once, more than five years ago. All my other encounters are purely sex based. But shit, I've been kidding myself, thinking I don't need anyone in my life. Thinking sex is enough.

It's not. Not even close.

"You've gone quiet, little elf." Santa states as he uses a white cloth to clean up the mess he made over his rippling abs. "What's going on inside your head?"

I consider giving him the truth, but think better of it. I don't know this man. The game we are playing is about nothing more than sex. Emotions aren't welcome here.

But I need to answer him, so I go with a partial truth.

"I'm just feeling a little needy. That's all."

"How so?" he asks quickly, and I bite my lower lip before answering in a near whisper.

"I want to touch you."

The rumble that comes through the speakers isn't a growl of frustration or anger. It's a growl of arousal.

"I want to touch you, too." He rasps. "All in good time."

I nod, knowing he's not going to give me anything else, so I slip back into my robe.

"Do you like exhibitionism, little elf?" He asks, and my eyes widen, my mood perking up as I nod and shrug at the same time. "Do you like public sex where there's a big chance you'll get caught?"

I nod again. This time without the shrug.

He chuckles. "Good. Tomorrow, I want you to drive to the city. Wear the toy I got you, and the choker as well. Go to the La Trobe Street entrance at Melbourne Central by 12pm and wait for my call."

And just like that, I'm ready for today to be over so tomorrow can begin.

Santa

I've been watching my little elf service her clients for a few weeks now, but from the position of the camera, it doesn't show what exactly is going on very well. So asking her to wear a camera so I could get a better look worked well. I could see just about everything she could see.

I didn't enjoy watching her client, but I loved seeing my little elf's hands and fingers at work, stimulating the woman until she came undone. I can't fucking wait to have Aggie's hands on me.

Suggesting she go on webcam wasn't planned. I have meetings to attend, and emails to respond to, yet I wasn't ready to leave my little elf. Not until I watched her come.

During my time studying her through the cameras installed in her rental, I noticed that she occasionally goes online and does sessions, which is why I knew to send her to her laptop so I could see her better.

I have one monitor picking up the live feed from her choker, and another monitor linked up with her laptop, so it was weird when I agreed to go online with her, and I saw what my little elf saw.

My hard dick.

It does look pretty fucking enticing, if I do say so myself. And fuck, the way her eyes lit up, growing wider when her eyes studied my manhood, made me feel like beating my chest like an alpha gorilla.

Coming by my own hand is not the same as sinking inside the hot damp heat of a cunt, but hell, I'm willing to wait. I'm not done playing with my food yet. By the time I sink into my little elf, she will be quivering with need… and fear.

Chapter Six

Public Play

Agatha

Predicting traffic when you go into the city is virtually impossible. Even though I give myself extra time by leaving half an hour earlier than I needed to, I'm still late by the time I arrive at the rendezvous point.

There are people everywhere, and my eyes dart to man after man, wondering if my Santa is here. No one looks at me expectantly, or with any familiarity, and I worry that my tardiness means Santa has already left.

Then my phone rings.

"You're late." His voice is gruff and laced with annoyance through the phone.

"I'm sorry. The traffic was crazy."

"You should have allowed extra time. You will receive your punishment when you get home later today."

I could argue my case, but that may mean an extra punishment, and if it's anything like being deprived of the luxury of electricity again, I'm happy to avoid it.

"Yes, Santa." I pout, feeling a bit pissy that he's being all dominant and shit, even though that's his role. He was more playful yesterday during the cam session. I enjoyed that side of him.

"Check your bank account, please."

I frown at his words, but do as he asks, opening my banking app and logging in. Then my brows lift off my head all together.

Holy shit. There's a grand in there that wasn't there earlier. I press the phone back to my ear, about to protest, when his voice cuts me off before I can even speak.

"Go shopping. Buy whatever you want. I'll be watching."

He hangs up before I can ask how he got my bank account details, and I'm left baffled, staring at the phone for a moment before my head kicks in.

He'll be watching. Is he nearby, or is he watching through the camera embedded in the choker he insisted I wear again today?

I feel like I'll never know for sure if this man is in my vicinity or not, so I give up stewing on it, and do as he demanded. I go shopping.

I don't normally indulge in a lot of new clothes. I typically shop at opportunity shops most of the time, scoring some amazing finds, and I keep the purchase of new things to a minimum. I'm more likely to buy sex toys and lingerie with my money than new clothes.

By the time I've spent some money in a couple of stores, and a huge chunk in Mecca, I feel the soft vibrations of the toy deep inside me start up.

I can't hold back my grin, suddenly not feeling so alone in my shopping spree. I have no idea where my Santa is, but through this wireless toy deep inside me, we are connected.

I continue to shop, and each time I enter a new store, the vibrations get stronger. It works quickly to send heat prickling over my skin from head to toe, building pleasure as I try to keep a straight face.

I take my phone out of my pocket numerous times, checking to see if he's called or messaged, and basically having to talk myself down off the ledge and stop myself from calling him. That's a big no no.

When I take the phone out once again, it starts to ring in my hand, so I quickly answer it.

"What do you want, little elf?" His voice is calm and almost seductive and adds to the lubrication surrounding the toy inside me.

"What do you mean? You called me."

He chuckles. "Yes, because you keep checking the phone. Were you tempted to call me?"

"Yes." I say quietly, hoping it won't bother him.

"Why?"

"Because I need you." I admit, and he hums.

"And?"

"And I want to come." I whisper into the phone.

"No." He hangs up.

What?

No?

I stop walking, nearly causing the group of people behind me to crash into me. I mutter an apology and ignore their glares as they pass.

My eyes dart around me as hordes of people brush past in a hurry to get to their destinations. The centre of my chest aches as the reality of my lonely existence creeps in, and suddenly, I feel like crying.

Why is he being so mean to me?

And is he being mean, or am I just being precious?

Why the hell am I being so damn precious lately?

Fucking Christmas!

I huff and bite back my unshed tears before heading into another store. As I walk, my shoulders roll back, and I stand taller as anger rises inside me. I'm angry at myself, and I'm angry at my arsehole Santa for denying me a release.

As I move about the stores, the vibrations get stronger, and the brat in me kicks in, letting my defiance take over as I pick up a random article of clothing and head to the fitting rooms.

I ignore the shop assistant, beelining for the furthest fitting room, and lock myself in.

Hanging the top on the hook, I ignore it completely and glare at my reflection in the mirror, knowing if Santa is watching, he'll be able to see my face right now through the choker cam.

Then I flip the mirror off.

Bad move, but I was expecting retaliation, so I'm not surprised when the vibrations inside me increase tenfold.

I buckle forward, bracing my hand on the mirror as I hold in a moan, my lips sealing shut in the hopes it will help.

"Fuck you, Santa." I whisper, making sure my lips can be read in the mirror, and then I press my hand between my legs, leaning against the back wall of the cubicle so he can watch me pleasure myself.

When the phone starts ringing, I debate whether to let it ring out, but I'm weak, desperate, and my need to please this stranger controls me.

So I answer the call.

"Did I say you could touch yourself?" he hisses.

"No," I pant, glaring at my own reflection.

"Then why are you doing it?"

"Because I need to come," I pant quietly, again.

"No! You don't come until I allow you to." He snarls low, "Remove your hand and leave the store. Go across the street to the State Library and go inside. Find the La Trobe Reading room and the dome viewing balconies. Stand on one of the balconies that is quiet and watch the people below. Wait there for further instructions."

What the hell is he doing?

He hangs up before I can agree to anything, and in frustration, I bare my teeth at the mirror in a hiss that he can probably see but not hear.

I could probably ignore him and get myself off already, but I'm a sucker for his games.

I hurry out of Melbourne Central, making my way to the State Library, barging past people on the street, my mind only focused on one thing. Pleasing Santa.

Inside the State Library, I take a map, studying it for a moment, before going in search of the viewing balconies. It's an impressive dome-shaped room with six levels of viewing balconies. I make my way to the top where it's quieter, and find a vacant balcony. And then I wait.

As I stand there looking over the railing down at the reading room below, the pulsing toy inside me increases again, and my hands curl around the railing as I bite back a moan.

Then a warm body presses against my back.

I stiffen, readying myself to turn around, but firm hands gripping both of my shoulders keep me in place.

"Stay right there, little elf."

Shit.

It's him.

He's here, in the flesh, with his hands on me. Touching me.

I moan and relax back into him, feeling his hard bulge at my backside as his spicy scent wraps around me. I fight the urge to disobey him and turn so I can finally see him. Instead, I keep my eyes trained on the room below.

"Santa?"

"Yes, little elf. Is your pussy still aching?" The rasp of his voice against my ear has me ready to explode.

"Yes," I pant as my heart thrashes in wild excitement.

"How badly do you want to come?"

I moan and breathe, "So badly."

"Lift the front of your skirt."

Shit. I have to mentally stop myself from rushing this. I try to calm my pounding heart, taking in slower breaths. It doesn't help, so I quickly tug up the fabric of my skirt, bunching it in my hands.

"Whatever you do, *do not* take your eyes off the people below. Understand?"

I nod. "Yes."

The speed of the toy increases deep inside me, and I whimper right before his large warm hand reaches around and glides up the front of my thigh. I jolt under the sear of his hand, but melt into him when his strong body presses firmer against my back.

His hands and fingers move torturously slowly as they sear a path higher, and as soon as his fingers brush the soaking lace of my panties, I jerk, releasing a gasping moan.

"Don't come until I say." He breathes against my ear. "You are a tantra specialist after all. I know you can hold on to it."

I whimper again, but nod and he presses his fingers to my needy lace covered bud.

My breathing quickens as the thrill of this situation races my heart so fast that I fear it might explode. But I remember my tantra training and suck in slower breaths, taking control, and slowing it down as I let myself feel the pleasure.

"You smell so good." He mumbles against my ear. "And you *feel* even better."

I moan again as the friction of his fingers increases.

"I want to touch you." I whimper, desperate for him.

"No, little elf. Today isn't *that* day. Today *I* touch *you*."

I want to scream at his refusal, but the way he's touching between my legs, finally making contact with me, is something I've been longing for in the short time we have been playing this game. I almost fear that he's going to stop touching me at any moment and disappear.

The toy's intensity hasn't let up, and his friction over my clit is making it impossible to hold back what my body truly wants. He must sense this, because he brushes my blonde hair off my shoulder and presses his lips to my neck before rasping against my ear.

"Come now, beautiful."

I crash hard, slapping my hand over my mouth to muffle any sound as I explode, the force spraying into my panties and quickly seeping through to run down my legs and drip to the floor.

"Fuck, that's hot, Aggie."

My legs shake and turn to jelly, which he notices, tightening his grip on me to help hold me up as I sink back against him. His erection is straining hard against my back, and I desperately want to touch it, but I'm pretty sure I don't even know my own name right now. Moving to do anything is not a good idea.

As my hearing returns, I wonder if I was loud when I came. Did I catch anyone's attention? I glance over the railing, but all seems to be normal in the reading room below.

"Are you alright?" he asks, and I nod, too scared to speak yet. "I need to go, little elf. Do not, I repeat, do not turn to look at me, or go in search of me. I want you to remain here for another five minutes before leaving."

I nod even though my heart sinks a little. I don't want him to leave. I want him to stay.

"I need to hear you acknowledge it." He rasps quietly against my ear.

"Yes, Santa."

"I'll talk to you soon." He whispers, pressing his lips to my ear. He stays that way for a long beat, almost as if he doesn't want to leave me. Hell, I don't want him to leave me. I have no idea who this man is, but it's like my soul knows his soul, and they are yearning to connect and never part.

Which is just ridiculous.

Right?

Santa

Walking away from my little elf there in the library was harder than I thought it would be. Finally touching her. Feeling how soft she is almost made me cave and spin her around to face me. I don't think I've ever wanted something as much as I want to consume this woman.

I fucking yearn for her. But I can't have her yet. I need to see if she can survive this game.

She didn't see me following her through the shopping centre. There were so many people, making it easy to stay hidden. Hell, at one point she went into the jeans store, and I fucking went in, too. While she browsed the clothing on the female side of the store, I pretended to browse the male side.

It was risky getting so close to her, but fuck, I just couldn't help myself by pushing the boundaries a little.

Sending her to the State Library was always my plan. I wanted to see how publicly she'd let me have my way with her. She didn't even seem scared.

Nervous, but not scared.

And fuuuck she was so wet. When my fingers finally pressed against her panties, my dick jerked at how much she had already ruined the fabric from her arousal.

So I helped her completely destroy them.
And in time, I will completely destroy her.

Chapter Seven

Losing My Senses

Agatha

Tears began streaming from my eyes the moment Santa left me. I felt like we were in our own little cocoon on that balcony looking down over the readers, and the moment he stepped away from me, it burst, and so did my control.

I stay on the balcony for longer than five minutes, trying to calm myself down from the sobbing mess I'd become. I've never been clingy after sex. Quite the opposite, really. Yet now, a faceless man has me all worked up over something I don't even understand.

When I eventually leave the library, I give up on shopping and head back to my car, my eyes flicking to every male I pass, my mind wondering if he was my Santa.

On the drive back to Redfield Lake, I contemplate picking up Santa's phone and calling him. For what? I don't know. But instead, I pick up *my* phone, and call the one female friend I have that I should be keeping a distance from.

Rhys George. AKA, Kitten.

"To what do I owe the pleasure?" Rhys practically purrs after accepting my call.

"Hey Kitten. Just thought I'd check in with you. See how things are going."

Lies! I'm lonely and need a friend!!

"Oh, you know, I'm fan-fucking-tastic getting worshipped by my guys on the daily. Life's pretty sweet right now."

Kitten may have had a sex addiction and been the 'toy' for everyone to play with at the Vixen's Lodge Feast Nights, but things have turned out well for her. She found a way to have a relationship, and although it's not normal in the eyes of society, Rhys and her boyfriends care about each other so much, they don't care what other people think.

To say I'm jealous is an understatement.

What I'd give to have just *one* person want me that much.

"I'm glad they're treating you well," I say honestly. That poor kid deserves all the happiness life can bring. "How are you doing after the whole Master getting murdered thing?"

"Hmmm." She hums, taking a moment to choose her words. "I'm a little disappointed it wasn't me who butchered him in his hospital bed. I would have enjoyed seeing him take his last breath. But knowing he's gone from this world has made me look over my shoulder less lately."

"The world is a better place without him and his brand of toxic in it." I agree. "Are you really doing ok though? Like in all seriousness?"

Rhys is quiet for a beat before she responds, her normally playful tone now gone. "I have my struggles, but the guys are helping me with that. They are patient. Loving. They make me feel worth being loved."

My eyes well with tears as I hear the pain in her voice. For so long, she wore a mask of confidence to hide how she never felt good enough to be loved. She even tried to hide from herself. I'm so glad she doesn't have to live like that anymore.

"You *are* worth being loved, Rhys. So much." I don't normally call her by her real name. The few times we caught up outside the Feasts, we still referred to each other by our sex club names, so by using her real name, I hope she hears how true my words are.

"Thanks, Aggie." She says quietly. Almost a whisper.

"Can I ask you a serious question?" I ask, keeping my eyes focused on the road and the busy freeway traffic as I drive and try to see past the blur in my eyes.

"Of course, Foxy Moxie." She giggles, her playfulness returning, which is probably a coping mechanism for her.

"The time we spent together… Did you ever feel… forced? Or like you didn't really want to go *there* with me, but did it anyway because that was what was expected?"

"Fuck no." She blurts quickly. "Girl, you do remember who you're talking to, right? Most of the time I felt like I was the one forcing myself on others and they were too kind to refuse me."

I scoff. "No one ever felt like that with you, Kitten. Especially me. I just put your age to the back of my mind and pretended like it wasn't illegal as fuck. I'm sorry for that. I should have stopped it. You should never have been there."

"Mox! What are you talking about? Stop this nonsense." She scolds. "You know and I know that if it weren't for the Feast Nights, I would have gotten myself into trouble some other way, in a not so controlled environment. Hell, I'd probably be dead by now if I didn't have a place like that to be… me."

"Maybe," I say softly and Kitten sighs.

"Are you ok, Mox? You don't sound like yourself."

I swallow the lump that forms quickly in my throat and bat the tear off my cheek that escapes. "Yeah. Just been reflecting a lot lately. That's all."

"Do you need me to come for a visit? I can get Ty to sneak me to you." She giggles and I grin.

Ty is her fifth boyfriend, but he also used to be her sponsor at Vixen's Lodge. Kitten had blackmailed him to get her in to the exclusive club as a member, and I watched for a few years as he internally tortured himself over that decision.

Kitten didn't see what I saw. He hated her being there. Not because he didn't like her, but because he did. Way too much for a schoolteacher to like his student.

That part of their relationship had shocked me when I found out. I was angry that as a teacher he hadn't protected her, but then I realised I was just as complicit. Every adult in the club was.

Ty loves her, though. Fiercely.

He lives across the lake from me, and I often stare over at his house, wondering if Kitten is there with him.

"No, it's ok. I'm keeping busy with work and preparing for Christmas." I lie, and that's when she goes into a whole new conversation about what sexual presents she's going to give each one of her five boyfriends.

I let her ramble on for another half an hour, enjoying the light conversation and the way her energy and playfulness lightens my mood a little.

When I eventually arrive home, I slip the toy out and wash it, and remove the choker, placing it in my dresser drawer, before taking a long hot shower, my body sinking to the floor as I silently cry. Again.

At this point, I'm thinking perhaps it's time to visit a doctor. My emotions are crazy out of whack, and I can't remember the last Christmas that affected me quite like this. They've always been hard, but this is on a new level.

Before bed, I decide to try some self-love, and go to my toy drawer to find a willing participant. Only the drawer is empty. My vibrators are gone, and so too are the toys I have specifically put aside for my clients in the spare room.

That's when I remember Santa promised a punishment for arriving in the city late.

A laugh bursts from my mouth without warning as I nod to myself at what a good punishment it was.

Touché Santa.

I should congratulate him on his cunningness, but then it dawns on me that to get to my toys, he would have had to come inside my house, and I quickly turn anxious.

He can see me through cameras I can't seem to find. He knows intimate details about me, yet I know nothing about him. And now, I know for certain he has access to this house.

Am I safe? Is he really someone I can trust?

These are the things I stew over well into the early morning hours, and I struggle to determine how exactly I feel about it. Clearly, he knows I'm a sexual person, and if he's been watching me all this time, he would know my toys are a nightly routine for me. It's almost like a bedtime ritual which helps me to relax and have a better night's sleep.

Giving myself some self-pleasure is the only thing I can think of to turn my anxious feelings off and try to find some peace, so sleep will come. So without access to my toys, I use my fingers. It takes me a little longer than my vibrating toys would, but the buildup means I get an intense orgasm that leaves me both satisfied, yet hungry for more.

So, I do it again. Three times, all before 3am, which is when I receive a text from Santa.

Santa

Touch yourself again, and there will be consequences you don't like.

Fucker!

"Cock block!" I yell in my dark empty house, my voice bouncing off my bedroom walls. My sour face only lasts a minute though, because his simple message reminds me that even though I can't see him, I'm not alone. He's always watching.

I relax, sinking into my mattress with a small grin at that knowledge, and that's how I finally fall asleep.

Once the sun is up a few hours later, and I've dragged myself out of bed, I go about my normal routine. On Saturdays, I do groceries, so I do that, checking the phone Santa gave me every fifteen minutes as I eagerly wait for him to contact me.

When back at home, I try to meditate and do yoga, only to fail in the concentration department, and shift my attention to my cleaning chores, ignoring the fact that I check the phone every ten minutes.

The day is long and drags as I wait for him to make contact, and I'm about to get changed into a nice dress and hit up O'Connor's or the Red Room strip club to find myself something or someone to do, when I get a message around 9pm.

Santa
Go to your bedroom, take your clothes off and put the blindfold mask on. Then sit on your bed and wait for me. Don't move off the bed, no matter how long you have to wait.

My brows shoot up as I read over his message again.

A blindfold mask?

Leaping up off the couch, I dash to my room to find a mask on my bed. How the hell did that get there? I think over the last time I came into my bedroom, which was probably about an hour ago, and note that there wasn't anything I can recall on the bed then.

Has Santa been in here? And if he has, when? I didn't hear anything.

And what does he mean by *wait for him*? Is he going to call?

Anticipation has me moving instead of bothering to ask myself more questions I have no idea the answer to, and I strip out of my clothes, tossing them in the corner of the bedroom before going to the toilet to empty my bladder. Since he said I can't move off the bed no matter how long I have to wait, I get the feeling he's testing me, so there's no way I'm going in unprepared.

Once done, I dash through the house stark naked and grab a water bottle from the fridge before returning to my room. I toss the bottle on the bed and pick up the mask, slipping it down over my face, plunging me into darkness.

I'm not a fan of darkness, but it feels different with my eyes closed, so I keep them shut as I blindly feel in front of me, patting the blanket on my bed to help find my way. I crawl up on the mattress, my hand knocking into the cold bottle of water as I get myself comfy. I sit cross-legged in what I assume is the centre of the bed, and I wait.

And wait.

And wait.

At first, I try to count the minutes, but then my thoughts stray, and I completely lose track of where I'm at. If I had to guess, I've been waiting for over thirty minutes when my ears pick up a noise somewhere in my house.

Footsteps.

My heart thrashes wildly, knowing he's actually in my house. It's unnerving really, knowing he can get in here, which just raises more damn questions. And perhaps some red flags I'm not willing to acknowledge.

"You look positively delicious." His deep rasp startles me, making me jump, and he chuckles as my senses pick up that he's right in front of me. "Hold your hand out."

I do as he asks, holding out my hand and his fingers clasp it as he presses something squishy into my palm.

"Put them in your ears. Tonight's game is Sensory Deprivation."

My breath hitches with excitement, and I suck my lips in, trying to stop my expression from showing. I don't know why, but I don't want him to know how excited he's making me. I don't want to seem too willing. Too submissive. Too desperate.

As I close my palm, I squeeze the objects in it and realise they are earplugs.

I've done something similar before, but at the time, I already knew who I was doing it with. Nervous butterflies flutter in my tummy as I'm reminded that I don't even know who this man is. He's now inside my house, in my bedroom, and he wants to take my senses away from me.

I get that this could be dangerous. I won't be able to see him, or anything he uses. I won't be able to hear his approach or the sounds of things that might give me clues as to what he's going to do.

Still, the excited, curious cat in me inserts the earplugs.

He takes my hands, kissing them one at a time, then pulls me off the bed to stand. He lifts me in his arms and carries me and I inhale his spicy scent, which helps me to relax.

I have no idea where he is carrying me, but a moment later, the soft mattress of my bed is under my back, and he positions me the way he wants me on my bed.

I fear he might be able to hear my heart beating like a drum in my chest, but all worries of that are forgotten when he takes my arm and secures something around my wrist before doing the same to my other wrist. Once done, I feel the press of his lips against my forehead before my arms are quickly tugged taut, removing my ability to touch him.

My breath hitches in surprise, and I chew my bottom lip as my breathing deepens, a little fear seeping in as I feel him doing the same thing to each of my ankles. In the end, I'm left completely bound to my bed like a starfish, unable to see or hear, completely at his mercy. My only senses left are smell and taste.

The mattress dips on each side of my chest before I feel his warm breath hover over my lips. I wish I could see him right now. Look into his eyes, whatever colour they may be, but all I'm met with is darkness.

Something brushes over my lower lip. His thumb maybe. He parts my lips with it and then the unmistakable press of his lips is finally on mine.

My heart skyrockets as Santa kisses me for the very first time. I moan. I can feel it vibrate in my chest as he deepens the kiss and I give myself completely to this stranger. Our tongues meet and dance, getting familiar with each other, while his lips, which are softer than I imagined, meet mine in fevered urgency.

Before too long, he breaks the kiss, his lips trailing down the column of my neck before paying attention to my pebbled nipples. The heat of his mouth over my straining buds is intoxicating. I want my hands free so I can hold him there, but there's no need. He's in no hurry, taking his sweet time, getting to know them intimately.

I can't tell what noises I'm making, but I *can* tell I'm making some. I'm pretty sure they get louder as he travels down between my legs, and I feel his fingers glide over my seam before parting my lips wide and gliding the hot silk of his tongue up my centre.

I think I call out 'Santa', but for all I know, it could be a low groan. Either way, it doesn't matter, and I don't care if I sound ridiculous. Right now, he is everything, and I know that if he is a murderer, I'd happily die at his mercy.

His fingers join the party between my legs, sinking in to give me a good stretch. It's intoxicating to have him buried between my legs like this, my eyes and ears not able to join in, but my sense of feel is blooming like wildfire.

I know I'm not going to last much longer, so I give myself over to the pleasure, revelling in the feel of him touching me, eating me, and filling me with his digits.

The stretch is divine, and fuck, this man knows how to stimulate, sending me crashing over the edge before I even realise it's about to happen. My inner walls clamp and pulse around his fingers, and I can't tell if I squirt or not, maybe a little given the rush of heat between my legs, but his tongue doesn't let up, lashing at my nub over and over until a second wave hits, and I'm pretty sure I scream.

Slowly, he eases me down from my high. His fingers slipping free, and his tongue no longer lashing, but slowly lapping to clean me up.

I can feel beads of sweat over my skin, the air cooling me as he moves from between my legs and off the bed.

I instantly miss his presence, wondering what he's doing right now. Hell, he could have walked out and left me here, and I wouldn't be able to do anything about it.

"Santa?" I call, I think, still not able to hear a damn thing as I wait for some sort of sign that he's still here.

A hand touches my foot then, slowly travelling up my leg as I feel his weight climb on the bed, between my legs.

Is he going to fuck me now? Oh man, I really want him to fuck me now. I want his cock inside me, filling me, but I also wish I could see and hear him, too. I desperately want to see if I affect him the way he does me.

The familiar nudge of a dick between my legs tells me that this is it, and a moment later his thick girth eases inside me. My back arches as he fills me to the max, his arm coming around my back, holding me there as he starts to thrust.

"Yes." I think I cry out before his warm lips claim mine.

Something you don't get at most sex parties is kissing. It's a thing a lot of people have a rule about. Kissing being too personal and stuff, and I'm reminded why now.

It's not only personal, but feels more intimate than the dick sliding inside me. I can't actually remember the last time I've been thoroughly kissed like this. If ever.

Santa speeds up his pace before something vibrating gets pressed to my clit.

Fuck. He really does know all the moves to send a girl wild.

My hips buck, my pussy filled to the brim with his dick as the vibrations tease my nub and I explode quickly. Embarrassingly so.

He doesn't stop though, his dick slamming harder and harder inside me as he keeps the toy pressed to my nub. Unexplainable pleasure soars through me, something more than I've ever felt before. My whole body starts to tingle, sparks of numbness igniting over my flesh from head to toe.

With one last hard thrust, Santa stills over me, his hips jerking as he reaches his climax, and a few moments later, he collapses on top of me. His lips press to my ear, my neck, my cheek, my nose and then my lips.

The only word I can use to explain how I feel right now is worshipped.

He stays on top of me for a minute or two, his fingers stroking lazy circles on my shoulder before his weight slowly eases off me.

I miss him instantly, but he doesn't disappear completely this time. His hand touching my arm, leg, foot or tummy at all times, letting me know he's still there. Eventually, his fingers come to my ears, and he slips the earplugs free, and my hearing comes back loud and crisp.

"You taste as sweet as honey, little elf." He rasps against my lips, nipping them before sucking them into his mouth. "And that tight, hot cunt of yours feels like heaven." He kisses me again, hard and lustful, tongues clashing with more need before he pulls back.

Nipping at my lips again, Santa's kisses veer away and travel to my earlobe. "I'm sorry to do this, but I have to go."

"You do?"

Shit. Why do I sound so needy? I want to slap myself for being so pathetic.

"Yes. I wanted to stretch this out longer, but I received a call before. Duty calls, I'm afraid." He runs his thumb over my bottom lip, much like he did earlier. "Fuck, little elf. I could kiss these lips all night."

I moan, wishing my hands were free so I could touch him.

"I want to touch you." I whine, and he chuckles.

"Not tonight. But soon. I promise." He starts to untie my right foot, and I pout like a little bitch. "Don't forget your aftercare." He reminds me, moving to untie one hand, and then the other. "I'm going to leave now. I've left one ankle tied. You can take your mask off and untie it in five minutes. Ok?"

Damn it.

I nod, still pouting. "Ok."

He lifts my hand, placing a kiss on the back before I hear him walk away, leaving out the front door.

Part of me is tempted to get up now and run to the door to get a glimpse of who he is, but a bigger part of me doesn't want to ruin the mystery.

I realise I don't care what he looks like. Not when he feels so amazing and knows exactly how to take care of me.

Santa

I hadn't intended to fuck my little elf just yet. I wanted to save that part for the grand fucking finale. As much as my dick has been aching to have her, my main goal has been to make her bend to my will and torture her with pleasure.

The little minx is like a fucking siren. She had me in a trance tonight, my dick with a mind of its own as it sunk into her tight, hot heat.

And fuck. Those lips. Both sets tasted so fucking sweet. Both are as addictive as each other, and I found it hard to leave my little elf. I could have happily unleashed my monster on her right then and there.

But, lucky for her, that side of me will have to wait for a different day.

Chapter Eight

Guess What?

Agatha

For the first time in a long time, I sleep in on a Sunday. I'm not normally so lazy. I typically get up when the sun rises and do yoga on the deck before breakfast, yet this morning I was too happy staying in bed.

Yes, I was daydreaming about my Santa and how good he made me feel last night. He even came to me in my dreams, although he was still faceless, but his voice had the deep rasp to it that sends chills up my spine, and his touch kept me on the cusp of arousal all night.

When I crack open my eyes, the room is bright, filled with the summer sun streaming in through the windows, and I take a moment to glance around my small bedroom, trying to picture Santa here last night.

I remember then that he could be watching me via a hidden camera, so I throw the covers off me to reveal my naked body and I start running my hands down over my breasts, down my abs before I find my aching clit.

My lids fall shut as memories of Santa's touch swarm me, and I grind my hips up against my fingers to cause more friction. My other hand comes up to find my breasts, my fingers rolling and pinching my nipples as I work myself over, wishing like hell that Santa was here with me. Just the thought of him sends me over the edge, and I come hard, not squirting this time, but it's still magical and leaves me nearly legless.

The chime of my phone tells me I have a new message, and I slowly roll over, reaching for the bedside table to grab it.

Santa

It looks like you're having a good morning, my little elf.

I have the day off, so I will be there in an hour.

Make sure you are washed, dressed in something with easy access, and sitting on the couch by 11am wearing your mask.

Today we are spending the day together.

That last line sends a rush of butterflies right through my entire body, and I sit up abruptly, grinning.

Little Elf

Ok Santa.

I scramble out of bed to quickly shower and dress in a cute little mint green sundress before taking the mask to the couch. At 10:59am, I put the mask on.

At 11am, the front door clicks open, and just like last night, my heart races with anticipation.

"Hello again, my little elf. You look stunning."

I grin. "You can hardly see my face."

"True, but I know what it looks like under that mask. And your body is just as stunning as your smile."

I can't help it. I beam.

The couch dips next to me, and I shift in my seat, tilting my body towards where I think he is.

"How are you feeling after last night?"

I smile. "Wonderful."

"Were you dreaming of me? Is that why you needed to pleasure yourself this morning?"

I can feel my cheeks flush red, but I push down my nerves. "Yes. I can't seem to get you out of my head. Well... Your voice, and lips, and... well, you know what I mean."

"Yes. I do." He chuckles. "So, today's game is a guessing game. We will play two rounds. One before lunch, and one after lunch. Does that sound ok with you?"

"Yes, Santa."

He lifts my hand in his before I feel the press of his lips to the back of it. I instantly feel my cheeks burn again, and damn, I feel like a teenager.

"Let's move to the dining table." He suggests, his deep voice fanning warm breath against my ear before he tugs me to stand. I feel awkward trying to move without the use of my eyes, but his hands stay on me as he leads me to the dining table, helping me to sit down in one of the chairs.

"Stay right here. I need to grab a few things."

"Ok." I say breathlessly, feeling his warm touch disappear. My ears pick up his movement in my kitchen, and my fingers twitch to tug my mask free and reveal his identity.

"Sit back and relax, little elf." His deep rasp causes me to jump, not realising he is as close as he is.

Nodding, I relax back in the chair, dropping my shoulders to help ease the building tension inside me. My ears pick up a few sounds. It sounds like he is placing items on the surface of the table before I hear the scrape of another chair. At first, I think he must be taking a seat too, but then the press of his denim clad knee sliding between mine tells me he is still standing.

"Open your mouth." His voice is quiet, but no less demanding, so I do as he asks. "Stick out your greedy little tongue."

Again, I do as he commands while my heart just about breaks my rib cage, it's beating so hard.

"Taste this and tell me what it is. Think carefully before answering, because a wrong answer will mean a punishment."

My brows shoot up in surprise, and then I pout.

This doesn't seem very fair, but his chuckle keeps me compliant, and I wait for him to give me a taste. The flavour of salt bursts my tastebuds to life as what I can only imagine is a potato chip is placed on my tongue. I close my lips, sucking off the salt before crunching on the chip. Enjoying the texture and flavour.

"Potato chip," I say, licking my lips after swallowing the chip.

"Good girl. Let's try another one." He rasps, sounding pleased. "Open."

Again, I open my mouth, sticking out my tongue. The moment the cool, wet, sour food is placed on my tongue, I cringe, the citrus of a lemon turning my expression into a cringe.

"Lemon," I balk, darting my tongue out to spit it free. It falls to my lap, and Santa chuckles, low and deep and panty-meltingly hot.

"You don't like that one, little elf?"

"Ew. No." I shake my head, wishing I could have a drink to wash away the sourness.

Santa chuckles again. "Fair enough. Let's try another one. Open."

I smirk before obeying. Parting my lips and sticking out my tongue. Something cold is placed on it, and I draw it in my mouth. Running my tongue along it. It tastes familiar, so I bite down, feeling the crunch before the sweeter flavour explodes on my taste buds.

"Red capsicum." I rasp, enjoying the flavour.

"Good girl. You're good at this."

I grin. "I like things in my mouth."

"Hmmm. I bet you do." He chuckles, and I feel his legs shifting against mine again. "Open."

This time the unmistakable taste of mayonnaise hits me, and I swallow it down quickly. "Mayonnaise."

"Well done. Let's see if this one fools you."

I can tell he wants me to slip up so he can punish me, and shit, I find myself wanting his punishment just as bad even though I may not like it, which makes no damn sense, so when I taste Coca-Cola drip into my mouth, I answer quickly, deliberately saying the wrong thing.

"Pepsi."

He growls, and a moment later, his hands fist in the top of my dress before it's forcefully ripped down the front. I gasp at the loud tearing sound, and the way my tits spill free as the cooling of the air conditioner pebbles my nipples.

"That was Coca-Cola, little elf. Why do I get the feeling you deliberately said the wrong thing?"

"I don't know," I lie, my chest rising and falling with my excitement.

"Hmmm. Do you want me to punish you, little elf? Be honest now."

I lick my lips before answering. "Maybe."

He growls again. "Open."

I instantly recognise the smooth round surface of the cherry before sinking my teeth in for the flavour to ooze out over my tongue. I bite and chew around the pit before sticking my tongue back out with the pit on it, and let it fall into my lap.

"Cherry." I grin and again, he chuckles.

This goes on and on.

I taste the sweetness of whipped cream, the tang of mustard. Then I come across something I can't figure out, and my panties are ripped from my body when I answer incorrectly.

He doesn't stop, though. More and more flavours fill my mouth, but now as he feeds me, he tweaks my nipples, or flicks his tongue over my breasts, cleaning up a trail of strawberry syrup and honey that spills free.

"Little elf. You are so incredibly sexy when you eat." Santa rasps before nipping my lips. His voice is filled with lust, and it sends electrical currents to my clit.

Every so often, I hear him gasp a little, or grunt, and my mind conjures images of him standing before me with his hand wrapped around his cock. The thought that he could be getting himself off while he feeds me sends heat washing over my body from head to toe and I begin to pant with anticipation of something I have no idea is actually happening.

"Open." He grunts, almost as if he's in pain, and I open, desperate for what he has to give, sticking my tongue out. Then I hear a strangled type of moan, and a moment later warm salty goodness squirts onto my tongue and I leave it out, leaning forward as a moan rumbles in my chest and my mouth begins to fill.

I swallow and cry out. "More." And more of his seed comes. "More," I cry again, and the silk of his tip presses to my tongue. I lick over it, the tip of my tongue pressing into his slit before I close my mouth around his girth and suck.

"Fuck, Aggie." He groans, his hand coming to the back of my head as he fists my hair.

I love it when he calls me Aggie, and not little elf. It feels more personal, and I wonder if he realises he did it.

"My turn." His cock pulls from my mouth, and I whimper, nearly tumbling off the chair as I lean forward in search of it.

His large hands come to my knees, spreading them wide before he tugs me forward in the chair a little. I fall back, my hands whipping out to the base of the seat to steady myself, and before I know what's going on, I feel the silk of his tongue glide up between my folds.

I cry out, my head lolling back as I spread my legs wider, giving him full access to my pussy. He laps at me like a man starved, his tongue flicking my needy bud before diving as far as it can reach inside me.

I'm helpless not to grind up to meet his mouth, desperate to swallow him whole. Without thinking, my hand reaches forward, my fingers sinking into thick silky hair, and I grip it tight, holding him captive in between my legs.

A low growl rumbles from Santa, and I almost expect him to pull back and scold me for touching him, but his hands grip my thighs tighter, and he picks up his pace, eating my pussy like it's a delectable dessert that he needs to devour.

"Yes." I pant. "Just like that." I grind harder against his face, feeling the scratch of longish stubble from his jaw.

My pleasure builds quickly, and before I can ease it back to make this last longer, I explode, both hands clinging to his head as I mash myself against his face.

"Oh. My. God." I pant as I start to come down and my body falls lax.

I release his head slowly, revelling in the way his chuckle teases my sensitivity, and he kisses a trail up my front, over my breasts before claiming my lips. It's a searing kiss, and I taste myself on his tongue, wringing yet another moan from me.

"Fuck, Aggie." He pants as he nibbles on my lips. "I can't seem to get enough of you."

I feel his forehead press against mine, and the urge to pull my mask free is almost too overwhelming. The game we are playing is fun, but I'm desperate to know who this man is. I'm scared that once the game is over, he will disappear, and I'll never know who it was that took me to the place I've been longing to reach for so long.

"I want to see you." I whisper, letting my emotions show a little.

"Not yet." He pulls back from my forehead, and I worry I've said something wrong. Is he going to leave now? He said we were spending the day together, but has he changed his mind now?

"Am I ever going to get to see you?" I push a little more because I can't help myself.

"If you're a good girl." His breath flutters over my ear as he whispers his reply, and then he's gone, stepping away from me.

My fear that he is going to leave is quickly dashed as I hear him cleaning up before coming back to me and pulling me to stand. He tugs my torn dress all the way free, leaving me to stand completely naked before him.

"Let's make some lunch." He takes my hand, leading me carefully through my house to the kitchen where he presses his bare chest and jean clad hips against my back, and guides my hands from behind to help me blindly make a sandwich.

As we work together, he whispers in my ear, instructing me on what we are about to do, and I find myself relaxing and giggling like a giddy schoolgirl through most of the process. When the food is made, he leads me to the couch, where he slowly feeds me the sandwich, and he lets me blindly feed him his.

I know I'm making a mess of things, but he doesn't seem to mind, his warm chuckle making me feel at ease. He's letting me touch him now, which is new. Sure, I gripped his head before, but now, as I reach out, I cup his stubbled jawline to help guide me to his mouth. When the tips of my fingers move up to his cheeks and forehead, they are met with soft, smooth skin that hints of a well-groomed man.

I briefly worry that he is well groomed because he is taken care of by a girlfriend or wife.

The thought makes my heart sink.

"Santa?" I ask, biting my lips in worry.

"Yes, little elf."

"Can I please ask you a question?"

He's quiet for a beat, and I brace myself for a new punishment, but it never comes.

"One question." His voice is calm. Not angry, but firm.

"Are you married? Or in a relationship of some sort with another woman... or man."

He chuckles. "Definitely no man relationship going on."

I release a small smile.

"And no Aggie. I'm not married or in a relationship with another woman."

I'm sure he can see how I visibly relax at hearing that news. I don't know why I'm even affected by it at all. This is just a game we are playing. A sex game. Nothing more. I know that, yet somehow, my heart is grasping for more from this man. Which is ridiculous right? I don't know him. How can I even consider something more with someone I don't know and have never seen?

Again, I put my emotional rollercoaster of feelings down to it being Christmas. It's the most obvious conclusion. It has to be. I'm not normally this needy and emotional.

Santa cleans up our lunch, and I sit back and relax, still completely naked, while I wait patiently for him to return to my side. After a few minutes, soft music meets my ears before I hear Santa's feet on the timber floors as he returns to me on the couch.

"Time for round two, little elf."

My heart races at his words, and when I feel his hand slip into mine, I let him tug me up to stand and lead me somewhere else. My arse falls to my bed when Santa gives me a little nudge, and he presses his hand to my chest, easing me back onto the mattress.

Just like last night, my wrists and ankles are bound as I'm spread wide for him.

"We played 'guess the taste' earlier. Now you need to guess what is penetrating you."

My brows shoot high as a gasp escapes me when his words sink in, and heat instantly pools between my legs.

"I see you like the idea of that." Santa chuckles. "It's why you're perfect for my games, little elf."

I don't have a second to respond before I feel something cold nudging at my entrance.

"Tell me what this is."

Slowly, the object eases inside me, and I relax, welcoming it. It's not as thick as my Santa is, but it's long, and still cold, so it must have come from my fridge.

"Are you fucking me with food?" I ask, even as I feel arousal flutter deep inside me.

"Yes. What food is it, little elf?" He slides it slowly out and eases it back in.

"Can I have a clue?" I pant before biting my lip at how good it feels.

"No." He growls. "Now what is it?"

"I don't know, but it feels good." I admit as my hips rise off the mattress to meet the thrusts. Then he pulls it free.

"Open your mouth."

I do as I'm told before the object meets my tongue, and all I can taste is myself.

"Bite it."

My brows shoot up in surprise, but I do it, letting my teeth sink into it as I take a bite. It's hard and breaks off in my mouth with a crunch, and then I grin.

"Carrot."

"Atta girl."

I moan at his praise, and he chuckles, returning the carrot between my legs to ease inside me again.

"Fuck the carrot for me, Aggie." He rasps, so I do, rolling my hips and letting the vegetable slide against my internal nerve endings.

I do this over and over, letting my pleasure build before he eases it back out.

"New object. What is it?"

Another object presses to my opening, and I feel what I think is some sort of rubber coating on it. It slides in easily enough, and I have to assume my Santa covered it in lube. It's thicker at the end that enters me first, giving me a nice stretch.

Moaning, I shake my head. "I have no idea."

He chuckles. "This game is a little harder than the last one, isn't it?"

"Yes." I pant, rolling my hips as he slides it nearly all the way out before pressing it back in.

"I guess I can give you a few clues." He presses his lips to the inside of my thigh as he steadily fucks me with the unknown object. "It's not food."

A laugh bursts free, and I bite my lower lip before responding. "That doesn't really narrow it down much."

He chuckles. "Fine. You would find it in a toolbox."

Fuck. My insides clench at the thought of a tool inside me right now. "Please tell me it's clean." I pant.

"Of course, little elf. It's brand new and thoroughly sterilised."

I nod, focusing on it. It must be the handle of something.

"A screwdriver?"

"No." He drives it deeper this time, showing me just how long it is.

"A h-hammer." I stutter through a pant, and he chuckles.

"Good girl."

Jesus. He's fucking me with a hammer. The handle of one, anyway. And why the hell does that make more heat pool from my already slick opening?

"You like that? Being fucked by something that isn't a body part."

"Yes." I pant.

"Fuck. I can't hang back anymore." He rasps, clearly affected by my arousal. "You want to come, beautiful?"

"Y-yes." I pant and he fucks me with the hammer harder and faster.

"Good."

The familiar buzzing noise of a sex toy meets my ears, and a moment later it presses to my clit. I don't even last thirty seconds. The thick handle of the hammer and vibrating toy skyrocket me over the edge.

I feel the gush of spray burst from me, and as soon as it's over, my pussy is empty and throbbing as Santa's heavy weight crawls up my body. And up. And up.

"Open your mouth." He demands and I do so as I feel his thighs press against the sides of my bare tits. The press of his cock nudges my lips further apart, and he eases himself inside me. I can picture him bracing himself at the head of my bed as he starts to fuck my mouth. I imagine him looking down his body at me, watching his dick disappear inside my mouth that is stretched painfully wide.

And fuck, I love it.

First, he moves slowly, my tongue pressing against his shaft as he eases in and out, but he quickly loses his control, his thrusts more demanding as he presses impossibly further almost like he's testing me to see how I'll react when he causes me to gag.

He moans when I do, and it fuels me on as I try to breathe through my nose, wanting him to dominate my mouth completely. He doesn't disappoint, his length breaching my throat as I nearly choke. As he fucks my mouth with vigour, my body bounces around on the mattress, and the feel of him unleashing his desires on me has me utterly consumed.

Santa's addictive assault doesn't last too long, and before I know it, I'm swallowing down his offering, desperate for more.

Santa

The sight of my cock disappearing in my little elf's mouth was intoxicating! It felt fucking amazing having her lips wrapped around it. The silk of her tongue pressing against it, gliding over my sensitive flesh.

With a hunger to push her boundaries, I eased myself in further, pressing into her throat to see if she'd accept me.

Her body jerked at my invasion, and as she gagged, I fucking moaned. Fuck, I felt my dick grow thicker from that gagging sound alone, and the fact that she couldn't breathe stirred the monster in me.

It's getting harder and harder to hold back. To keep my monster at bay and not give into it and just break her now.

I can be a patient man when I want to be, though. Lucky for my little elf. She has a little time left before I change her world forever.

Chapter Nine

Party Pooper

Agatha

Waking on Monday morning, I knew without any doubt that I'd have to cancel tonight's sex party. Anticipation of potentially having Santa here was what made me drag my feet until this morning, but knowing he's been watching me and the parties for so long breaches my agreement with my guests. It's meant to be secret, and a man whose identity I don't know has witnessed way too much. So, I make the calls I need to and cancel, explaining that I have a surprise guest staying with me and I will notify everyone of a new location in the coming weeks.

My other realisation, which I desperately wanted to ignore, but know I can't, is that I'll probably have to move to a new rental sooner rather than later.

Part of me likes that this man is watching me, because that's the part of me that is a little unhinged. But the other part of me knows that my safety and anonymity are at risk in this house, which clearly has security issues. For someone lying low, it's not good that I have eyes on everything I do, especially with the Vixen's Lodge scandal very fresh in the public eye.

Since it's only a few days until Christmas, I know it will be impossible to find a new place to relocate to, so for now, I will have to stay put.

My day with Santa yesterday was something else. I enjoyed his company, even though we didn't really discuss anything personal. I liked having him here and enjoyed that he didn't have to run off.

After fucking my mouth with his thick girth and coming down my throat, he released my wrists and one ankle again, and then slid onto the bed with me, pulling me into his naked side while stroking my hair.

I fell asleep, which was nice, but when I woke, I was bummed because he was gone, and all that was left was a note.

Little Elf
You have pleased me immensely.
I didn't want to leave you,
but staying isn't part
of the game.
I will be in touch tomorrow.
In the meantime,
remember your aftercare.
Xx Santa

I love the letter, but also hate it. The part about '*staying isn't part of the game*' is what I hate. It's a reminder that this isn't serious. That there is an expiration date to this arrangement, which is fast approaching.

I don't hear from him all day. Once again, I have the urge to pick up the phone and dial his number. Last time I did that, I didn't like the punishment, and I'm also scared the punishment might be to break off our arrangement, so I keep myself busy by doing some online shopping, and a top-to-bottom clean of my rental.

While cooking myself some dinner, I bake a batch of Christmas cookies, which is the only tradition I have, ready in time for Christmas Eve tomorrow.

At around 7:45pm, my Santa phone rings, and I scramble to answer it, not concerned that I'll get punished if I'm not fast enough, but concerned if I don't answer it, I may never hear his voice again.

"Where are your guests?"

His tone is curt, and not at all playful, which is why it takes me a moment to comprehend what he means.

"I cancelled tonight's party. No one is coming."

"You did what?!" His voice booms through the phone in anger, and my heart sinks.

"I thought you would have heard the phone calls I made this morning cancelling the party since you sit around all day watching me." I snap, letting my anger show.

"I work, Agatha. I don't have time to sit around all day." He snaps back and I flinch. "Why did you cancel the party?"

I consider hanging up because his snarky mood is pissing me off, but I don't, because also, I'm needy.

“I seem to be having some security issues. I can’t very well lie to my guests and tell them they aren’t being watched. Possibly recorded.”

He’s silent.

“As fun as this is, Santa. I have agreements to uphold, and your cameras are a huge breach. You really have no one but yourself to blame.”

Fuck. I’m playing with fire. I know he needs to hear what I’m saying, but I also don’t know how he will react since I don’t know more than how good it is to have his cock fill me.

“Get your mask on now!” He booms even louder down the line, and instead of complying, I hang up, defying him.

When my phone rings again, I don’t answer it, my chest heaving with my own frustration, but also worry because I’ve disappointed him. I want to please him, but I can’t put others' personal lives at risk just so I can get a bit of dick.

Suddenly, the lights go out.

I leap up from the couch as a squeal escapes me, my eyes darting around frantically before my phone rings again, shrilling loud in the silence.

I let it ring five times before I finally answer it with trembling hands.

“Don’t test me, Agatha.” He growls. “Put the blindfold mask on now!”

“Why?” I snap and he hisses.

“Because I’m going to come in there and punish you.”

Fuck.

My heart flips with excitement and my pussy clenches in anticipation. What the fuck is wrong with me? He is trying to control me. Practically threatening me. Hell, what's to say he won't get violent?

Even though I know these things, my mouth still parts and words still slip free.

"Fine."

He hangs up immediately, and I use the phone torch to find the mask in my bedroom before moving to the couch and slipping the mask on. I'm still pissy at him, feeling the need to be defiant when I hear the front door open.

My heart races even more, blood pulsing past my ears as his footsteps near. Then I reach up and tear my mask off. My eyes widen as they adjust to the suffocating darkness inside my house, until I can make out the dark silhouette of a man standing before me, his face covered in a black ski mask.

"Put it back on!" He roars, and I squeak in fear, leaping up off the couch and bolting for my room. His feet thunder behind me, and he catches me easily, tackling me face first into my mattress, his powerful hands securing my wrists behind my back until he manages to tie them with something. I scream, but it's muffled in my blankets, and I thrash, trying to buck him off. As soon as he has my hands tied, the mask gets dragged back over my head, and what little I could see in the dark turns to pitch black.

His rough hands roll me over, and I pant in frustration.

"What the fuck, Aggie?"

It pisses me off the way he uses my name, like we know each other.

I don't know who he is. I know nothing about him other than he's not in a relationship. Or so he says anyway. He could be a big fat liar for all I know.

"What has gotten into you?"

"You pissed me off. I'll submit to you when we are playing bedroom games, but don't think you have any control over my business life. I have no fucking idea who you are. You are basically stalking me, who knows for how long, and you expect me to still invite people into my home to unknowingly expose themselves to you, and whoever else watches what you catch on camera?"

"No one sees into this house but me." He hisses.

"So you say. But I don't know you. I wouldn't be able to spot you in a lineup, or even know your name to stalk you on Facebook. I will play your game, but I won't risk my guests."

He remains quiet for a few beats before speaking again.

"Fine. But you're still getting punished for being a brat."

He drags me off the bed and I slip and fall with a thud to the floor, struggling to find balance with my hands tied behind my back. His firm hands wrap around my upper arms as he manoeuvres me on the floor, pressing me back against the bed, and a moment later, the hot silk of his dick nudges my lips.

"Open. I'm going to fuck your mouth. And I won't be gentle."

Christ.

Heat pools between my legs at his words, obviously not getting the memo that this is a punishment, and I open my mouth wide to accommodate his girth, giving in way too easily.

He was telling the truth when he said he was going to fuck my mouth. That's exactly what he does.

From his first brutal thrust, I gag forcefully, my eyes instantly watering. I whimper around his thick shaft, the sound muffled as he pounds into my throat. I have little time to prepare for each thrust, and gag numerous times, his cock invading my throat, only letting me breathe occasionally as he punishes my mouth.

It's more brutal than yesterday, and done with a fierceness I'm not unfamiliar with. Many guys at sex parties like to fuck mouths this way. It's an ultimate domination. And because I'm a little sex twisted, by the time he's choking me with his cum, I'm weeping from my core, even as I tremble with fear that perhaps I don't know this man after all.

Once he's done, he leaves me for a few minutes, panting and gasping to fill my lungs with oxygen again, my body feeling weak from trying to hold strong.

I can hear Santa moving around my house, taking his time to do whatever the hell it is he's doing before he returns to me.

"Up." He demands, his voice hard but not filled with so much anger now.

I struggle to my feet, given my lack of hands to help me up. My trembling limbs not helping. Santa's large hand wraps around my upper arm, and he leads me somewhere not too far before attaching some sort of cuff to each of my wrists still bound behind my back.

Once they are secure, he undoes the binding around my wrists before holding each arm up above my head and attaching the cuff to something. Then he cuffs my ankles before they are pushed apart with the familiar click of a spreader bar, forcing my stance awkwardly wide.

"Would you like to come, my little elf?"

His deep voice startles me in the silence, and I jerk before nodding quickly.

"Y-yes."

"Why are you shaking?" He snaps, and I flinch a little.

Heat pricks the back of my eyes as my emotions battle to be set free, and I bite my lower lip, shaking my head.

"Aggie." His voice is softer this time, the harsh tone from moments ago now gone. "You can tell me to stop, and I will."

Shit. Can I? I'm not sure if he's just playing with me or not.

I'm struggling to understand the emotional chaos whipping through my brain. I like brutal hard-core fucking. It's not unfamiliar to me, so why does what he did make me want to cry?

The other question is, do I want him to stop?

I should want him to stop. I shouldn't want to let a stranger do these things to me.

Yet I do want it. I want all of it. Even if it hurts my body and my heart.

It's confusing. I like being dominated in the bedroom, but not in my everyday life. His attempt to control that part of me should have me running for the hills. So why am I staying? Why am I putting myself through this with the sure possibility that I could get hurt? Will get hurt?

My bottom lip trembles, and I suck in a deep breath as I try to get my emotions under control.

"Shit." He murmurs quietly, his hands moving to my wrist to undo the cuff.

"No." I blurt and his hands still. "Don't undo it. Don't stop."

I feel his hand fall away, and for a long beat, everything is quiet. Then, his warm fingers wipe over my cheeks, and I realise a tear must have escaped past the mask.

"Are you scared of me, little elf?"

I don't answer him.

"You should be." He whispers impossibly close to me. "You're right with what you said earlier. You don't know me. I could be anyone. So why would you let me do this to you? Why don't you want me to stop?"

"We need to finish the game." I whisper, hoping it's enough.

"You realise tonight's game is punishing you for being a brat, right?" He deadpans.

"Yes." I nod, and his fingers grip my chin roughly.

"You're at my mercy right now. I could do *anything* to you, and you wouldn't be able to stop me."

"Y-yes. I know." Fuck, why won't my body stop trembling?

"Why would you let me do that?" He growls, and I'd shrug if my arms weren't tied above my head.

"I-I don't know."

He shoves my chin away, and a moment later his hand slaps my right arse cheek hard. I cry out, feeling the sting of his palm before I feel him move in front of me again, his hands coming up to caress my tits.

"You *don't* know why you would let a complete stranger have their way with you?" His teeth sink into my nipple, just hard enough to cause a bite of pain, but also a ton of pleasure.

"No." I cry out, the tremble in my voice disappearing as lust begins to consume me.

"What if I call a friend to join us? Another person you *don't* know. Would you like that?"

My heart stutters at the thought, and I shake my head. "No."

"Why? You let multiple guys fuck you at the parties you go to. Girls too. Why wouldn't you like it if I invited someone to join us?"

I shake my head, knowing the answer, but not wanting to admit to it.

He runs his hands down over the curve of my hips before searing a path to my weeping core, where he begins to circle my clit.

"Why, Agatha?"

Again, I shake my head, and he hisses before sinking three fingers deep inside me while this thumb plays my clit like the strings of an instrument. His curling digits work at the sacred spot inside me, building pleasure quickly in combination with his thumb, sending a flush of heat over my skin. Then he stops, pulling his hand away.

"Why, little elf?"

When I clamp my mouth shut, the bite of cold fluid jars me as it's poured over my chest. Then he inserts his fingers again and fucks me with them, slow and soft, curling and stretching, building me back up until I'm sure I'm going to explode.

That's when he backs off.

I grin as I realise what he's doing. "I'm the queen of edging, Santa." I pant and he clucks.

"Is that so?"

"Yes." I nod.

"Then let's see how long we can drag this out. But just so you know, the safe word is answering my question."

Fuck.

He's too damn smart for his own good.

Sinking his fingers back in, he works me over, his lips trailing over the sensitive flesh on my neck, ears, and breasts, dragging it out for what seems like hours but is probably only minutes.

"Tell me why, Aggie. Why would you let me do this to you and not someone else?"

I shake my head vigorously, my emotions building with my pleasure as my body writhes, covered in sweat and filled with frustration as I try to beat him at his own game.

"Why me?" He whispers in my ear, and I whimper and beg.

"Please, Santa."

He chuckles. "Do you want to come, little elf?"

"Yes."

"Are you going to be disobedient again?"

Since tomorrow is the last day of this game, I figure I can handle that part. It's the other part I'm struggling with. The part where this ends.

"No, Santa. I'll be good." I rasp before begging. "Please."

"All you have to do," he says against my lips this time, "is tell me why you would let me do this. Say it, and I'll let you come."

Hot tears burst free as my punishment becomes unbearable.

"Because I only want you."

"Atta girl," he says before falling to his knees and replacing his thumb with his tongue.

I crash hard, like a bolt of lightning ripping through me and consuming me for a long, thrashing beat. Ripples of ecstasy hum through my body over and over, and when I finally come down from my high, my legs give out, leaving me to hang from my arms, wherever it is I am.

"This isn't over, little elf." Santa's rasp is next to my ear as he leans down to me. "I'm furious at your display of disobedience. And even more angry that you refused to answer my question for so long. When I ask you something, you answer, always, with the absolute truth." He moves away, his heat instantly vanishing. "Stand up."

I plant my feet on the floor, forcing my trembling legs to obey. As soon as I'm standing, he releases my wrist cuffs, and I nearly fall to the floor as my legs fight to keep me upright in the awkward position from the spreader bar.

Then he leaves, his footsteps fading as he lets himself out, slamming the door without another word.

Santa

I'm fucking furious. Not about her cancelling the party. That was a test. But her attitude and disobedience, combined with her lack of self-respect, has me fucking fuming.

Agatha Fiera better be fucking prepared, because if she isn't, she may not survive our last game.

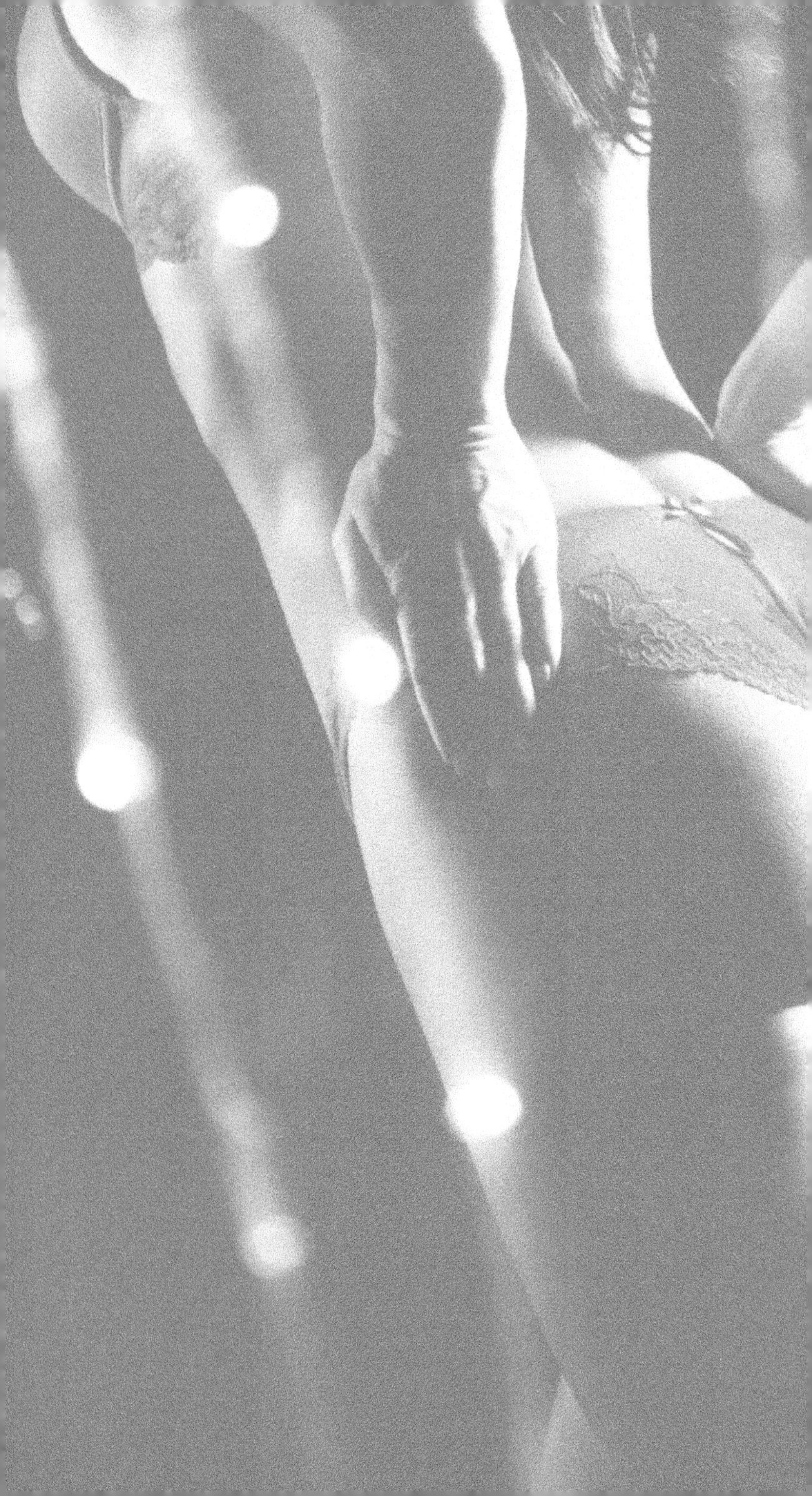

CHAPTER TEN

RUN!

Agatha

I'm at war with myself. On one hand, I'm still angry at Santa or whoever the fuck he is for the way he treated me last night. First, he assumed he had a right to control my sex party side hustle. Then he punished me, which, yes, I guess was called for, but then forced me to admit something I didn't want him to know. Then he said, *'When I ask you something, you answer, always, with the absolute truth.'*

What a fucking hypocrite. He knows so damn much about me and still I know jack shit about him. He expects me to tell him the truth, yet doesn't give me anything in return.

My head is messed up about this guy. Like crazily so. I should hate him for his behaviour, yet my core clenches with need every time I think about the punishment he dealt me. Even though it was brutal, I was totally there for it, loving the experience.

But then, I'm angry that he was so cold towards me, especially when he released my wrists and left me to fend for myself.

But stupidly, I miss him, even though my power is still out and there's still a huge fucking lock on my power box. Even so, my patheticness wins over as I continually check my phone every five minutes to see if he's called or sent a message.

Like seriously. I think I need my head checked.

Since today is Christmas Eve, I drive into town and pick up the ham I ordered from the butcher, get some fresh veggies and stock up on snacks for the next few days.

Christmas was only fun when I was a kid until my parents overdid their alcohol consumption. Now, I don't even know where my mum and sister are.

I know where my dad is, though. I'm happy I'm not anywhere near him.

Since I don't have anyone to spend Christmas with, I tend to celebrate alone. Or perhaps wallow alone is a better term.

I'm used to it. It's been that way for over ten years. It's just been me and my TV and the batch of Christmas cookies I bake.

I never get a Christmas tree, but today I stopped by the florist and picked up a huge flower arrangement which has a little battery-operated star in it. It's the first time I've brought any sort of Christmas decoration. The simplicity of it is enough. It's perfect.

As the sun goes down and my little rental plunges into darkness, I sit on the floor by the open glass doors that lead onto my deck, with my new flower arrangement next to me, and flick the little star light on. A faint warm glow oozes from it, doing little for seeing anything, but at least it looks pretty.

It's pretty here by the lake. I'd love to have enough money to buy this house. Well, I used to think that, but I'm not so sure anymore, what with the whole Big Brother is watching vibe. Then again, knowing my Santa is watching, whoever he is, kind of makes me feel less alone.

At 10pm, I still haven't heard from Santa, and I begin to feel like a caged animal, so I grab the phone and a candle and leave the dark house, strolling down the grassy hill to the jetty that sits out over the lake. With my feet dangling over the side into the water, I lay back on the weathering timber and look up at the stars, letting the beauty of the earth fill me with positive energy.

I'd lived such a calming routine life before I moved here. Before the Vixen's Lodge scandal. Now, I'm so on edge, teetering with fear of being exposed for my sinful ways, and fear of not experiencing such sin again. It's why I continued the sex parties, even though I was putting my location at risk. Even so, I haven't found the true peace I felt before. All the meditation and yoga in the world hasn't been able to get me back to that place. Although, sometimes when I'm subbing for my Santa, I feel more at one with myself than I have in a long time.

By 11pm, I figure the silence from the phone is an obvious message that Santa has bowed out of our game. After all, in one hour, our arrangement is over. The clock will strike twelve and Christmas Eve will turn into Christmas Day, and I'll be left to my loneliness for another year.

It's probably for the best. He's probably the baddest of men, and I've probably caught a lucky break to still be alive right now. I obviously never learnt that I shouldn't talk to strangers.

The vibration of the phone on the wooden surface of the jetty next to my head is loud as it starts to silently ring. I startle, bolting upright to grab the phone, instead knocking it to skitter across the jetty. I gasp as I lunge for it, catching it just in time before it tumbles over the edge into the water.

Shit. That was close.

On its third ring, I quickly answer the call.

"Cutting it close."

His voice.

Shit.

Why does its deep rasp have such an effect on me?

"We have an hour, little elf. Are you ready for the finale?"

No.

"Yes." I breathe, my heart racing with anticipation.

"Are you sure? I'll give you one last chance to back out now before I tell you what tonight's game is, because if we do this, little elf, we will see it through to the end."

What does that mean?

"Can I ask any questions first?"

"No. You decide here and now." He rumbles. "And just remember that I know everything about you, Agatha Marie Fiera, daughter of Roma and Dougal. Sister of Elizabeth." He chuckles at my loud intake of air. "You only know how I sound, taste, smell, and feel. You have no idea what my name is. Who my family is. Where I live. What I look like. What I do to earn a living." He chuckles again. "I could be butt ugly, Aggie. Really fucking ugly, either on the outside or inside." He clucks. "Or both. Be sure of what you want before you commit to our last game, my little elf, because it's the best one yet. But is it best for me… Or you?"

I get it. He's trying to scare me, right? Make me second guess things to create more anticipation. Well, I'm not that easily scared.

I think.

"I'll play." I say before I think too much, and this time I hear his audible intake of air before he growls through the phone.

"You have until midnight to try to get back to your house and lock the door before I catch you, because tonight, my little elf, I am the hunter, and you are my prey."

"What?"

"You heard me, Agatha. Now, you should be wondering what sort of hunter I am, and what sort of prey you are, because remember, you don't know me. I'm the man who has been stalking you, from the moment you moved in. I've watched you fuck men and women in your house. I've watched you fuck yourself. I've turned your power off, entered your house when you weren't there to remove your toys. Hell, I've even stood in your doorway and watched you sleep some nights."

"W-what?" I stutter as fear and confusion slaps me.

"Have you been subbing for Santa, or subbing for a *killer*?"

"I-I..."

"The clock is ticking, Agatha."

My heart thrashes as I fear I've made the biggest mistake of my life, and then I hear the menace in his tone as he says one last word.

"Run!"

Chapter Eleven

Prey

Agatha

I stare at the phone for a brief moment before my brain finally kicks in. And then I run. My feet pound against the jetty as I go, probably too loudly, giving my location away, but I don't stop. I run, because he's right. I don't know him, and even though I'm still alive now, he could well have been buttering me up for his final showdown.

His kill.

My blood thunders in my ears and I race up the grassy hill towards my pitch-black rental. Just as I make it to the top of the hill, I spot a dark figure looming on my porch. I can't see much, but I can just make out that he is wearing only a pair of pants. Jeans maybe, with what looks like a piece of fabric falling from the back pocket. His chest is bare. And so is his face.

I skid to a stop, a gasp flying from me as he takes the first step down off my porch. The moonlight filtering through the trees still isn't enough for me to make out any facial features, but his stance is all menacing. Ready to pounce. So, I turn and run into the thick scrubland.

I'm only wearing a summer dress. My feet are bare, and I'm quickly reminded of that when twigs stab into my feet as I try to escape. My ears pick up the heavy thud of Santa giving chase. I almost want to call his bluff by turning around and facing him. He won't hurt me. This is just primal play, right?

Wrong.

Something whizzes past my head and hits a tree beside me as I run, and I realise he's either throwing something at me or shooting something at me.

Holy shit! I'm going to die.

A scream rips from my lungs as he shoots something at me again, the whizz closer to my ear this time.

I leap over a fallen branch, but crash to the bush floor when I land, my foot getting caught in some sort of vines. A sob escapes me as I scramble back to my feet, deciding to take a different route back towards the water.

Maybe I can swim to safety.

The lake is big, but I'm sure I can swim it if I make it down to the water in time. Maybe I can get across to Ty's house. He will help me.

Something cracks against another trunk as I run, bits of bark or something flying over my head on impact. I scream again, not able to hold in my terror, hoping there are people out here that will hear me and come to my rescue.

Or maybe he will kill them, too.

Last night he said I should be scared of him. Why didn't I believe him?

The glistening reflection of the moon on the lake's surface comes into view between the trees, and I push my legs harder, ignoring the painful cuts on my feet as I run for my life.

As I burst through the thick scrub, out onto the grassy bank of Redfield Lake, the sound of heavy feet and snapping twigs behind me tells me he's nearly caught up. With my eyes trained on the water, I charge forward, desperate to escape, but I don't make it. Something heavy slams into my back and I fly forward, hitting the grassy ground hard, the wind flying from my lungs as he tackles me.

I try to scream again, but pain slices through my ribcage, the air trapped in my lungs as I fight to breathe. Clawing at the grass in front of me, I try to escape his heavy weight, but even as it lifts off me, my dress is torn from my body like it's made of nothing but paper, and a second later my panties are gone too.

Tears stream from my eyes, blurring what I can see of the lake, which is so close ahead, as a sob finally escapes me. I try to roll over. I try to kick. I try to swing a punch backwards, but his hands are too strong, fighting off my attempts easily, overpowering me as his mostly naked, heavy weight pushes me face first into the grass.

He growls like a wild animal as he manages to get my legs spread by using his feet and weight, while one of his hands wraps around both of my wrists, trapping them at the small of my back as he presses down, pinning me in place from behind.

Then I feel him pressing his dick between my legs.

"You're mine now, Aggie. I'm never letting you go."

With a single thrust, he impales himself inside me, and my gasp lodges in my throat as arousal slams into me. Years of rough play, pushing the boundaries, and ignoring my fears has conditioned my body to respond this way, thinking this is a game I want to play. Even as he releases my wrists and snakes his hand under the front of my hips, the moment he presses them to my clit, my body betrays me even more.

"Let's juice up this cunt some more, little elf. I promise it will feel good."

His words are confusing, my body already on board with what he's doing while my brain is screaming at me to run.

"That's it." He rasps, his voice as feral as a wild animal as he starts to thrust hard inside me from behind. "Give in to me, little elf. Let me claim you."

I don't know what comes over me, but I figure if he is having one last fill before he kills me, I may as well enjoy it. At least, that's what my body is saying, softening to accommodate his girth, and grinding against his fingers.

"Fuck, yes." He hisses, rising up to brace himself on one hand as he starts slamming hard into me. He forgets about my clit, but it doesn't matter. The way he's pressing me into the ground causes friction between my clit and the grass, and the way his dick hits the right spot so deep inside me causes an animalistic need of my own to take over.

Instead of fighting it, I accept his claiming while I fuck him right back.

His teeth latch onto my shoulder, and it's all it takes for me to explode, my body's reaction milking him of his orgasm too.

He roars up into the night like a possessed beast before collapsing over me again.

Our panting breaths are loud amongst the chirping crickets that have come out to enjoy the warm summer night air. As my heart starts to calm from the intensity of what we just did, it begins to pick up again, as my memory kicks in.

He was shooting at me. Or throwing something. He meant me harm.

This isn't over.

I need to get away.

Even as I think it, his weight lifts off me and his rough hands flip me over to face him. The moonlight is better here. It beams like a spotlight down on us, and I come face to face with my Santa for the first time.

I gasp as I take him in, his face not at all familiar to me, still leaving me with a thousand questions. His hair is dark, possibly a deep brown or nearly black shade. His eyes are dark too, most likely brown. Even in this dull light, I can tell his skin is tanned naturally, probably from a Greek or Italian heritage. The stubble I felt between my legs a couple of days ago is dark, running over a chiselled jawline, and once again my body betrays me as I remember how it feels to have his face buried in between my thighs.

If this man does mean me harm, showing me his face is probably the last thing I will see before he kills me.

"Who are you?" I whisper, and he smirks, a dimple caving in below his right cheek.

He doesn't speak, his dark eyes dropping from my face to my pebbled nipples before travelling down lower.

Then he growls. "I'm hungry."

Before I can even fathom what he's going on about, he shifts back to his knees before dropping his head between my legs. His tongue is searing as it licks from my arse to my clit, and my eyes widen as my brain finally kicks in.

With a hunger I've only recognised in myself, I watch his dark eyes remain locked on mine as he devours my pussy, eating me so thoroughly that there's no way he's left any traces of his cum behind.

Once again, I give in to this dominating man and I reach out, fisting my fingers into his dark hair as I grind and fuck his face. The noises that come from me are just as animalistic as the ones that came from him only minutes ago, and when my eyes fall shut as the pleasure takes over, he pulls back.

"Eyes on mine!"

My lids snap open, going wide at his command, but once they are on his, he returns to his task, devouring me completely.

My orgasm is a clenching explosion, and I cry up into the night sky as I let it completely consume me. I'd be happy to die right now if it weren't for my need to know more about this erratic man.

As the ripples start to ease, and I relax into the grassy bed under my back, Santa gives me a few last licks before kissing my mound and sitting up in between my legs.

"Who the hell are you?" I pant, taking in his lethal beauty as my chest rises and falls.

A smirk crosses his face as he looks at me, causing him to appear positively sinful under the moonlight.

"I'm Griffin Marx. Your landlord."

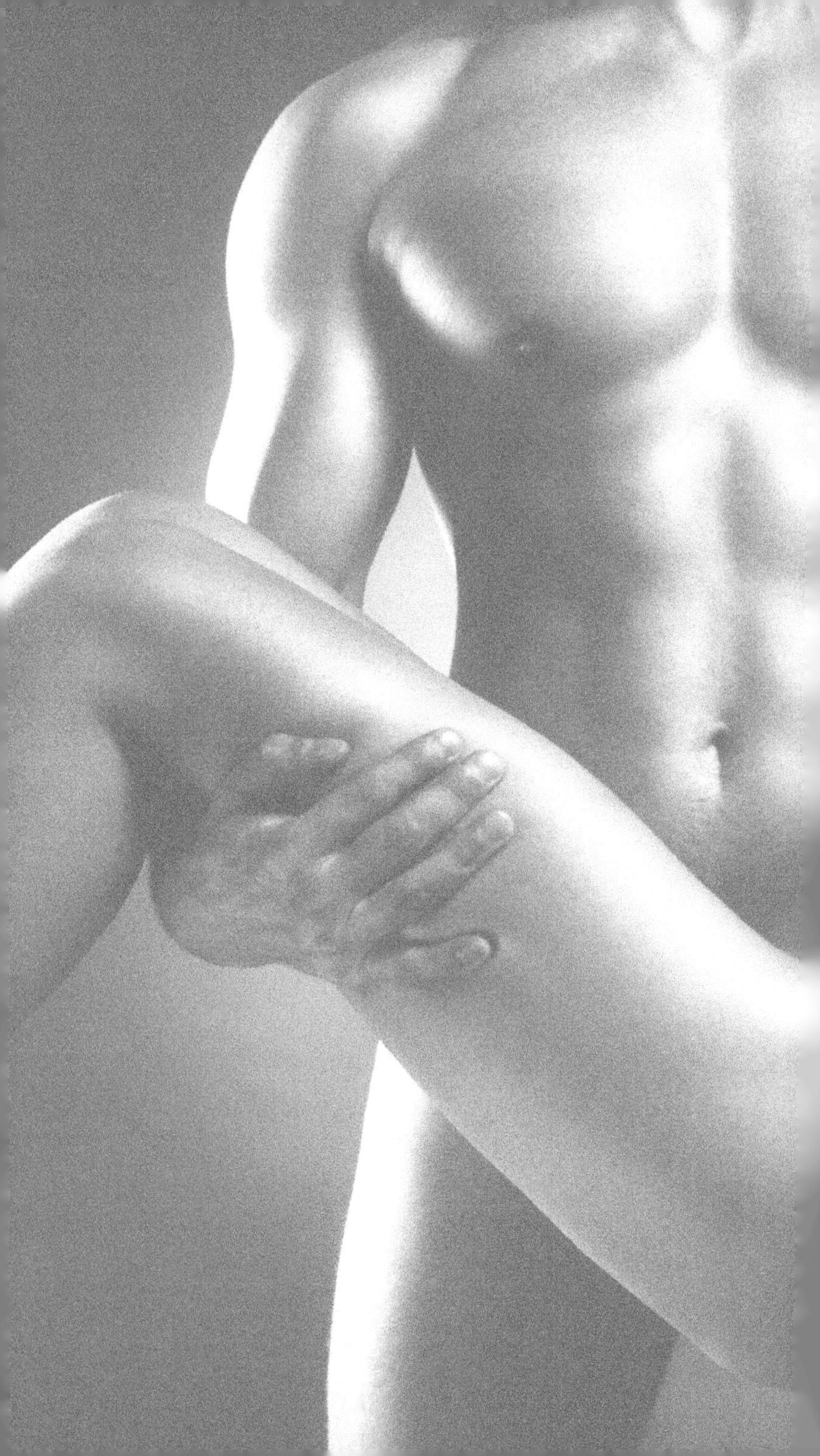

Chapter Twelve

Brave

Griffin

The blaring light of a spotlight takes me by surprise as it lights up my naked body.

"Is that you, Griff?" The voice of an elderly man meets my ears, and Aggie's gasp catches my attention as I watch her try to cover her naked flesh with her arms and hands.

She's still on her back on the grass, and lucky for her there's a bushy garden bed blocking our neighbour's view of my little elf.

"Yeah, Albert. It's me." I turn back to the glare of the light, giving the old guy a wave as I stand and ignore the fact that I'm butt arse naked. "How are you this evening?"

"Oh," Albert's eyes widen as he takes in my lack of attire, but quickly shakes it off. "I'm good thanks, Griffin. Was that you making all the ruckus out here?"

"Oh. My. God!" Aggie whisper-yells. "Kill me now."

"Yeah, sorry Albert." I suck in my lips for a moment, trying not to laugh at Aggie's expression. "Me and my girl were playing kiss chasey."

"Kiss chasey my arse." She mutters quietly, and I can't hide my smirk this time as I glance back down at her.

"Ahhh." Albert laughs. "How fun to be young and in love."

"It's the best." I chuckle, nodding at Albert.

"Alrighty then. I'll leave you two to have your fun. Have a lovely Christmas." He smiles, his eyes briefly dropping to my exposed junk that I made no attempt at covering.

"You too, Albert. Merry Christmas." I stand proud, knowing my body is worth gazing at given the work I put in to keep in shape.

Albert's chuckles fade as the spotlight disappears and I turn my gaze back to my little elf. "Busted." I snicker and Aggie rolls her eyes at me.

I step forward, offering her a hand, and she stares at it for a beat, her eyes portraying her racing thoughts. She's wary of me, and rightfully so. I unleashed my beast on her tonight and showed her my true colours. But her body knows me. She can't deny that.

"Come on, Aggie. You have to know after all that, I'm not going to hurt you."

Her brows furrow into a deep frown and she slaps my offered hand away, getting herself up off the grass.

"No, I don't fucking know that! I know nothing about you!" She snaps, her glare slicing as she balls her fists at her sides.

Even as she glares at me, I can't stop my eyes from travelling the length of her naked body and note how her nipples pebble under my scrutiny.

"What was that before? Primal play?" She snaps again, and I grin.

"Yes. Exactly." I tilt my head to the side to study her expression, taking in how flushed her cheeks are, even noticeable in this dull light.

"Primal play? Really?" She hisses this time between clenched teeth, and I nod even as her anger seems to grow. "What the fuck were you shooting at me? Because I'm pretty sure you were trying to kill me."

I release a sigh, my shoulders dropping a little as I gesture behind me. "I'll show you, little elf. Come on."

"Huh." She scoffs. "As if I'm going anywhere with you. You're fucking crazy."

I freeze at her words and tone, rolling my tongue in my mouth as my anger nudges at my control. Gritting my teeth, I suck in some much needed oxygen, hoping for calm before I drop my chin to my chest.

I remind myself she has a right to be angry. That was always going to happen, and right now she is confused.

Turning away from her, I take a few steps to where the t-shirt I had hanging from my jeans pocket lies on the grass, and I pick it up, flicking it out to remove any stray grass or dirt.

"I appreciate that you're a little pissed right now." I say quietly as I turn and stroll towards Aggie. "But it really is in your best interest to never call me crazy again." I step up to her, my gaze deadly serious before I slip the t-shirt over her head. I help her slip her arms in, and my t-shirt falls to her mid-thighs, working well to cover her naked flesh.

"Is that a threat?" She breathes quietly, suddenly losing her bravado.

Bending down into the bushes, I tug out my jeans and step into each leg. As I pull them up, covering my now lax cock, my eyes find Aggie's again. "Not a threat, little elf. Just a word of advice."

Her face falls soft, her lips parting a little as she studies me. I wonder if she's happy with what she sees. Are my looks to her liking? Was she hoping for something different?

"Come on, Aggie. Let me show you." I offer her my hand again, and this time, she takes it slowly, showing me her reluctance.

As her hand slips into mine, I gently rub my thumb over the back of her hand and watch how her brows furrow a little as she looks to where we are attached. She seems confused by my gentleness, which is understandable given the monster she's been playing with for the last couple of days.

I start walking toward the tree line that borders the thick scrub we had run through earlier. When we reach it, I stop, smirking down at Aggie, before I bend and sweep her up to cradle her in my arms. A squeak flies from her mouth, and I can't help it. I chuckle at how sweet it sounds as I step into the bushland.

"What are you doing?" She clings to my neck briefly, like I'm going to drop her, but then she relaxes in my hold, finally giving me her trust.

"Your feet are all cut up. I'm not letting them get worse." I state and glance down at her in time to see her brows shoot up at my admission.

She doesn't say anything, but as I step through the dry landscape, twigs digging into my feet as I go, I can feel her eyes on me. Watching me. Studying me.

Weaving through the trees, I stop by one and gesture my head up higher.

"Look."

She glances up to see the evidence on the tree. It's hard to tell exactly what it is in this dull light, but her brows quickly shoot up and she drops her eyes to mine.

"Is that paint?" She squeaks in disbelief, and I nod.

"Yes."

Her eyes widen. "You were trying to hit me with paint balls?"

I grin and shake my head. "No. I was trying to *scare* you with paint balls. There's no way one would have hit you. I kept my aim high."

Her eyes turn into slits, and my smirk drops.

"Come on, Aggie. You have to admit, that was fun. And fucking hot." The whole thing had me hard as stone, and fuck, my dick is growing again just thinking about it.

"I'll never admit that." She snaps, narrowing her glare at me, which just makes me chuckle.

"Your body didn't lie, beautiful."

Her glare deepens, and I continue to smirk as I start walking again.

Was I trying to scare her? Yes. Why? I could admit that having people scared of me comes naturally, and runs thick in my veins, but that's not what was happening here tonight. Primal play is better when the prey isn't sure if it's a game or not.

Is that fucked up? Yeah, it is. But do I care? Fuck no.

I knew Aggie could hack it, even if she was terrified. That's why I chose her.

Even as she struggles with her anger as I carry her, she watches me again, taking in everything. Her mind must be racing, but she doesn't speak her thoughts, instead keeping them locked tight inside her head.

Back at her house, I open the front door and carry her in, walking through the dark like it's second nature, knowing exactly where the furniture is to avoid running into it. This is, after all, a house I own and manage.

I lower Aggie to the couch, her eyes still staying on my every move as I press a kiss to her forehead before standing and looming over her.

"I'll be right back. Stay right there. Do not move off this couch." I point a stern finger down at her and she scoffs.

"The game is over now. I don't have to submit to you anymore." She counters, smirking like she's tripped me up, but I grin with a confidence that has her smile dropping from her face.

"We'll see about that, little elf."

Turning my back on her, I stride out of the house, quickly taking the path up to her meter box and find the key I hid nearby before removing the lock and turning her electricity back on.

When I return, I say nothing as I close the front door and stride back over to my little elf before scooping her up in my arms again. She doesn't fight me, instead wrapping her arms around my neck and drawing herself close.

Poor little thing doesn't even realise she's already mine.

Passing through the bedroom, I step into the bathroom, grabbing a towel from the rail and lay it over the stone benchtop before lowering Aggie to sit on it. Then I turn to the bathtub and start filling it.

Now that we are in full light, I can clearly see how much she is taking in every inch of my face, her eyes roaming over it, memorising my features in fascination. She can now see that the thick hair she clung to is a deep brown, almost black, and my eyes are a similar shade. She's probably wondering about my heritage, given my European appearance. And as her gaze travels over my arms, I watch her study my tattooed sleeve with interest.

As she continues to study me and the tub fills, I lean one shoulder against the shower cubicle, crossing my arms over my chest and pointedly study her back. My analysing eyes makes her squirm, and my lips quirk.

"You're quiet, little elf. I thought you'd have questions."

"I do." She practically whispers.

"Are you going to ask them?" I wag my brows at her, trying to show her I'm not the monster I was by the lake not that long ago.

She shrugs. "I guess."

Again, I chuckle and push off from the shower. "Let's get you in the bath."

Turning, I cut off the water, running my hand through the bubbles before shaking them off and moving back to her still perched on the benchtop.

"Arms up." I command, and she hesitates, her eyes staying locked on mine as she continues to study me.

I don't wait for her to obey. Instead, gripping the hem of the shirt, I tug it upward so she has no choice but to raise her arms. My eyes unashamedly fall to her chest, her nipples peaking to attention under my gaze. When my eyes travel further south, Aggie darts her hands to cover her pretty pussy and I throw my head back, laughing.

"I've already met your sweet pussy intimately, Aggie. There's no need to hide it from me."

"I don't care." She snaps, keeping her hands in place, and I suck my lips in, trying to hold back more laughter before I scoop her up in my arms again.

When I lower her feet into the hot water, she hisses out in pain as the scrapes and tiny cuts on the bottom of her feet react.

"Shit, sorry." I rasp, hoping she hears how genuine my words are as I change positions and lower her into the water arse first this time.

Aggie keeps her feet raised up out of the water, and I dart out of the room, grabbing one of the large throw cushions off the couch before returning to my little elf. I immerse it in the water, not caring if I ruin it. I'll just buy a new one.

I notice Aggie's expression, her brows shooting up as she watches on with curiosity, before I gently guide her feet to rest on top of the large cushion up out of the water.

"So, this house is yours?" she asks, and my eyes lock with hers before I nod and stand again.

"Yes."

"And that's how you were able to get in whenever you liked, and how you set up cameras?" she asks with no anger, just curiosity.

Again, I nod. "Yes."

"You know that's illegal, right?"

I smirk. "Of course."

"But you did it, anyway?" Her brows shoot up and again, I nod.

"Yes."

"Why?"

Slowly, I lower myself to my knees on the tiled floor next to the bath, with a washer in my hand. Dunking it in the warm water, I start washing it over her perfect breasts, giving them considerable attention for a few long stretched out moments before looking back up.

"I needed to see if you have what it takes," I admit, vaguely.

"Have what it takes for what?" she asks, her brows furrowing.

"To be my woman," I admit easily, and her brows dip further.

"You were testing me to see if I have what it takes to be your girlfriend?"

"Girlfriend sounds so juvenile. Call it woman friend instead." I grin, flashing my teeth, and she rolls her eyes. Fuck, I love it when she does that. It riles me up.

"Fine. Whatever." She waves me off. "Let's focus on the whole test part of things. Why were you testing me?"

"I thought I covered that already." I frown seriously as I watch her, my hand still washing warm water over her chest.

"Firstly, what makes you think I would want to be your girl? I don't even know you." She snaps and my dick twitches.

"You'll want to be mine. I have no doubts about that."

She scoffs. "Cocky much?"

"Naturally." I shrug, which just pisses her off because she bares her gritted teeth and growls.

Doesn't she know that just turns me on?

"Let's pretend I *do* want to be your girl." Her tone is laced with sarcasm. "What exactly does it take to be yours?"

"I need a brave woman." I answer quickly. "Level headed, especially when the going gets tough, but with just enough craziness to match my own. I need someone loyal, who has morals, and knows how to follow instructions."

She flinches at my words and raises her hand up to stop me from touching her with my talented washing skills.

"Hold up. You think I'm a submissive? That was just a game."

I sigh. "I know you're not a submissive, but I needed to confirm that you could do what I ask of you."

"But I didn't. Not always."

I smirk. "No. But that was within reason. You were protecting yourself and your clients. It actually worked in your favour."

She narrows her eyes. "How so?"

"Your refusal to continue with your sex parties showed me how loyal you can be. Protective of what matters."

"Yet I let you watch my tantric session with Meagan."

"That's different." I shrug. "She doesn't try to hide her identity when she meets with you. She hasn't signed a contract like your sex party guests."

"How do you know that?" She frowns and my lips thin before I give her a small smile.

"I told you, Aggie. I know a lot about you. I did my homework before I approached you."

Her lips part to say something, but she snaps them shut like she's not sure how to respond to me. I use her silence to begin washing her again, this time squeezing water over her shoulders.

She relaxes a little as she mulls over our conversation before she asks more questions.

"You said you need a brave woman. Why? Do you mean brave enough to be sexually adventurous?"

I like that she's interested enough to have so many questions. It means there's hope.

"I already knew you were sexually adventurous. I've been watching you from the moment you moved in." I shoot her a devilish wink, and her cheeks instantly redden. "I wanted to see if you were brave enough to embark on this game with me, even though you didn't know who I was. I wanted to see if you'd be brave enough to handle the punishments, even though they were pretty tame."

A loud incredulous laugh escapes her as her caramel eyes widen. "Choking me with your dick isn't that tame."

"No, but it was fun." I shoot her a wink and again, she rolls her eyes at me.

"For you maybe." She scoffs and her cheeks turn flaming red.

Did she just lie to me?

"You can't fool me, Aggie. I know you liked it." I shoot her a shit-eating grin as I call her out, and she huffs, wrapping her arms across her chest.

"Whatever."

I chuckle.

"So basically, you needed to make sure I was stupid enough to play with a stalker?" She throws her hands up, giving me another glimpse of her perky tits.

"I don't think you're stupid, Aggie. I think you're perfect." I say with honesty, and once again she scoffs at me.

"Perfect? You're a stranger to me. I played a game, handing over my trust to a complete stranger and put myself in danger."

This time, my brows shoot up as I prepare to stir the pot. "Well, now that you put it like that, it does sound kind of stupid."

Aggie shoots me a dagger and I try really fucking hard not to smile.

She's quiet for a few minutes, and I continue to wash her shoulders, arms and legs in the comfortable silence.

When she speaks again, her voice is soft, filled with curiosity.

“Why did you need to see if I am brave?” she asks, sinking lower into the steaming hot water.

I take a moment to study my little elf. My eyes darting between hers, hoping she’s ready to hear my next words.

“Because in my world, if you’re not brave, you die.”

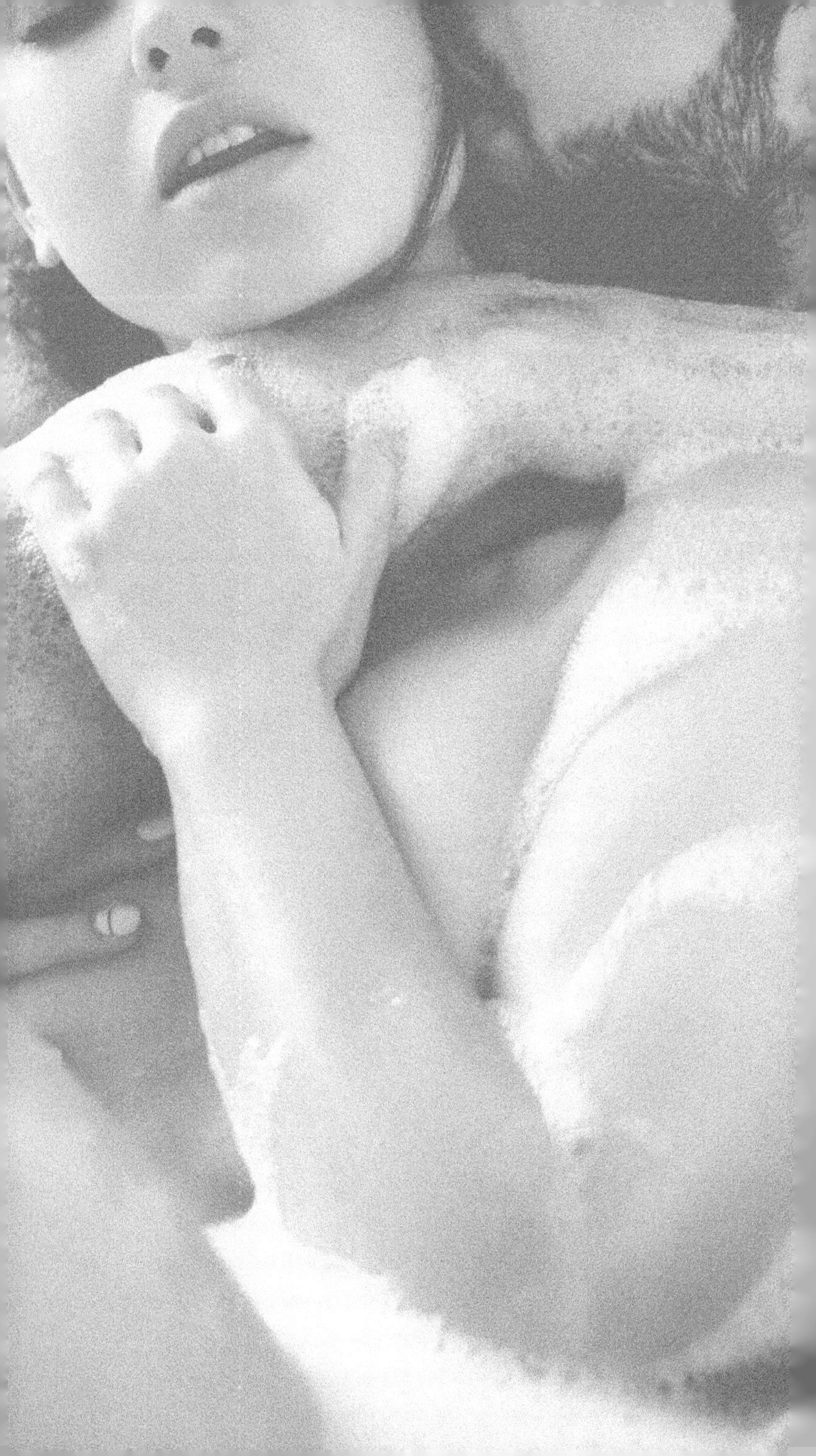

Chapter Thirteen

Curiosity

Agatha

Die? What is he talking about? My frown hurts my face it's so strong, and all he does is give me a soft smile before standing and undoing his jeans. I should tell him to leave, yet I don't. Finally, I've met my Santa, and even though there are little red flags waving in my mind, I can't bring myself to ask him to leave. For some reason, I want him to stay.

"I'm still confused," I admit, and he nods.

"It's understandable."

"I want to know what you mean about your world, but first, please tell me about this house. Do you spy on all of your tenants?"

"No."

My brows hitch. "Just me?"

"Just you." He nods, stepping into the bath behind me and sinking down. The water rises with his added mass, my feet sinking under a little, but this time it doesn't hurt.

"Why just me?" I shuffle forward a little to give him room, but his arms come around me, dragging me back flush with his naked flesh.

"I was curious about you." He admits, his breath warm against my ear, and damn, my cheeks heat again.

"Why?" My voice is breathless, and he nips at my ear before answering softly.

"I just was."

"That's not an answer." I grumble and he chuckles quietly.

"Spend Christmas with me."

I stiffen at his words.

"What?"

"You heard me."

"You're deflecting." I call him out. "Answer my question. Why were you curious about me?"

"If I answer, will you spend Christmas with me?" Again, he nips at my ear, effectively relaxing me into his embrace.

"Here?"

"No. With my family in the city." He presses his nose to my neck and inhales before moaning.

And there I go, stiffening again.

Family?

I don't do families. I don't know how to do families. They will hate me.

"Your family?" I squeak, exposing my internal freakout.

"Yes." He sounds amused, but he doesn't laugh.

"But I only just met you. I can't meet your family yet." I remind him, and he presses a gentle kiss to my neck before answering.

"You met me a week ago, Aggie."

"Not really." I frown.

"Kind of." He rasps, squeezing me tighter to him as he leaves his lips to linger on my neck.

"A week ago, you stood outside my car window and watched me come from the toy you were controlling. That's not meeting you." I scoff, and again his lips press firmly before grazing the sensitive skin just under my ear. Fuck. He's making it hard to think straight.

"Hmmm." He rumbles quietly in my ear. "You have a point."

"I know I do," I say softly, letting my eyes fall shut to the sensations he's stirring to life.

"Even so. I want you with me tomorrow. And the next day."

"Why?" I ask, confused. Is this man crazy?

"Because you're mine."

My eyes snap open at his deadly serious tone.

"No, I'm not." I shake my head, but I stop as soon as I feel his fingers pinch my nipple. How did he manage to get his hand there?

"Yes, you are. I won the game. I caught you and fucked you like an animal under the moon. You're mine, Agatha."

Jesus. How does he make that sound so hot?

"Were you ever told *no* as a child?" I snap, and I can feel his shrug behind me.

"Sure. Quite often."

"I doubt it. You don't seem to understand the meaning."

He chuckles. "Oh, I understand. *You* just don't understand how determined I am to make you mine."

Sighing, my shoulders drop. "If I agree to spend Christmas with you—"

"And the next day." He interrupts and I roll my eyes.

"And Boxing Day, too. Will you tell me why you were curious about me?"

"Yes." He agrees quickly.

"Fine. I'll spend it with you. Now spill."

"So bossy." He presses his lips to the sensitive spot just under my ear again before continuing. "I was curious about the beauty who was desperate to rent a property with the request for the information not to be disclosed to anyone. In my line of work, I make sure to background check everyone. There are reasons why people want to remain hidden, so either you were hiding from a toxic relationship, or you were in trouble with the law." I stiffen at his words, but he continues. "I couldn't find a lot on you myself, so I had a consultant of mine do a search on you, and I found some interesting information."

Shit. I need to run. Now.

"Your name was on an original list we had in our possession but had been removed from the new version by special request. Do you know what list I'm talking about?"

My heart stops beating as realisation dawns, and I prepare myself mentally to flee. Because hell no. He can't have gotten his hands on *that* list.

"You were a member of a very high-class exclusive sex club."

That's all I need to hear. As fast as I can, I try to stand, but his hand wraps around my wrist. Spinning me in the water, he tugs me back down, straight onto his lap, and I hiss at the sting coming from my feet. Now face to face, I have nowhere else to look but at him.

"Don't run from me." He growls, his expression dark and serious as he directs his stern domination towards me.

"I'd like you to leave." I say on a shaky breath, and he sighs.

"That's not going to happen, Aggie. We are having this conversation, and then we are going to fuck again."

"N-no." I stutter as fear grips me. "I need you to leave. Now."

"Do you think I'm judging you for being a member at that club?" he asks, his head tilting to the side as he studies me.

"Are you a cop?"

"Hell no. I'm the guy cops wish they could catch."

My brows reach my hairline at his admission, whatever it means, but I shake my head, still needing to get away. He could be telling me anything just to get the information he wants from me.

"I don't know you. I'm not talking about this with you." I rush out in a panic, and he sighs.

"Fine." He reaches over the edge of the bath and grabs his phone, unlocking it and handing it to me.

"Do an internet search on me. Griffin Marx. That will tell you enough to know I'm not here to turn you in to the police."

I eye him warily, a silent standoff of sorts happening between us before I finally accept his phone and drag my attention to the screen. Opening the web browser, I type in his name and do a search.

The first hit tells me all I need to know.

Fuck.

Slowly, I glance up from the screen to his heated gaze. "You're part of a crime family?"

"I wouldn't call it crime, exactly." He shrugs.

"What would you call it, then?" I ask, and he smirks.

"Business."

My eyes just about bug out as my head swims with this knowledge.

What the fuck have I gotten myself into?

"I think you should go," I whisper, my gaze dropping to his chest as I suddenly feel unsure of the man I'm straddling.

"Hey." He lifts my chin, drawing my gaze up to meet his. "This is why I needed to test your courage."

I shake my head, still confused. "Are you going to blackmail me or something? Is that why you chose me, knowing you had leverage with my part in the sex club scandal?"

"No. The Vixen's Lodge Sex Club scandal is what drew my curiosity. It was watching you on camera from the moment you moved in that stole my attention. I do need to know though..." He hesitates, and I know I'm not going to like what he says next. "Are you into underage sex?"

"What?! No! You need to leave!" I surge up, but he comes with me, once again trapping my wrists in his grip.

"I'm not leaving, Aggie. I've already told you that. I just needed to know since the scandal involved a minor."

"That minor is my friend, and that's the last we will ever talk of it!"

He studies me for a long, drawn-out moment as my chest rises and falls with my emotions. "Ok." He releases my wrists and pretends to button his lips.

I eye him for a long time, both of us standing with rivers of water dripping from our naked flesh in the bathtub.

"How did you get that list?" I whisper, almost too scared to know the answer. "It was meant to be destroyed."

"Yes. By my family."

My brows shoot high. "The Marx family are the ones covering my arse?"

"Yes. Your arse and the arses of some others on the list." He nods. "Like the name of the minor involved in the scandal and her underage boyfriend that attended the club. The teacher who she is in a secret relationship with. Oh, and the cop and his secret boyfriend. I believe you had dinner with them last week when we played our first game."

"Shane and Ben?" I gasp, worried he knows all about them, too.

"Yes. Police officer Shane Kent."

Holy shit.

"Does he know it's your family who stepped in to hide our identities?" I ask, concerned for my friend.

"Yes, he does." Griffin nods, running his hands down my arms. "He also knows why my family recently moved into the area."

"Which is why, exactly?"

"That's not information you need to know yet." He frowns and my brows shoot up.

"Right. I'm on a need-to-know basis, am I?" I hiss through clenched teeth, and he gives me a single nod. It's not enough. "You need to leave."

"No. I need to fuck you again." He deadpans.

"Like hell! Get the fuck out!"

He doesn't let me say anything else, instead his lips slam into mine as his arms wrap around me, pulling me flush against his naked skin. I fight it for a moment, fear causing me to react, but then his tongue breaches my lips, and I forget my fucking name.

As I relax into his embrace, his arms loosen, and I grip his bare back as a frenzy takes over us. Griffin's hands come down to cup my arse, and a second later, he lifts me, my legs automatically wrapping around his waist before he steps out of the bath.

I momentarily worry he may slip, but with the press of his erection against my core, I quickly forget all rationality.

My arse meets the benchtop he perched me on earlier, and I feel him positioning himself at my entrance. I should make him stop, but this feels too good. Too right.

With a brutal thrust, Griffin impales me. I throw my head back, breaking our kiss as he fills me and starts thrusting. I release a moan as his lips sear a path down my neck, his hand slipping between us to start working on my clit.

"You're mine." He rasps, nipping at my nipple, but I ignore his words, keeping my focus on the tantalising sensations building inside me.

"Tell me you're mine, Aggie." He growls, this time fisting my hair with his free hand to direct my gaze to his.

I shake my head, closing my eyes as my hips meet his thrusts, desperate with need.

"Aggie!" He hisses again, and my eyes fly open. "Say it."

"No." I pant, barely able to speak.

Growling, he tears his magical fingers away from my clit and stills, and like the desperate bitch I am, I whimper.

"Why won't you say it?" He rumbles and I stare back at him with wide eyes.

"Because I don't know you."

"Your body knows me, Aggie. I know you can feel it too." His thumb brushes over my lower lip, his eyes watching its path. "The way we connect like a puzzle piece. The pull our bodies have on each other. The way we fit together just right." His eyes lock with mine again. "Tell me you can feel that."

"Just because I feel it doesn't mean we are meant to be together. It's just attraction. Lust. My body might know yours, but you're a stranger to my heart."

"You're not a stranger to mine." He rasps, frowning.

"Maybe, but I'm still playing catch up here. You've been getting to know me before I even knew you existed. I can't just give myself to a man I don't know."

"Shit." He whispers, leaning forward to press his forehead to mine. "Will you let me in so I can show you who I am?" His hand leaves my hair and comes to rest over my heart, and hell, emotions rise in me that I'm not the least bit prepared for.

Griffin begins to thrust again, slowly, his eyes remaining locked with mine. "Please let me in."

Gone is his demanding tone. His voice is almost pleading, and I'm helpless to refuse. Biting my lip, I give him a single nod, and it causes a small grin to lift his lips.

"Fuck, Aggie. I've waited a lifetime for you to come into my life."

His words take me by surprise, and so does the kiss he plants on me, not giving me a moment more to dissect just how serious he is about this.

We quickly fall back into our frenzy. His fingers, dick, and lips all knowing exactly what to do to set me ablaze and shoot me to the stars. By the time the echoes of my screams dissipate, we are left in a tangled panting heap on the benchtop in the bathroom.

"Fuck. I'll never get enough of you." He groans, nipping at my ear, before I push at his chest.

"Stop trying to hypnotise me with your dick."

A laugh bursts from him, causing him to slip free from between my legs. "Is it working?"

"No." I shake my head, falling serious. "You still need to leave. This is all... too much."

Griffin's laugh dies as his expression morphs into a frown, and a hint of disappointment flashes across his eyes.

"I know I have sprung this on you, and I know you don't like the fact that I know your secret, but I really hope you give me a chance to prove to you that we could be good together."

Leaning forward, he cups my face and presses his lips to mine for a gentle peck. When he pulls back, his dark gaze penetrates mine, locking me in place.

"I'll be outside on your porch at 10am. If you haven't come out by 10:05, then I'll know you've made your decision and I'll leave you alone." He runs a wary hand through his hair. "Maybe."

I grin. He couldn't help himself. He just had to add that maybe in.

With one last glance, he presses a kiss to my forehead before scooping up his jeans and walking out.

Chapter Fourteen

Blushing

Agatha

Sleep was hard to come by and in the end, I only got a few hours in before dragging myself up out of bed. By the time Griffin left in the early hours of this morning, and I stopped stewing over what to do, I was left with little time to re-energise. My mind wouldn't stop racing, going over everything he said and did.

He'd been spying on me for a while, which is just a gentle term for stalking.

He knows about the most recent skeleton in my closet that I thought I'd hidden. Strangely, despite that, he still set his sights on me.

Let's not forget that he's part of a well-known crime family. I did some more online stalking of my own after he left. The Marx family isn't to be taken lightly. Their involvement in organised crime, mostly in the state of Victoria, has them sitting at the top of the organised crime hierarchy according to my research. And somehow, I managed to snag the attention of one of them.

What will happen to me now that I know this information about him? If I refuse Christmas with him, will my body be found in a week's time decomposing in the lake?

Although, I don't think I really believe that. Hell, at this point, what the fuck do I know? I don't even know Griffin Marx. Even as I think it, it feels wrong. I feel like I do know him. A part of him anyway, which is just absurd given the situation. What I'm almost sure of, though, is that I don't believe Griffin would hurt me.

Sure, he's unconventional, but then, so am I.

It's for that reason, and the fact that my stupid heart misses him, that I shower and dress myself up pretty, stepping out of my front door with an overnight bag at 10:04am.

Yes, I was cutting it fine, but I had to let him sweat it out a little.

"That was payback, wasn't it?" His deep voice is instantly calming. I've been so used to hearing it of late, I hadn't realised just how strongly it affected me.

"Maybe." I smirk and he grins wide. Holy hell, in the bright summer daylight, he looks so different. Soft. Gentle. But still mouth-watering, and panty melting. "Here." He holds up a small, wrapped gift. "Merry Christmas."

"Oh." I frown. "I don't have anything for you."

"Stepping through that door is my gift, little elf." He nudges the gift towards me, and I reach out and accept it while he takes my bag from me.

Biting my lower lip, I open the red and gold foil wrapping to find a long black velvet box. When I glance up at Griffin, he's watching me with a smirk, waiting for me to continue.

My cheeks heat as I look back down, opening the box to find an exquisite gemstone necklace.

"Oh." My breath whooshes from my lungs. "It's beautiful."

"It's a rainbow iris agate, encased in a gold pendant with an amethyst at the top. I got it because agate—"

I cut him off. "Is linked to the name Agatha."

He grins and nods.

"It's truly beautiful." I take the stunning gift from its case and ease it over my head.

"Just like you."

I redden even more at his compliment, causing him to chuckle as he reaches out his free hand to me. I take it, loving the feel of his fingers linking with mine, and I easily let him lead me to the black Mercedes parked in the driveway.

Like a gentleman, he opens the door and helps me in, shooting me a wink before he closes the door and places my bag in the boot before slipping into the driver's seat.

I'm nervously quiet for the first few minutes of the drive, unsure of where to put my hands, so I clasp them in my lap, picking at my fingernails.

"You ok over there?" Griffin's deep rasp snaps my attention to him to see his eyes darting from the road to me a few times. I nod and offer him a small smile. "Hmmm. You're very quiet. I've never seen you so timid before."

"Sorry." I bite my lip, focusing on the road ahead.

"No need to be sorry, Aggie." He states, and I can't help myself. I look back at his smouldering brown gaze. "Is something wrong?"

"No. I'm just nervous. And I have a lot of questions."

He grins, looking back to the road. "Ask them. I'll answer what I can."

I stew over what to ask him first. I want to know about his family, but I also want to know more about him. Just him.

"Where do you live?"

He chuckles at my question, and I'm confused as to why that would be so funny, until he answers.

"Next door to you."

"What!" I screech, which just makes him laugh more. "You live next door? Which house?"

I already know the answer to that, even though I still ask. My friends rented the house to the west for a weekend not long ago, so he must live in the house to the east.

"Looking at the lake, I'm on your left side." He responds, sounding amused.

"No wonder you were able to cut my power so quickly."

"You nearly busted me the first time I cut it." He chuckles. "When you came out to check, I was hiding in the bushes just near your garage."

My mouth drops open at his admission. "Holy shit! You were like, right there?!"

"Yep." He beams, proud of himself.

"So you own the house I'm renting. You installed cameras that I can't seem to find, just to watch *me*, and the whole time you have done that from next door?"

He nods. "Yep. Although I don't own the house. My family does."

"Same thing." I shake my head as things click into place.

"You're actually lucky to be renting that house. We don't normally let that particular property to tenants. We typically keep it for Marx crew members that come to town."

"Marx crew?"

He nods. "Yes."

"That sounds like a gang."

"It is, in a way, I guess." He shrugs like it's no big deal.

Jesus.

"I'm sure you've come across a lot of women in your… what? Thirty years?"

"Thirty-four." He corrects and I nod.

"So, in thirty-four years of searching for a woman, you come across me and think, hell, yeah, I want her to be mine?" I ask with a grin, and Griffin chuckles, shaking his head at me.

"I'll admit, your stunning tall and curvy body, perky tits, sun kissed skin, and luscious long blonde hair definitely caught my attention. *But* it was the sex party stuff that sucked me in."

"So you're just after a girl that can fuck?"

"What?" He darts his eyes to mine as he frowns. "No. It's not like that."

"Then what is it like?" I ask.

He flicks on the indicator, slowing down and pulling the car off the road before shoving it in park. Then he turns to me, one hand braced on the headrest of my seat, the other on the dash in front of me, caging me in.

"I want a woman that's not scared to ask for what she wants in the bedroom. I have no interest in a woman who thinks all she needs to do is please me, and then in ten years' time feels deprived because she's never asked for what she really wants and is still too fucking scared to do so."

"So, you think I'll ask for what I want, and it will mean there will be no secrets or disappointments?"

"Maybe." He shrugs. "I hope that's the case."

"So, if I say I want to go to a sex party and fuck other people, is that going to be a problem?"

He smirks. "Not a problem as long as I'm invited, too."

My brows shoot up at his admission. I'm not sure why this surprises me. He did say he wanted to come to my sex party before I went and cancelled it.

"So you're after an open relationship? Is that it?"

He growls, leaning in close. "No. Let's get one thing straight. *You are mine*, Aggie. You will not have a relationship with anyone else, and I will only be with you, but a sex party where we are both attending is nothing more than meaningless sex that we are both witness to. To me, it will simply be another form of a sex toy."

"Oh." I breathe, feeling my cheeks heat. "So, you would sit back and watch me in a gang bang?"

He smirks. "Maybe. Hell, I might even join in."

Jesus. That sounds hot.

"So you see. Sex may be a big part, but as long as we are open and exploring together, then we could have a happier relationship than most."

It's a little unorthodox for most people, I'm sure, but it feels kind of perfect for me.

"I get it," I admit, and he grins.

"Good." Leaning forward, he presses his lips to mine in a soft, sensual kiss that has my core clenching.

Everything about this man is alluring. His scent. His lips. The way his tongue dances with mine. I could easily get lost in everything Griffin Marx. Easily hand myself over to him for all eternity.

After a minute of teasing me with his lips and tongue, he slowly pulls back, breaking the kiss, his dark eyes studying my face for a moment before he offers me a slight smile. This version of Griffin is different from the animal that claimed me by the lake last night, but I can tell that monster still lurks just under the surface. Maybe I should be afraid of it. But I'm not.

"What other questions do you have?" he asks as he pulls the car back out on the highway.

I consider the thousands of questions darting through my mind, and decide to move onto his family.

"You have a big family."

"Yes. Very big." He nods, keeping his eyes on the road.

"Is your family like the mafia or something?"

I expect him to laugh and shake his head, but Griffin remains neutral.

"Mafia is an overused term."

My eyes practically bulge out of my head. "You're mafia?"

"We don't use that term." He still keeps his eyes on the road.

"What term do you use then?"

This time, he glances at me. "We are a family. A crew. An organisation. There's no need for labels."

"But you're a family that does business through organised crime?"

"Not always." He shrugs, his eyes back on the road.

"But mostly."

Sighing, he glances back at me. "Is it a deal breaker?"

My brows shoot high, and I shrink back into the seat. "I don't know. If it is, is my body going to be found dismembered next week?"

Griffin's laugh is loud in the confined space of the car. His beaming smile and laughing eyes dart to glance at me. Then he falls quiet when he realises I'm serious, and maybe a little scared.

"Shit. Sorry. You're being serious?"

"Yes." I frown and he shakes his head.

"Many people know who we are, and they don't turn up dead. You're safe. I promise."

I want to believe him, but right now my mind is blown.

"Have you killed people?" I ask reluctantly, and my question must take him by surprise, because he flinches a little. His lips thin as his eyes dart back and forth between the road and me, and I sit patiently waiting for him to answer.

"Is that really something you need to know, little elf?"

"Yes." I nod.

"Why?" He frowns, and I shrug.

"Honestly, I guess I can't be involved with someone who keeps secrets. So if you kill people, I need to know."

His brows shoot up, but he nods too, momentarily distracted by his thoughts before responding.

"If I say yes, is *that* a deal breaker?"

"No." I whisper, and his head snaps to me.

"It's not?"

I shake my head. "I just want honesty."

His face softens. "This is why you're perfect for me, Aggie. You're not judging me."

"So you have? Killed someone, I mean." I ask, and he nods.

"I have."

"How many?" I ask and he frowns, and his expression turns regretful.

"Too many."

"Were they bad people?" I ask, and his face turns to stone in a serious expression.

"Yes, Aggie. I'm not in the business of killing for sport or because someone stole my lunch. Death is delivered by my hand only to the worst of the worst."

"Rapists?"

"Yes." He nods.

"Child sex offenders?"

"Yes." He nods again.

"Do you see me as a child sex offender?"

He frowns, darting his eyes back to me. "No."

"But you know I was involved with a minor, right?" I feel sick as I say those words, hating that I'm guilty.

"I've been made aware that Rhys George was consenting, and the circumstances were very different, given her experience."

"It still doesn't make it right." I mutter, dropping my gaze to my lap.

"She's your friend, though, right? I heard your phone call with her in the car the other day. She doesn't seem threatened by you."

"You heard that?" I dart my wide eyes back to him.

"Yes. And I heard the regret in your tone. So let me ask you this. Do you think she sees you as a predator?"

I shrug.

"Do you think she sees the master of the club and his wife as predators?"

"Yes." I answer quickly, and he offers me a warm smile when I glance back at him.

"She wouldn't be your friend if she thought you were a bad person, Aggie. How about you cut yourself some slack?"

Sighing, I nod and glance out the window, watching the trees pass by.

"Does your family know?" I ask, not looking at him.

"About your involvement at the sex club?" he asks, and I nod. "No."

Relief washes over me, lifting the heavy weight that had settled over my chest.

I have my demons, but so does Griffin Marx. Perhaps that's what draws me to him so easily. It's a nice feeling to know someone accepts you and all of your flaws and mistakes.

Griffin

She's hard on herself. It's not necessarily a bad thing, but I wish I could take all her worries away. Life isn't that simple, though. Especially my life. Which is why this Goddess will fit in so well. Because her life hasn't been easy either.

I admit, I was worried that she'd want to run screaming in the other direction when she learnt that I do in fact kill people, but she seemed comforted by the fact that they are always the scum of the earth that need to be sent straight to hell. Those fuckers deserved the death I delivered, and when I join them in hell eventually, I'll be sure to make them suffer again.

I won't ever admit this to Aggie, but when I first found out about her involvement in the Vixen's Lodge scandal, I was ready to deliver her to hell like the others, but the more I investigated her, the more it didn't add up. She's no predator. And after a thorough investigation into Rhys George's involvement in the club, it became apparent that the minor had a small group of members that tended to stick by her most of the time, which, in a twisted way, helped protect her.

My Agatha was one of them, and she *did* form a friendship with the girl, even if they sometimes crossed the line. It was probably better it be Aggie than some of the other sick fucks out there.

It sounds all kinds of wrong, which is why I've tried to do everything I can to make sure Agatha Fiera's name never comes up in relation to the scandal. I don't want people to judge her. She doesn't deserve to be put in the same class as other predators.

My little elf wants honesty from me, so I plan on giving her that, and hopefully it will help her to reveal the other skeletons in her closet. I know there's more about this woman that I don't know and can't find through my investigative channels, but I fully intend on breaking down her walls so that one day she trusts me enough to reveal her real self to me.

Chapter Fifteen

Family

Agatha

The long drive from the Timber Valley region to the large Marx estate, north of the city, leaves me a mix of tired and anxious about meeting Griffin's family. I'm not all that accustomed to being in a relationship, but I'm pretty sure meeting the family this soon is irregular. Let's not forget that his family is a crime family.

A fucking crime family!

The lavish Marx mansion is set on sprawling green acreage, a mix of grey stone and render on the house's façade, partially hidden behind large trees that provide some privacy from the road.

Griffin drives his car through the large black cast iron gates, up the cobble stoned drive to park behind an array of expensive cars that sit, framing the fountain in the centre.

"You like?" Griffin asks, and I realise my jaw has dropped open in awe.

"Yeah. It's amazing."

"Wait until you see inside. The walls are panelled, and the floors are a mix of herringbone timber, marble, and the softest damn carpet you'll ever walk on."

"Shit. Maybe bringing me here wasn't a good idea." I mumble, my eyes scanning over the manicured gardens.

"Don't be silly, Aggie. You belong here. With me."

I don't look back at him, but I hear him get out of the car, and a few beats later, he's opening my door.

"Come on beautiful. Come and meet my family."

I let him pull me up out of his car, even though I'm about ready to lock myself in, and he tugs me along the driveway to the front door. I don't speak as he leads me, my heart thumping wildly in my chest as he pushes the large glass door open, and the sound of laughter meets our ears.

My eyes dart everywhere, taking in the grand foyer with the intricate herringbone timber floors Griffin told me about. The walls are lined with white panelling on the ground level but changes to mirrored panelling on the second story where a large crystal chandelier hangs down from the timber panelled ceiling.

"Fucking hell," I whisper, and Griffin chuckles.

"Beautiful, isn't it?"

"Beautiful is one word for it," I say quietly as he leads me through to the main living room.

My hand instantly feels sweaty in his hold as so many eyes turn our way, most of them male.

"Oh! This must be Agatha." A woman cries, pushing through the tall wall of males, beelining in our direction.

"Yes, Selena. This is Agatha." Griffin grins.

I'm about to drop my hand from his grip to offer Selena a handshake, but she reaches forward, pulling me in for a hug. My eyes dart to Griffin over her shoulder, who's wearing a beaming smile before he speaks.

"Aggie. This is my stepmother. Selena."

Selena pulls back from our hug, her dark hair in long smooth waves, her expression delighted as she studies me.

"Uh. Hi." I offer, because I'm a woman of many words, apparently.

"It's wonderful to meet you, honey. When Griff told us he was serious about a girl, we simply had to have you over for Christmas."

Again, when I glance at Griffin, he's beaming.

"Thank you for having me." I offer, not knowing what else to say, and she offers me a warm smile in return.

"Ok, let's get the introductions over with. I'm starving." Griffin rubs his hands together as masculine chuckles fill the room.

An older man steps through the crowd, his eyes trained on me as he approaches. Instant chills run up my spine as I realise who this man is. After all, his face came up in a lot of my internet searches last night.

"Welcome, Agatha. I'm Ewan, Griffin's father."

Holding his hand out to me, I eye it quickly, before deciding that being rude to the head of the most notorious crime family in the country isn't wise.

"Hello." I smile at him, taking his hand for a brief shake.

Shit. Can he feel my sweaty palms?

"Let me do the introductions." He smiles warmly, dropping my hand and I smile and nod, hoping it doesn't look as forced as it feels. "Let's start with my oldest children." He gestures his hand, and my gaze follows. "This is Leo, my oldest and second in charge. And this is Conrad, Bernadette and Kendrick." The four he gestured to smile and nod back at me in greeting, and I'm pretty sure I've already forgotten their names. "Their mother, Audrey, passed some years ago from breast cancer."

"Oh." All of a sudden, I don't want to smile, but no one else seems sad or affected by Ewan's words, so I focus on where he is gesturing now.

"My second marriage ended in divorce, however Caroline gave me three beautiful children, so in my eyes, it wasn't a failure."

Again, I have no idea what to say to Ewan, but he continues his introductions, so I don't have to stand awkwardly for long.

"Barrett is the oldest of Caroline's children, but fifth in line." He chuckles, and I'm pretty sure if there was a joke in his words, it went straight over my head. "He's currently overseas, so you'll have to meet him a different time. Cassandra is older than Griffin, leaving him to be Caroline's baby."

"Hey! I'm no baby. I'm seventh in line." Griffin playfully scolds, and everyone laughs.

What was his sister's name again?

"And of course, my radiant Selena has been very busy over our time together. I'm sure you will forget everyone's names, but from oldest to youngest, this is Liam and Fallon. They are twins. Oswald, Brennen, Haile, Quinlan, Chance, Dustin, Anders, Everett and Ethan."

They all nod or wave and I laugh.

"Wow, that's a lot of children."

Selena smiles proudly, nodding. "Unfortunately, my body can no longer produce more heirs for Ewan, but I figure eleven children is enough."

"Yes. Absolutely." I laugh, a small part of my brain freaking out because, holy shit, that's a lot of childbirth.

"And let's not forget Gracie." Ewan chuckles, looking around before calling her name. "Gracie!"

"Yes, Ewan. I'm here." I frown at the blonde haired, blue eyed girl that bursts through the men, looking so completely different to everyone else in the room.

Wait. Did she call him Ewan? Not dad?

"Hey Agatha. I'm Grace." She offers me her hand and I shake it, giving her a warm smile as I study her features, which are so different to everyone else's. "You're confused, I see." She grins, and my eyes dart to Griffin in panic.

He chuckles, wrapping his arm around me and tugging me to his side. "Gracie isn't a Marx, but she's been living with us since she was little."

"Oh." I say in surprise. "I'm sorry if I was rude. You just look so different from everyone else."

"Girl, don't I know it. Not only don't I have the Italian-Australian blood running through my veins, but I'm way less uptight than the rest of them."

"Hey!" A few of the men complain, but Grace doesn't cower, a laugh slipping from her lips.

"Come on. Let me give you all the family gossip." Grace snatches my arm, tugging me from Griffin and further into the room.

"Not too much gossip please!" Griffin calls, and a laugh escapes me as I finally relax.

These people aren't so bad.

After some fussing in the kitchen, we all sit down to eat at the longest dinner table I've ever seen, and the family settles into fun banter as we devour our Christmas dinner.

I spend most of my time observing. I've never seen anything like this before, and it's hard not to be fascinated by how well they all get along. Well, most of them anyway.

The female twin, Fallon, has kept her gaze on me for most of the day. I can tell by her assessing eye that she doesn't trust me. Which is totally understandable. I'm a stranger in their home. Everyone here are siblings, aside from Grace, who acts just like a sibling despite not being one.

One thing I've noticed is that I'm the only plus one. Surely, the older family members have wives or husbands. The oldest boy, Leo, I think his name is, has to be well into his forties. So where is his wife or partner? Or children?

It seems odd to me, but I keep that thought to myself as I learn what it's like to be part of a family on Christmas Day.

My mind wanders to my mum and sister often, this year being one of the worst in a long time to notice their absence. Did their lives improve after I left? Do they have families to spend Christmas with? Are they even still alive?

"You ok?" Griffin's deep rasp against my ear snags my attention from my plate, and I turn my head, his nose brushing over my cheek, he's so close.

"Yes." I nod.

"What were you just thinking about? You seemed to go somewhere in your head."

Mr Observant, isn't he? How frustrating, yet also… nice.

"Just thinking about family. How nice it must be to have such a wonderful family to spend your Christmases with."

He brushes my golden waves back off my face, tucking a few strands behind my ear. "It is wonderful, yes. Family is very important to me."

A lump forms in my throat then. I can't relate to that, but I desperately want to.

"Do you want a family, Aggie?" Griffin asks quietly so no one else can hear our conversation. "Kids someday?"

The question takes me by surprise, my brows shooting high as I consider it. "I guess. Someday."

He smirks. "I already know what I want for Christmas next year."

"Oh, really?" I grin at his playful tone. "And what's that?"

"To be announcing your pregnancy."

I choke on my own saliva, my hand flying to cover my mouth as I cough.

"Oh my god, Griffin. Did you just say something gross to her?" Grace whines while the others start hooting and laughing.

"Shit. Do you need a drink?" Griffin starts fussing over me, but I shake my head, pushing him back a little so I can get a bit of space between us. He's been attentive to me all day. Some part of him touching me at most times. But at the mention of pregnancy, I'm about ready to bolt. I've lived such a solitary life and never thought I'd ever find someone to spend my years with, let alone have children.

"What can I do?" Griffin asks, but my coughing subsides, and I take a sip of water, trying to compose myself. "Do you need some fresh air?"

"No, but let's not discuss the P word again."

He frowns. "Ever?"

I shrug. "If I'm here with you this time next year, then we can start discussing it again then."

Slowly, his lips spread wide and his teeth flash as the biggest damn smile I've seen him wear morphs his face. "Deal."

After lunch, we all move outside, where most of the boys play cricket. Griffin joins in, and I enjoy sitting back in the warm sun and watching him joke around with his brothers. I learn a few things from this.

One is that he's very competitive. Another is that he looks downright sinful when he tugs his t-shirt off and sticks it in his back pocket, reminding me of last night when I thought he was going to kill me. Now I just think it is insanely hot.

I also learn that his brothers are all cut from the same sinful cloth. Jesus, they have good genes. I can only imagine they have women throwing themselves at their feet most days.

After a few glasses of wine, my bladder makes itself known, and I excuse myself to go and relieve it. After I've done my business and open the door to step back out of the lavish powder room, I jerk to a stop, nearly running into Fallon, who is standing in the doorway, blocking my path.

"Sorry," I laugh awkwardly. "Didn't see you there."

She raises a single dark brow at me and steps forward, which means I take a step back to avoid her running into me. This happens a couple of times until she closes us back inside the powder room.

"How'd you do it?" She snaps, and I flinch back.

"Do what?"

"Convince him to see you after finding out your involvement in the sex club scandal?"

I pale, my brows shooting up. "What? I don't—"

"Don't talk shit to me, Agatha. You know what I'm referring to. Griffin isn't in the business of letting child sex offenders take another breath, so why the fuck are you still alive right now?"

"I-I..." Shit. I need to go. "Excuse me, please. I'd like to leave."

She scoffs. "You think you'll ever get to walk away from him? He will kill you before he ever lets that happen."

The door behind Fallon flies open, and a monstrous Griffin reefs her back, shoving her against the wall in the hall, his hand wrapping around her throat.

"What the fuck did I tell you Fal? Huh?" He roars and Fallon doesn't even flinch.

"You're thinking with your dick and not your head, Griff. You know what she is." Fallon spits back in his face, not the least bit scared of her brother.

"You don't know anything. Things aren't always black and white!" He hisses back, baring his teeth, but Fallon doesn't flinch. Instead, her expression turns to rage.

"No? Aren't they? I'm pretty sure they were black and white when you pressed the gun against Marshall's head and pulled the trigger!"

"Enough!" The boom of Ewan Marx makes me squeak like a timid fucking mouse, my natural instinct sending me backwards into the powder room, ready to shut myself in. "This conversation has no place in this house!" Ewan steps up beside his children, looking between them. "Griffin, remove your hand from your sister's neck right fucking now."

Griffin hesitates, tutting like he's fighting an internal battle, but he does as his father requests, releasing Fallon's throat.

"Fallon, I specifically told you to keep your mouth shut. Be in my office at 9am tomorrow."

"And if I don't show?" She turns her snarl to her father and his lip curls.

"You know what will happen."

"Wait. Hang on a minute. Let's not get carried away." Griffin holds his hands up, waving them between his sister and father.

"Are you questioning how I do things, Griffin?" Ewan snaps and Griffin huffs, his eyes darting between them as he struggles to form a response.

"Uh..." I squeak. "I'm sorry Mr Marx. This is my fault. Please don't be angry at them. Fallon is just trying to protect Griffin from me, and Griffin is just trying to protect me from everyone else. I'll leave and give you all some peace to continue sharing your Christmas together."

"You're not leaving, Aggie." Griffin frowns, taking a step towards me.

"Griffin is right. You're not leaving. Stay. Eat. Drink. Enjoy. Tomorrow, you and I will also have a talk."

I shrink back at his words, ready to argue, but he walks away, effectively ending the conversation.

"Huh." Fallon grins menacingly. "I guess we will find out tomorrow if she has what it takes."

As she walks off, looking smug as fuck, I don't miss the worry that mars Griffin's face.

Fuck. What have I done?

Chapter Sixteen

Sharing

Griffin

Fuck! I'm going to kill Fallon for confronting Agatha like that. And then I'm going to find out how the fuck her and my father know about Aggie's involvement in the sex club scandal, because I was pretty fucking sure I'd destroyed all the evidence.

As I watch my dad's retreating back, Aggie pushes past me and Fallon, and runs.

"Aggie!" I call, and Fallon laughs.

"Huh. She's just proving my point. She can't hack it, Griff. Get rid of her."

If I didn't love my little sister, I'd fucking put a bullet through her skull right now.

When Aggie doesn't stop running, I watch her disappear around the corner and know she's heading for the front door. Fuck.

Leaving my sister's snickers behind, I take chase, my heavy feet pounding on the timber floors as I try to catch up to my woman.

When I round the corner, I see Aggie bolting out the front door, leaving it wide like she can't waste any time closing it, and her feet carry her down the front steps.

"Aggie!" I boom, and I hear a squeal fly from her lips as she disappears from sight.

Fucking hell, Aggie. Don't do this.

I continue my chase, reaching the front door and leaping down the front steps as I see Aggie's head over the top of the cars, darting between the parked vehicles.

"Stop, Aggie!" I yell, but she doesn't stop or even look back. She keeps running.

Leaping over the front of Oswald's car to take a shortcut, I run towards my car, knowing that's where she's headed, and I see her panicked face as she darts out from between the cars, reaching my driver's side door.

As she grabs the handle, I reach her, my hands gripping her shoulders and spinning her to face me before I push her, not so gently, against my car.

"Stop!" I growl, her caramel eyes wild with fear and tears. "Don't fucking run from me, Aggie. Don't you get it? That's exactly what they expect you to do. If you leave, you prove them right, and fuck me, Aggie. I was sure you were brave enough to handle this."

"Handle this? Are you serious? I'll be lucky to leave here alive." She screeches, and I frown.

"What are you talking about?"

"Your dad wants to see me tomorrow. He's going to kill me, isn't he?" Aggie whisper-yells.

"What?" My brows furrow before I shake my head. "No, baby. He just wants to chat with you. Granted, it may be an uncomfortable chat, but he's not going to kill you. My family isn't like that."

Her brows shoot high. "Really? Your family isn't like that?" She points back towards the house as anger consumes her. "Your psycho sister just bailed me up in the fucking bathroom. She knows about the sex club, Griffin. Let's not forget how she said you would kill me if I tried to walk away from you!"

Fucking Fallon! I'll make her pay for this.

"They were just words." I try to gentle my tone, hoping she hears my honesty. "She's testing you. She's pushing you to flee to prove you don't have what it takes to be in my life. She's trying to see how brave you are." I reach out and take her hand in mine, bringing it down between us.

"Newsflash. I'm not that fucking brave." She snaps, and I smirk.

"Yes, you are, baby. I know it in my gut that you're the right woman to stand by my side."

Her shoulders fall at my words and she shakes her head. "What if I'm not? What if you've invited me into your life and I see too much? You know, and I know, I'll end up dead."

"You watch too many movies." I grin and she frowns.

"How do you think the movies get written? By research and facts." She deadpans and I shake my head.

"Please don't leave me." I say softly, hearing my voice break a little, and I reach over and cup her face. "I need you. By my side. Please."

Aggie's big caramel eyes study mine for a long, drawn-out moment, and I feel like she can see into my soul.

"Does your whole family play head games?" she asks quietly, and I shrug.

"Newcomers are always tested." I brush some of her golden blonde strands off her face before cupping it again, and she finally relaxes into my touch.

"You should have warned me, Griff."

"I didn't think it would come to this. I'm sorry," I say honestly.

She studies my eyes for a moment, as if she's looking for the slightest hint of a lie, but she won't find one.

"Things were easier when you were a stranger with no face," she whispers, and my lips thin.

"You wish I didn't reveal myself?"

She considers that for a moment.

Our subbing for Santa game was fun. The anticipation was off the charts. But it was just a game, and now I'm asking her for more. For something real.

"Actually, I'm glad you finally showed me who you were." She offers me a small smile. "Easy is overrated."

Fuck.

Relief washes over me at her words, and a grin tugs at my lips.

"So, will you stay?"

"Are you sure I'll walk out alive?" She asks in all seriousness, and I hate that she even considers being killed an option.

"I'll burn this place to the ground and everyone in it if anyone so much as touches you with a feather." My growl is menacing, and the look in her eyes tells me she believes every word.

"I guess that will have to do." She grins, and fuck, I love seeing her smile.

Pressing my body flush against hers, I steal a kiss and she instantly melts into me. Her dainty hands fist in my hair, dragging me closer, and I moan into her mouth, wrapping my arms around her slim waist, not able to have her close enough.

When my dick joins the party, I pull back reluctantly, my eyes dropping to her pink swollen lips, before staring into her caramel gaze.

"Fuck, Aggie. I know we are new, but I feel like I've known you longer. So much longer." I press my forehead to hers, and her lashes flutter with emotion as she stares back.

"Griff." She breathes. "I still have so many questions, but I'm too exhausted to think about them tonight."

"Shit, I love it when you call me Griff." I admit, and a laugh spills free from my woman.

"Well *Griff*. Any chance we can get drunk and forget our worries for the rest of the day?"

"Absolutely." I beam, pulling her in for a hug. "And later, I'm going to make you come, and then fuck you so hard the entire house will hear."

"Oh my god, no!" She pushes me back, slapping my shoulder and I chuckle and snatch her hand, slowly leading her back towards the house.

We wander back inside, and I lead her to the kitchen where I pour us another drink. Given Fallon's attempt to cause trouble earlier, I have no interest in exposing Aggie to that shit again, so I stay attached to her for the rest of the day. I keep our bodies linked, either by our hands, arms, or legs, as we both pretend that Fallon isn't staring daggers into the side of my woman's head for the rest of the afternoon.

Fucking Fallon. She's not normally a troublemaker, but I'll be fucked if I sit back and let her torment the woman I'm going to make mine. She can fuck right off.

Thankfully, she keeps her distance, and we can relax somewhat, watching my brothers hang shit on each other, and Gracie talks Aggie's ears off with stories of me from when I was in my early twenties.

Dinner is leftovers, and afterwards everyone pitches in to do the dishes and clean the living area and kitchen before dispersing into different groups throughout the house.

Upstairs, just off the landing through double doors, is the rec room, which is more of an adults' retreat. Sports memorabilia hangs on the panel walls, which are a rich charcoal, giving the room a dark and sultry feel. An extensive bar runs along one corner, with a wide screen TV and sofa nearby. The centre of the room features a black timber pool table topped with red felt, and at the other end of the room, sitting before large glass doors which are open letting in the warm night air, is an oval poker table.

It's probably more of a man's retreat than anything.

Following my brothers, I lead Aggie to the poker table, taking a seat before tugging her down onto my lap. Kendrick, Liam, Oswald and Brennen take their seats too, and Kendrick starts shuffling the cards, while the other three pretend like they aren't checking out my woman.

Sneaky fucks!

We all chat and take the piss out of each other as Kendrick deals the cards, and we sink into a comfortable flow as we play against each other. Something we do every year.

I whisper the rules in Aggie's ear as we play, and at times, I get her to move chips into the centre—which gives me a good view of her arse—and I ask Aggie what she thinks I should do. She doesn't really have a clue how to play, but I want her to be involved, and the expressions she makes while she thinks over what to do are fucking adorable.

About an hour in, once Aggie has relaxed into the atmosphere and gotten comfortable with my brothers, I decide to make my card playing a little more fun.

Aggie is relaxed back against me, her head resting against my shoulder and her arse sitting right over my hard dick. She has to be able to feel it, because it certainly feels her. Reaching under the table, I brush my fingers over Aggie's bare thigh and slowly run them up towards heaven.

"Griff." She whispers, turning her head to my ear, her breath warm.

"Yes, my little elf." I say, not keeping my voice quiet, and she stiffens, which only presses her harder against my straining cock. I guess using her sub name came as a surprise.

"What are you doing?" She whispers, and a smirk tugs at my lips.

My fingers travel higher, moving to the inside of her upper thigh, and I feel a warm flush travel over her skin.

Using my nose, I nudge her head, so she turns it to face my brothers, who are still pretending not to sneak glances at her, and I whisper in her ear. "I wanna do some public play. Are you going to obey, little elf?"

As I say the words, I brush my fingers over her damp panties, feeling the shape of her hungry lips underneath. Aggie's breathing deepens, and I notice her head dart to each of my brothers, checking to see if they are aware of what's going on.

They are. But she doesn't need to know that just yet.

Even though the lower half of Aggie's body is hidden under the poker table, I worry she may not be so keen given the close proximity of my brothers, but when she subtly spreads her legs wider, I know she's happy to play this game with me.

The thrill of the situation has my cock weeping, and as I continue to gently brush teasing fingers over the panty clad seam of Aggie's pussy, the rush of wet heat that pools there shows me just how into this she is.

Fuck yes. She is perfect.

"You're so wet for me." I rasp against her ear, inhaling her sweet vanilla scent.

Turning her head back to my ear, she sucks in a deep breath like she is working hard to remain composed. "We can't do this here, Griff. They'll notice."

I grin, turning back to her ear. "So? That's half the fun, little elf."

She glances out the corner of her eye at me, and her brows shoot up. She knows I'm being serious about this. That I want to do this to her with my brothers in the room.

As I press firmer against her clit this time, I feel her hips do a slight roll under the table, her willpower to fight her arousal practically impossible now.

She turns her head to the side again, her lips practically kissing my ear. "You want me to come in front of your brothers?"

"Fuck yeah I do." I growl, not bothering to keep my voice low.

All four of my brothers glance at me, their brows furrowing just the slightest as they try to figure out who I'm talking to, but just as quickly, they drop their eyes back down to their cards.

I don't give Aggie another chance to deny me. My fingers starting their assault, rubbing with more pressure over her sensitive nub.

Aggie's eyes move back to the other four around the table, but all she will see is my brothers playing cards. She won't see that the game is at a standstill.

She rolls her hips again, this time not as subtly, and a small gasp escapes her before she presses back against me and bites her lower lip.

"Fuck, Aggie. I want to throw you down on this table and eat you in front of them."

My words cause her to whimper, and she doesn't even realise I said them loud enough for my brothers to hear.

It's at that moment that Liam, the fucker, decides to make a point of watching Aggie as he wears a small smirk, placing his cards face down on the table before relaxing back for the show.

Aggie gasps, but I pick up speed, circling her clit so she can't think straight, and a moan escapes her as she turns her head into my neck again.

"Stop, Griff. Liam is watching."

I chuckle before surprising Aggie by speaking the next words loud enough that she has no doubt everyone can hear them.

"Liam can look, but he can't touch."

All four of my brothers chuckle, giving away that they were already aware of what I'm doing to my woman under the table, and Aggie stiffens, her eyes darting around to see their unfazed smirks.

"Part your legs wider, baby." I instruct, no longer bothering to whisper, and she's helpless not to obey.

"Is this your way of trying to win the game, Griff?" Oswald asks. "Because you know we'll fold, needing to run off and have a tug after this."

"Oh my god." Aggie whimpers, and I take that moment to slip my fingers under the fabric of her panties.

"Just give into it, baby. Let yourself go."

As two of my digits slide inside her tight hot heat, she watches as my other three brothers lay their cards on the table, rearrange their dicks in their pants and relax back in their chairs for the show. I can tell Aggie is a little torn about what to do. Part of her loves being watched. It's part of what drew me to her in the beginning, because I fucking love me some exhibitionism. But there's another part of her that wants to shy away from what's happening.

"Fuck." She moans, giving in and using one hand to pinch her nipple through her dress, and the other to circle her clit under the table as my finger works her from the inside.

"Hella-hot." Liam grins, his eyes on her face as his hand disappears under the table.

"You're soaking, baby. Are you gonna squirt?" I ask, grinning.

"What?" Brennen sits up in his chair, his eyes wide. "She squirts?"

"Yeah. Sometimes." I admit as my woman closes her eyes and gives in to the building sensations.

"I've never been with a girl that squirts. I wanna see!" Brennen demands, showing his immature twenty-six-year-old age, but he can fuck right off. So, I make sure he can tell by my tone that I'm serious when I speak next.

"No! That part is just for me."

Aggie is now writhing in my lap, teasing the fuck out of my dick, which feels like the skin is going to split any moment. I don't think she'd even notice if she was naked and spread bare before my brothers right now.

I can feel her walls squeezing my fingers tighter as she chases her orgasm, so I speed up my fingers, curling them and pressing against her upper wall, telling my little elf what I want. I want her to squirt. The pressure and pace I'm applying to just the right place will ensure her orgasm isn't just muscle contractions but accompanied by female ejaculation.

Aggie thrusts her hips up, eagerly meeting my fingers, and a moment later she starts convulsing. A cry of ecstasy rips from her throat as wave after wave crashes over her, and the warm feeling of wet spray shoots from her, all over my hand and right into her panties.

When she's done, her panting breaths aren't the only ones in the room, and when she pries her eyes open, it's just in time to see my annoying younger brother, Brennen, standing up from peeking under the table.

"She squirted alright. There's stuff dripping from the chair."

"Fucking hell, Bren. You really had to go there?" I hiss and Brennen shrugs.

"I wanted to make sure she wasn't faking."

Grinning, Liam stands, pulling his hand from his pants and holding it up for us to see the evidence of his own release sticking between his parted fingers.

"Looks like I need a shower." He laughs, shooting me a wink. "Welcome to the family, Aggie."

"Come on, Bren, let's leave the lovebirds to have some time alone." Oswald stands, nudging Brennen's chair, who nods and follows Oswald out of the room with a smirk.

"Well, you finally found your match, Griff." Kendrick stands, shooting me and Aggie a shit-eating grin. "Welcome to the Marx family, Aggie. I promise we aren't all perves like Griffin here."

"Hey, you could have left, bro." I tease my older brother, and Kendrick nods. "Yep, I probably should have, so Aggie knows some of us are gentlemen."

"Actually. I probably would have felt insulted if you left." She says, letting the naughty part of her take over.

Sexy little minx.

"Which is why I stayed." Kendrick bows. "Good night, you two."

The moment we are alone, Aggie stands from my lap awkwardly, turning to face me with fluid still dripping down her legs.

"Is my Santa happy?"

"Very." I smile. "Were you ok with what I just did?"

"Yes." She nods, even as she blushes. "I like being watched."

"Oh, I know. You've given me many shows once you knew the cameras were there."

She giggles. "The best thing about what we just did was knowing you wanted me to do that too. It was hot."

"Yes, it was. I'm so fucking hard right now," I admit, and she nods.

"Well Santa, before we go and sort out your hard cock, can I ask one thing?" She says in all seriousness, and I sit forward in the chair, ignoring the mess she made.

"Of course."

"Don't ask me to fuck your brothers or anyone else outside of a sex club. And even then, don't ask me to fuck one of your brothers there, either. Or sisters. They are off limits."

What we did pushes a lot of boundaries. Sometimes things can get misinterpreted, and lines can become blurred. I'm not interested in being intimate with anyone else but Aggie, and I'm glad she is setting this boundary. It shows that her interests only lie with me, and that she's not fair game to my family.

I'd fucking kill them, anyway. No way do I want them to touch her.

Slowly, a grin tugs at the corners of my lips. "I'm actually really glad you asked that. And I won't ask that of you. Ever. I'm the only Marx that is allowed to have access to your body. No exceptions."

"Thank you." She smiles, relaxing her shoulders.

This is exactly what I need. A woman who will speak up no matter how uncomfortable it makes her. She's fucking perfect.

Chapter Seventeen

Connection

Agatha

Cleaning up the mess I'd made doesn't take too long. Griffin insists on taking care of most of it, and minutes later he retrieves our bags from the car and leads me upstairs to a bedroom.

The house has eight bedrooms, so some of Griffin's siblings are bunking in together, and some went home since they don't live too far away.

The bedroom Griffin closes us inside has off white timber panelling wrapping the walls, and a platinum velvet royal looking bed covered in crisp white sheets, with an array of neutral toned throw pillows. As I step further into the space, my eyes fall to the carpet, a beige colour that almost looks like it sparkles, and I feel my feet sink into its cushioned texture with each step.

"I feel like I'm going to make this room dirty." I say, not realising until it's too late how my words can be misinterpreted.

"I hope so." Griffin grins wickedly, wagging his dark brows.

Smirking, I shake my head, moving to the bed to glide my fingers over the top sheet as I work up the courage to have a new conversation with my Santa.

"I need something from you." I turn to watch Griffin's brows shoot up.

"Anything. Name it."

"Tonight, you're my bitch." I keep my face neutral, watching him closely.

"What?" He laughs, and I grin back, stepping towards him until we are toe to toe.

"Tonight, we do things my way. You play *my* game."

"And what is your game?" His rasp is low and filled with lust, making it hard not to climb him like a tree this very moment.

"Tantra."

"You want to do what you do with your clients?"

"Not exactly." Reaching up, I lace my arms around his neck, pulling him closer. "I give my clients tantric massage therapy. With you, I want tantric sex. You've spent the last week basically testing me to see if I'm compatible with your needs, right?"

"Kind of." He frowns.

"Well, now I need to see if you're compatible with me."

"By doing tantric sex?" He tilts his head, studying me, so I nod.

"Yes. Some people find it very confronting and exposing. It's not for everyone."

"Is that so?" He grins.

"Yes."

"Why?" He brushes some of my hair back off my forehead, his eyes filled with desire. "Isn't it just sex?"

"No. It's more about making a connection with your partner and the energy your body creates."

"Connection?" He frowns and again, I nod.

"Yes. Do you think you can hack it, Mr Marx?"

He grins. "There's only one way to find out."

His lips claim mine then for a searing kiss. I let him take this moment to relax and enjoy the kiss before I pull back and explain a few things.

"We need to set the mood in the room."

"How do we do that?"

Grinning, I slip away from him and move to my bag, pulling out some candles I packed in preparation for this. Placing them around the room, I light them before switching the light off to plunge us into the low amber hue that is instantly calming and romantic.

Griffin is leaning against the wall, his arms crossed over his chest while he watches me, a light grin tugging at his lips every now and then.

From the other side of the room, I start popping open the buttons on the front of my dress and his eyes flare with heat and excitement.

"Get naked, Mr Marx."

"Fuck, Aggie. I like hearing you call me that." He pushes off the wall, tugging his t-shirt over his head in that sexy way guys do, before he starts to work on his jeans.

"Of course you do. You're a man that rules over others. You like the power it gives you." I drop my dress to the floor, and he nods while his eyes rake over my near naked flesh.

"It feels like more than that when it falls from your lips." He rasps, and my cheeks heat.

"How so?"

"I'm not sure." He shrugs. "For some reason, I don't feel like I have the power when it comes to you. You honestly have the power to bring me to my knees."

Shit. His tone is so serious. He means more than the tantric experience we are about to embark on, and it ignites butterflies in my chest.

Obviously, his demand from last night that I say I'm his, is a sign that whatever this is between us means more than some casual fling to him. Surprisingly, I want it to be more, too. But just because I want it, doesn't mean it's right. We are in the very early days. Anything could happen.

When his jeans pool around his ankles, I move forward across the plush carpet, the pads of my feet sinking into its luxuriousness. Griffin kicks the denim away from his feet and moves forward to meet me in the middle. When he reaches out to touch me, I hold my hands up to stop him, shaking my head.

"No touching." I whisper, and he freezes, his eyes going wide.

"No touching?"

I shake my head, trying to fight back my grin at how cute he looks right now. I reach behind me, unlatching my bra and watch his eyes devour me and I ease it down to drop to the floor.

"A huge part of tantric sex is about energy. About movement and anticipation." I hook my fingers in my soaking panties and tug them down, keeping my eyes trained on Griffin's face. "You can do that by engaging in your chakras and exploring the essence with each one. Although maybe not all in one sitting."

"Chakra?" He asks absentmindedly as he too tugs down his jocks, his eyes taking all of me in. "What's that?"

"Chakras are energy points in your body. A good way to think of them is spinning disks of energy that connect to nerves and organs. By focusing on one at a time, you can enjoy very different experiences."

"Is my dick one?" He smirks, and I laugh, not able to hold back.

"No, Griff. Your dick isn't one, but that's not to say that your dick won't get enjoyment from it."

He sucks in a deep breath, his dark eyes locking with mine to study me for a beat.

"I don't know how long I can hold back from touching you, Aggie. You're like a drug to me."

Shit. I understand his words completely as the urge to simply leap on him and sink down on his hard cock is almost overwhelming. But I refrain. I want to see if he can do this. I know he will enjoy it if he gives it a chance.

"We can touch soon, but for now, let's focus on energy." I gesture my head to the bed, and he follows on the other side, his eyes staying locked on me the whole time.

We both climb onto the soft sheets, kneeling before each other, and I offer Griffin a warm smile.

"Let's focus on our breathing first. Close your eyes and slow your breathing a little until you feel calm."

Nodding, Griffin closes his eyes, following my instructions, so I do too, turning my focus on my breathing.

"I can't focus." Griffin's voice is loud in the space, and my eyes fly open, startled a little to see him looking adorably concerned.

Grinning, I reach down and take his hand, guiding it to my chest and pressing his palm flat against my skin, right over my heart.

"I thought you said no touching."

"I'm modifying it for you. Now focus on my breathing and synchronise yours to mine."

Griffin frowns, but nods, his eyes falling to where his hand is pressed against my skin. I take slow deep breaths, watching how his chest starts to sync with mine.

"Close your eyes." I whisper, and his lids fall shut as he continues to focus on our combined breathing. "We are going to do this for a few minutes. Let your mind drift a little, but not too far that you forget about your breathing."

"Can you touch me too?" Griff whispers and I smile, watching one of his eyes crack open to peek at me.

"Is your love language touch, Mr Marx?" I ask, and he shrugs. "Ok, I'll touch you, too. But close your eyes and focus."

Fighting back a smirk, Griffin snaps his one eye shut, so I reach forward, pressing my hand to his chest, too. Instantly, heat travels up my arm like a sponge in water, and my lids fall shut as I enjoy the contact. Since Griffin is more about touch, I decide to revert to that form of tantra, and I slowly start running the pads of my fingers over the smooth skin of his chest.

"Keep your eyes closed," I whisper, "but let your hands explore my chest, neck and head."

As soon as the words are out of my mouth, Griffin's fingers are gliding over my skin, travelling up to my collarbone, neck, ear, and back down again. My hands follow a similar trail on his skin, and to make sure he is obeying my rules, I peek, cracking one eye open to see that he still has his eyes closed as he explores me.

When I move my touch to his arms, he moves his to mine too. When I start grazing my fingers over his face, he follows suit. Next, I sink my fingers into his hair, and his digits delve into mine as well.

I crack an eye again, but he's still in his zone, his eyes closed, his face looking relaxed and blissful, so I close my eye again and enjoy the feel of his touch. Slowly, I run my fingertips back down the side of his face and start to travel south. When I get to his chest, I can feel how deep the rise and fall of his breathing is. He is affected by this, which is good.

"Open your eyes." I whisper, prying mine open to see him do the same, a lazy look of lust meeting my gaze. "Eye contact plays a key part, as well."

"So we just stare at each other?" He asks, his face neutral as our fingers roam over each other's nipples lightly.

"Not stare. Look." I smile. "Look into my eyes and get comfortable there."

"I could drown in your eyes, Aggie." He admits, and my heart does a little flip thing in my chest.

"Then drown in them. Open yourself up to me." I keep my voice low as I speak, and I swear, even though he already has dark eyes, they darken even more.

"I understand what you said earlier about how it can be confronting." He rasps, and I smile.

"Some people find it extremely hard to let someone really look into their eyes. After all, it's the window to your soul."

"My soul belongs to the devil." He grins, but I shake my head.

"Incorrect. Your soul belongs to me."

He relaxes and smiles. "Ok, Aggie. I'm yours."

I believe him too. Which is just weird since we only met last week, and not even properly until last night.

Maybe there's some truth behind soulmates being naturally drawn to each other. Is Griffin Marx my soulmate? It certainly feels like I've known him for longer than I have.

"Breathe with me." I whisper, trying to steer us back on track. "Nice and slow. Let yourself completely relax."

As Griffin does what I ask, my hand comes away from his skin to hover over his abdomen. When he frowns, I hurry to explain, not wanting him to get too side-tracked again.

"Can you feel the heat of my palm?"

His eyes dart down to where my hand is hovering, and he nods, his eyes coming up to meet mine again as he too eases his hand away from my skin, bringing it to hover over my navel.

"There's energy flowing from my hand into your skin. It's a kiss of a caress. Tell me if you can feel it as it moves, but don't look anywhere but into my eyes."

He nods, and I start moving my hand. After a beat, his hand starts moving too, and I feel it travel the same path as my own hand, as if we were actually touching.

"Holy shit," he whispers. "That's crazy."

"It's tantra." I smile, continuing my exploration until I hover over his cock. It must jerk, because it taps my fingers, and his eyes widen.

"Shit. Sorry. I couldn't help that."

Sucking in my lips, I bite back a laugh before I move my hand up and down, hovering over his shaft as if I were actually touching him.

"Now you're just teasing me." He pants, his eyes breaking contact with mine to fall to his lap. He watches as I mimic wrapping my hand around his shaft, not letting my hand actually touch him, and again, his dick jerks.

"It's like I can feel you. Like a feather or something."

I grin, knowing it's the combination of his mind, anticipation, and the heat from my skin.

My tantric sessions aren't usually like this. There's normally less chatting, but I don't care. I love that he is trying this with me, even though I know I'm about to change it up and move it along faster. Maybe it's because we are new and desperate for each other, but I'm struggling to keep my willpower in check. I'm so ridiculously drawn to him. I think I understand what he meant when he said I was like a drug to him. I feel the same way. It's like I need him. Like if I don't have him close right this second, I will die.

Which is stupid. Of course I won't die. But hell, my heart aches like I will.

"Sit with your legs crossed in front of you." I suggest, shifting back a little to give him room.

"Like I'm a little kid sitting on the mat at school?" He smirks as he asks, and I grin back.

"Like yoga. Pretend you're about to do yoga."

He nods, sitting cross-legged before me.

"If it's ok with you, I'd like to move this along a bit. I'm having a little trouble holding back."

He beams, his grin way too sexy for the way he's sitting on the bed with his dick at full mast. "Fuck yes. No complaints from me."

"Ok." I nod, rising to my knees. "Let's do the Lotus position."

"There are positions in tantra?" His brows hitch high, and I smile, nodding.

"Yes. Many. The Lotus position is a very intimate position, though. Do you think you can handle it?"

"Yeah. Why wouldn't I?" He frowns and I shrug.

"It's less like fucking and more like…" I suck in my lips before I finish the sentence. "Love making."

Again, his brows hitch. He's going to get a headache at this rate. I worry for a beat that it might be too much, but then his lips spread wide, and a devilish grin contorts his face.

"You wanna make love to me, beautiful?"

"If you think you can handle it?" I jut my chin up, hoping to hide the momentary drop in confidence I'm hit with.

Reaching forward, Griffin picks up my hand and lifts it to his lips, pressing a kiss to my knuckles before speaking. "I can handle anything you throw at me, Aggie."

I move then, climbing onto his lap to wrap my body around his, crossing my ankles together behind his back while my arms weave around his neck.

"The idea behind this position is to be limited with how much movement can happen. I can either dry hump your bare dick or slide you inside, but we need to stay locked together like this."

Griffin nips at my ear. "Not much room for thrusting, but I don't really care, as long as we stay together like this."

"You like it?" I ask, pulling back a little to look into his eyes.

"Fuck yes. I need you close. Always."

His lips close over mine, and on instinct, our bodies start pressing against each other, hungry for more. I wasn't sure that Griffin would be interested in anything that wasn't a good hard fuck. Don't get me wrong, I love that, but this I also love. And for some reason, it feels so much more with him than with my tantra coach I learnt it from a number of years ago. He'd warned me at the time that it can be a powerful experience, and outside of training really should be with someone you feel safe to reveal all your secrets to.

I don't know if I can ever admit all of my secrets to Griffin, especially the one about my family, but if I did, I get the feeling he'd be able to handle it. Especially given his line of work.

Letting myself fall victim to the sensations building between us, I move my hips slightly, grinding my pussy over his hard straining cock and we both moan into each other's mouths, breaking our kiss.

"You feel amazing." Griff rasps next to my ear before sucking the lobe into the warm heat of his mouth.

"You wanna keep going like this, or you want to go inside me?" I ask as I grind a little harder, hungry for more friction.

"Stay like this. I wanna come on your clit."

"Fuck." I moan, my grip around his neck going tighter as we hug impossibly close, our hips the only parts of us moving the slightest.

"I like hearing you swear." He pants, nipping at my lobe this time. "I like knowing I have the ability to make you lose your inhibitions."

Moaning louder at his admission, my skin prickles with heat as Griff chuckles at my lack of control.

"Fuck, Griff." I pant, grinding harder. Faster. The silken feel of his stiff cock sliding between my folds, sending me into a frenzy.

"Look at me." He rasps, and I pull back a little so my eyes can meet his.

"How did this..." I pant, sucking in some much needed air, "turn into you taking control?"

He chuckles. "I'll always give you what you need. And you need me to dominate. Don't you?"

"Yes." I admit, looking into his eyes, showing him how much I need him without saying it outright.

"I need you, too." He grunts out, his face turning almost pained. He's not in pain, though. Quite the opposite.

We don't say anything else. Our eyes locked as our pelvises chase the high we are giving to each other. As we both draw closer to our ecstasy, Griff's hands grip my arse cheeks, his fingers digging into my flesh and pressing me harder against him. His dick slides through my wet folds, hitting my needy bundle of nerves with each stroke, and I start to soar. He must see it on my face, his friction picking up in pace until my internal walls start clamping onto thin air, and an explosion of pleasure detonates my nerve endings. The moment I feel the hot wet heat of his cum jet from his dick to hit my clit, I forget to breathe. Tiny zaps of electricity shoot over my skin from head to toe, heating my body from the inside out until I'm almost positive I'm about to self-combust.

Never have I felt this. Never has my body undeniably claimed another in such a way that I'm pretty sure our souls just merged.

My body has decided for me. This man is mine, whether I think it's a good idea or not.

Griffin

Aggie was right. Tantric sex can be confronting. I'm normally into rough, throw her around and show my dominance type of sex, making sure to pleasure her over and over before I take, but this. Tantra. It was something else.

The way her body wrapped around mine like we were going to melt into each other and form one being was a new experience. I found myself getting pleasure just from her closeness. From the smell of her skin just under her ear. From the way her eyes spoke the words she can't seem to find yet. And from the way her hands clung to my back like she never wanted to let me go.

I barely needed her to touch my cock, even though the press of her core teased that too.

Fucking epic.

I hope that one day she can teach me how to hold in my ejaculation, so eventually, I can legitimately fuck her all night long until we both pass out.

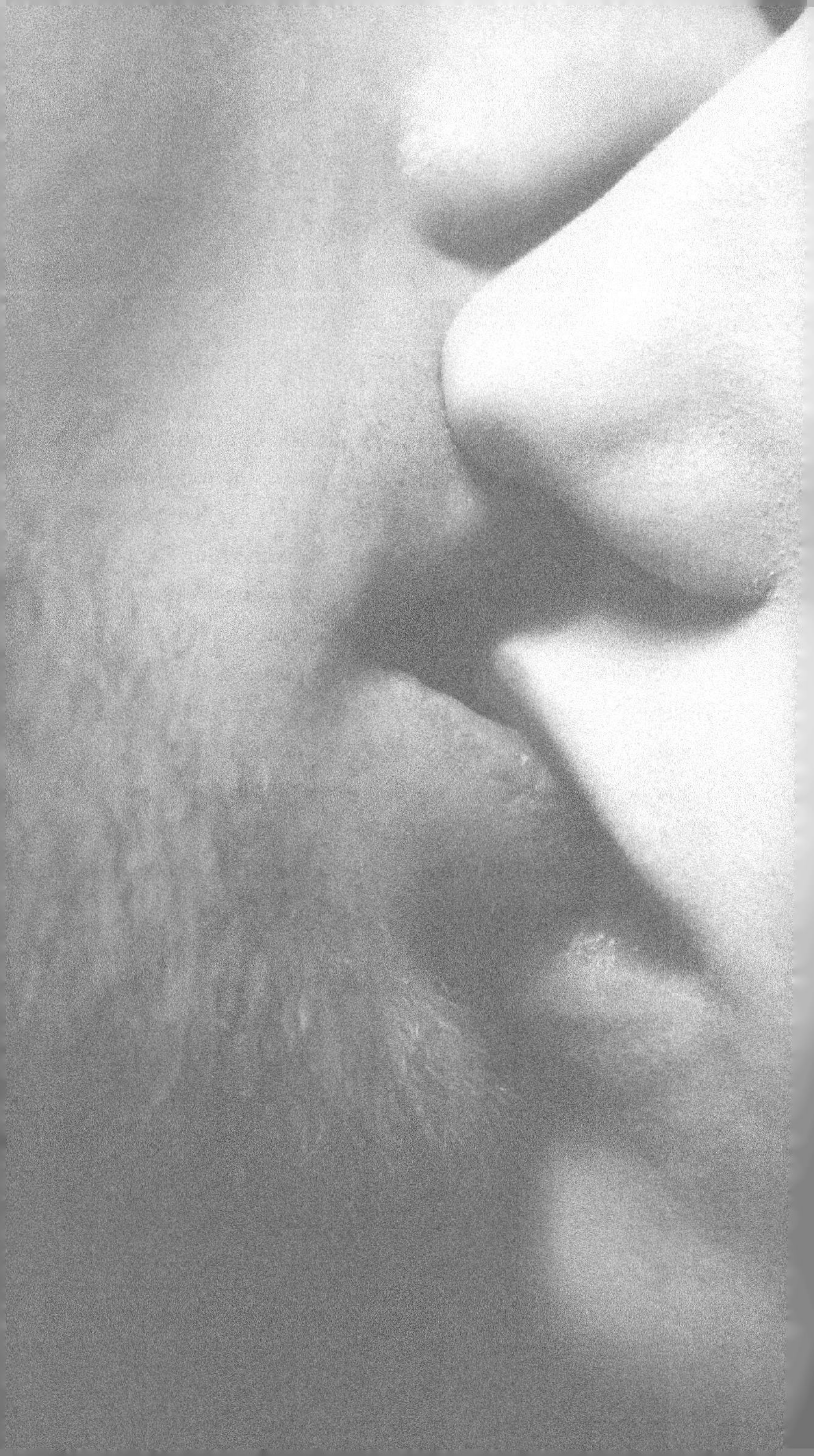

Chapter Eighteen

Truths

Agatha

Boxing Day is usually the first part of the Christmas season I like, because everything goes on sale. That's typically how I celebrate my Christmas, going shopping and buying myself gifts, which mostly consist of the lacy lingerie variety.

This year, however, there's no shopping. This year there's a big arse boat that looks like something David and Victoria Beckham would own. The boat is called *The Audrey*, after Ewan's first wife, who passed away from breast cancer, and Griffin price dropped on the drive to the bay; it cost over five million dollars.

Seriously, who has that sort of money to just go and buy a damn boat?

I guess organised crime pays well.

I push that thought aside, because I don't want that part of Griffin's life influencing how I see him. There are so many wonderful things about this man, which makes it hard to remember what family he belongs to.

The boat has a crew of six staff today, all uniformed up like it's a cruise ship, and we set sail by mid-morning.

Earlier this morning, at breakfast, we were getting some funny looks from Griffin's brothers, plus the typical glare from Fallon, until finally Grace revealed that Griffin and I were a little loud in our bedroom last night. I was sure my face lit on fire, which was surprising given what we had done in front of some of Griffin's brothers earlier in the evening.

Thankfully, not all of them have joined Griffin's parents on the boat, so I only have to suffer embarrassment from Oswald and Brennen, even though they haven't said anything.

The boat is divine, with three levels of decks and two levels of cabins below.

Grabbing a bottle of champagne, an ice bucket, and a platter of cheese and crackers, Griffin leads me to the front of the boat, which he tells me is called the bow, where there is a lounge and small table. There is no shade up here, but with the cooler ocean breeze, it's beautiful sitting in the warm summer sun.

"I was thinking we should play a game to get to know each other better." Griffin smirks at me and my brows lift.

"What sort of game?"

"Something simple, like twenty questions. I found a list on the internet of things you should know about your partner six months into your relationship. I figure we can skip ahead and just ask the questions."

I study Griffin's face as he speaks, noticing that he almost seems nervous, which is a first. He holds up his phone to show me he has a list, and I smile, giving him a nod.

"Sounds interesting. Do we both answer the same question?"

He nods. "Yep."

"Ok. Let's do it."

Grinning at me, Griffin pours us each a glass of bubbles before sitting back on the sofa-like sun lounge and tugging me back with him. I get comfy, curling into his side a little despite the heat.

"Ok. First question. How do you like to celebrate your birthday?"

"Oh." I glance up at his face. "I was waiting for you to ask what my favourite colour is or something."

"Not yet apparently." He grins, and I nod.

"Ok. Well, my birthday is usually cold, and yuk given it's in July, so I usually go out for dinner with friends, and head home before midnight. It's too cold to be waiting around for taxis that time of year."

"Ok, I'm rephrasing that question." Griffin grumbles and I laugh, glancing back up at him.

"Why?"

"Because we can do better than that for your birthday." He presses his lips to my forehead before pulling back and rephrasing the question.

"If money was no barrier and you could do anything you wanted for your birthday, what would it be?"

I consider that for a beat, my mind stuck on an answer since I've never had the luxury of considering it before.

"Maybe something just like this." I gesture around me. "Warm sun, the ocean, a boat, and you."

A low growl rumbles in his chest, taking me by surprise before he leans forward to nibble on my lips. "Done. I can make that birthday wish come true."

I shake my head, grinning wide before I ask him to answer the same question.

"Your turn, Mr Marx."

"Hmmm. Well, my birthday is in September, so it's still a little cold here in Victoria, but I think I'd like to take our private jet to the Maldives. Rent out a villa over the water and get lost in your body for an entire month."

I giggle. "I can help with the getting lost in my body part."

"Yes, you can, my little elf. You do that so well." He nips at my lips again, turning it into a searing kiss that nearly causes me to spill my champagne.

"Ok, next question." I urge pulling back, and he grins, his eyes moving back to focus on his phone.

"Do you like alone time, and if so, how much do you need?"

"Wow, these are quite personal." I point out and Griffin nods.

"Like I said, a good way to get to know one another."

"Ok, so yes, I do like a little alone time. I like to do yoga in the mornings, and as much as I enjoyed our bath together a few nights ago, I do really enjoy a quiet soak in silence."

Griffin grins and gives me a nod. "Noted."

"And you?" I ask, and he shrugs.

"I'd prefer to take a shit alone. Other than that, I'm good."

My head falls back as a laugh rips free, and Griffin grins, pleased with himself.

"Next question." He chuckles. "What is your favourite food?"

"Oooh, that's easy. Anything with chocolate."

Griffin chuckles. "A sweet tooth, hey?"

I nod. "A little food play, too. With chocolate." I smile, shooting Griffin a wink, and he throws his head back laughing this time.

"My favourite food is a ribeye steak, but I think I'm going to revise that now. Eating chocolate off you sounds way better."

"It really does. I think we should do that soon." I grin and he nods.

"Later today. I'm pretty sure there's a whole array of chocolate on board."

As we laugh, I snatch Griffin's phone off him and read out the next question.

"How long do you need to get ready to head out the door for the day?"

He grins. "Thirty minutes max, but honestly, I can be up and out in less than five."

"That doesn't leave very much time to iron your suits." I counter, and he scoffs.

"Woman, my suits are pressed and ready to go."

"Of course they are," I smile before including my answer to the question. "I can be up and out in fifteen minutes if I have to be, but I usually allow myself an hour and a half after I wake to do my yoga, eat a decent breaky and organise my daily to-do list, and then I take a quick shower and make myself presentable."

"Are you part of the 5am club?" Griffin asks in all seriousness, and I shake my head.

"More like the 7am club."

"Good to know." He leans forward and presses a kiss to my forehead, and I swear such a platonic kiss has never felt more intimate.

"Ok, next question." Griffin pulls back, stealing his phone off me.

We go through the list of questions, learning more about each other and spending a lot of our time laughing, or finding our answers open up a whole other conversation, steering us off track for a while.

I learn that Griffin's closest friend is actually his brother Liam, with Liam's twin sister Fallon a close second to his nearest and dearest. Something that shocks me a little after he nearly strangled her yesterday.

He prefers TV shows over movies because he doesn't have the ability to sit still for longer than an hour at a time. He can't help but laugh when someone falls over, which he admits has gotten him into trouble a number of times over the years. His guilty pleasure, beside me apparently, is buying new shoes and belts. The best way to support him when he is stressed or upset is to be patient and remain nearby so he can lose himself in me at the snap of his fingers. His words, not mine.

His biggest fear used to be dying alone, but now it's losing me. He is a dog person, wanted to be a fireman when he was little, and if he could travel back in time to change something he did in the past, it would be to never make his first kill, because once he stepped over that line, there was no going back.

We sit in silence after he reveals that truth, and my heart breaks for him knowing that once upon a time, he was a kid that had dreamed of a different future, but was dragged into the family business to become a completely different person.

"Your turn." Griffin's voice is a quiet rasp as his dark eyes lift from his lap to lock onto my gaze. "If you could travel back in time and change something you did, what would it be?"

My heart leaps in my chest as a hot sweat rushes over me, memories of my past slamming into me like a freight train. Griffin and I aren't that different. Not when it comes to answering this question, and while I'm sure he'd understand if

I admitted my past to him, I can't bring myself to reveal it. So I go with one of my more recent regrets.

"If I could go back in time, I wouldn't have stood by and let a minor join the sex club. I knew it was wrong, but I didn't want to get kicked out for having that opinion, so I kept my mouth shut and befriended the girl, hoping I could at least keep her relatively safe by taking her under my wing. Never again will I make a decision because it's the easier option."

Griffin's eyes soften, his fingers brushing back my flyaways as we stare into each other's eyes. "One last question."

I blink at him, offering him a smile as I try to refocus my attention.

"Aggie. If I asked you to marry me tomorrow, what would your answer be?"

Chapter Nineteen

Nowhere to Run

Griffin

She's looking at me like I'm nuts. In all fairness, I probably am, but that doesn't mean I'm not fucking serious. I meant every single word.

'If I asked you to marry me tomorrow, what would your answer be?'

I've completely stunned my little elf, and she reminds me of a fish out of water as she stares at me, opening and closing her mouth.

"Griffin! Agatha! We are anchoring here to go for a swim. Come and join us!" Selena yells from the top deck.

Great fucking timing, Sel!

Aggie takes that moment to bolt. Like actually bolt. By the time I stand from my seat, the back of her head is disappearing around the side of the boat, for fuck's sake.

A low growl rumbles from my chest as I make my way to follow my woman, and by the time I catch up to her, she is already bobbing in the water.

If it weren't for the way her eyes turn to pools of regret, I would have already been in that water with her, but as she looks frantically for me, and her shoulders only relax when she sees me on the back of the boat, I know I shouldn't take her reaction personally.

She cares for me. That much is evident. But she's having trouble processing the seriousness of what is between us.

Nevertheless, the brat ran from me, and for that, she must pay.

A sinister smirk tugs at my lips as I peel my t-shirt off over my head. I keep my eyes on Aggie as she treads water, and her eyes widen when she sees the look in my eye.

Yes, my little elf. You are in trouble.

The others are splashing around in the water, but I ignore them, only having tunnel vision for my woman. I dive into the water, propelling myself under the surface until Aggie's treading legs come into view. When I breach the surface right in front of her, she gasps as I flick my wet hair back off my face before reaching for her.

"You know, little elf. If you had asked me that question, I would have said yes in an instant."

"Griffin, I'm sorry, I just—"

My hand wraps around her throat, ceasing her words as I pull her against my body, my legs doing all the work to keep us afloat. She gasps as I squeeze at the sides a little, my eyes piercing her caramel pools with a dominating fury that has her cheeks instantly flushing.

"I wish we were alone right now." I growl, nose to nose with her. "I'd fuck you so hard for running off on me... again." The rumble in my chest is all animalistic, the beast in me thrashing to be unleashed. "Stop running from me, Aggie."

As if her pussy has a mind of its own, it grinds over my hard bulge, and she wraps her legs tighter around me. My brother starts splashing towards us, and I take Aggie's distraction to release my hard cock from my shorts and give it a squeeze.

"Jesus, are you two fucking again?" Brennen asks quietly as he swims around us, his eyes trying to peer down through the water, but the darker hue of the southern ocean gives us the privacy we need.

"Not yet." I grit out and Brennen's grin grows wide right before I reach between me and Aggie and peel her swimmers to the side. Her eyes widen, but I give her no time to question what I'm doing, and in one swift move, I impale her.

A gasping moan falls from her lips as her eyes go wide and Brennen starts coughing like he's trying to cover up the sound she made.

"Fuck, Aggie." I rasp, relishing the way her inner walls squeeze my dick. "Your cunt is so hot." I start to slowly thrust in and out, and my woman grips onto my shoulders as her body jerks each time I hit home. "Bren, go keep Gracie and the olds busy." I instruct my nosey brother, who's still treading water next to us.

"But my dick is so fucking hard. Can't I stay here?"

"No!" I hiss and Brennen splashes water at the both of us.

"Whatever." He complains, swimming away, and my eyes stay locked onto Aggie's, not letting her break the contact.

"Rub your clit." I demand, my face a mix of anger and lust.

She does as I demand, moving her hand between us to help build her pleasure.

"Don't make a fucking sound when you come, Aggie. If you do, I will fuck you up on deck in front of everyone, regardless of their age or relationship with me."

Even though we are both keen for some exhibitionism, I can tell by her wide eyes that she has no interest in putting that show on for my dad and Selena, or my teenage siblings. Hell, neither am I. So, when I feel her walls squeezing my dick tighter, I kick my legs in the water, turning us so Aggie's back is to everyone else.

It's then that she lets her face express what her voice isn't able to, and she lets go, biting hard into her bottom lip as she starts convulsing around my cock.

"That's it, beautiful. Milk me." My voice is husky as I speak, and a moment later my own release hits as I follow my siren over the edge, too.

With my chest rising and falling to try to get air in, my hips stop their underwater thrust and Aggie's body falls slack. I pull her against my chest and press my lips to her ear.

"We are made for each other, little elf. All you have to do is accept it and embrace it."

My words must do something to her, because she wraps her arms around my neck and doesn't let go. Then, she kisses me, her lips and tongue saying what she isn't willing to admit yet. I squeeze her so tightly against my bare chest that I'm almost certain we are going to morph into one.

We don't say anything else after that, instead, letting our bodies express our emotions silently as we bob in the water. We stay that way for a long time, ignoring the playful splashes of my family members until we are advised it's time to get out of the water to sail back to shore.

I swim us back over to the boat, and as we climb out of the ocean, my dad looms over us, his shadow menacing as he frowns.

"Agatha, get dressed and meet me inside. We need to have a chat."

Fucking hell.

Aggie stiffens at my dad's words while he walks off, giving us his back, and I desperately wish we were back at Redfield Lake playing subbing for Santa in our own little world where no one else fucking existed.

"It's ok, little elf. I'll come with you." I tell her when I see the fear in her eyes.

She glances up at me with so much concern that I just want to sweep her up in my arms and run away with her. I can't though. If she's to be part of my world, then she'll have to get used to my dad, even though I'd rather keep him away from her.

He can be a fucking prick. Totally ruthless at times which is why he holds so much power, but at the end of the day, I am his son, and I know he loves me. Just like Fallon, he'll be trying to make sure my little elf can hack this lifestyle.

Fallon was meant to join us on the boat today, but after her brief but brutal 'chat' with our dad this morning, she stormed out and sped off in her car. Apparently, dad demoted her to baby-sitting duties of some of our special guests in the city that get the type of hospitality that involves pulling out fingernails and waterboarding.

It's a notable hit to her position within the family business, and our crew will know immediately that she's being punished.

I feel fucking bad for Fal. I love my sister, I really do, but she was out of line yesterday. I wish our dad hadn't intervened, though. I never wanted such a punishment for her.

Aggie hasn't asked again about her, so until she does, I'll keep this information to myself. Aggie has a big heart, and even though Fallon threatened her, she will feel to blame for what's happened.

"Just picture him naked." I tug Aggie to my chest, sweeping her wet golden blonde tendrils off her cheek. "He has a beer belly and all. Surely that's not scary."

My words have the desired effect, and Aggie laughs.

"There it is. That perfect smile." I cup her cheek and she relaxes into my hand like she never wants to move away.

I help Aggie dry off, mostly because I can't seem to handle not having my hands on her every fucking second, and I deliberately stall, taking longer than needed as I try to avoid the inevitable of my woman having to deal with my dad.

Leading her below deck, I take her to my designated bedroom with its own private bathroom, where we shower together. There's no sex involved in this shower, but I hold her close as we remain quiet, helping to wash the salt water out of her hair.

After we dry off again, my eyes remain on Aggie as I dress, watching her slip back into her dress before she gives her hair a quick comb. I love the domestic-ness of this situation. I can imagine watching her do this in thirty years' time and loving the look of her just as much as I do now.

With reluctance, once we are dressed and can no longer avoid my father, I take Aggie's delicate hand in mine and lead her to my father's office. Stopping in front of the door, I turn to face her, my eyes remaining on her caramel gaze as I tap on the door.

"Enter." My dad barks, his tone gruff, and I have to fight the urge to roll my eyes at his intimidation tactics.

Aggie isn't the threat here. I wish he'd give it a rest.

“Remember beautiful. He’s naked with a big old round belly.” I smirk at my woman and her pretty pink lips quirk up in one corner.

Then I open the door.

Chapter Twenty

Threats

Agatha

Ewan Marx is sitting behind a small desk, focused on writing something before looking up to see us enter.

"Thanks, Griff. She'll be out in a few minutes." He grunts sternly, and I stiffen.

"I think I'll stay." Griffin advises his dad, who simply dismisses his statement.

"Nope. Out."

"But—"

"Out Griffin!" Ewan bellows and I flinch, my heart just about leaping out of my throat at the menacing yell of Griffin's dad in the small space.

My wide eyes lock onto Griffin, and I see him gearing up to argue with his dad.

"It's ok, Griff." My voice gains his attention, and he turns his frown to me. "I'll be ok. You go. I'll be out soon."

"But I said I'd stay with you." He says quietly, shaking his head.

I can see he would clearly fight for me, and I don't want that. Not with his dad and family. So even though I'm scared shitless right now, I slip on a fake smile and give him a reassuring nod.

"I'll be fine. I promise."

His dark eyes analyse me for a few beats, probably knowing I'm lying through my teeth, but he gives in and nods.

"I'll be right outside this door." He points his thumb over his shoulder, and I give him a nod. Then he pulls me to his chest and hugs me, pressing a kiss to the top of my head.

I can feel how hard it is for him to leave me in the room with his dad, which is worrying. Is he concerned because he doesn't trust his dad or concerned about my discomfort?

"You certainly have him twisted in knots over you." Ewan's deep voice draws my attention from the closed-door Griffin just stepped through, so I focus on Ewan, trying to appear unaffected.

"I think it's the other way around," I admit, and he nods.

"Maybe." He picks up a piece of paper from the desk and holds it out to me. Frowning, I slowly accept the small paper article, only to find it's a cheque, made out to me in the amount of one million dollars.

"What is this?" I ask, dragging my gaze back to Ewan.

"Take it. Relocate and make a new life for yourself. Forget about Griffin."

"What?" My eyes bulge as I comprehend his words.

"You're not cut out for this life, Agatha. It's no sex game like you two have been playing. It's brutal and deadly, and no place for someone like you."

My eyes narrow. "What do you mean, someone like me?"

Ewan sighs, scrubbing his hand through his silver hair. "Just take the money, Miss Fiera. Start a new life. Maybe try to stay away from sex clubs that allow minors."

Anger fills me at his words and without a second thought, I tear up the cheque and let the pieces fall to the desk. His salt and pepper brows hitch, and I lift my own challenging brow at him.

"I don't want your money, Mr Marx, and I'm not involved with Griffin for anything other than his love." I suck in a quick breath, balling my fists at my sides to hide their slight tremble. "Paying me off to stop seeing your son won't work."

"What will work then?" He growls, leaning forward in his chair.

"Nothing." I say with confidence, finally realising it's true.

"Everyone has a price, Miss Fiera. Name yours."

I shake my head. "I'm not ending things with Griffin, especially not because you insist or try to bribe me, or even threaten me, Mr Marx. I would like the opportunity to see where this relationship goes. If I break things off with Griffin, it will be because we weren't compatible. So unless you're planning to kill me to keep me away from him, we don't have anything else to discuss."

Ewan smirks in a sinister way that sends a chill up my spine.

"The only reason you would end up dead by a Marx hand is if you are a traitor, Miss Fiera."

I swallow the golf ball sized lump in my throat, hoping that when I respond, my voice is calm.

"What or who do you class as a traitor?"

"A traitor is someone who does the family wrong." He admits, relaxing back into his chair again.

"If things don't work out between me and Griffin, will you see me as a traitor?"

"That depends on why things didn't work out, or what you do afterwards." His vagueness riles me, and I shoot him a glare.

"Care to elaborate?"

He chuckles, linking his hands together in his lap. "Well, Miss Fiera, going to the authorities about any of our family secrets is a sure way to find yourself six feet under." His jaw ticks then, and my need to flee is almost overwhelming. "So will fraternizing with our enemies, killing one of us, or being unfaithful to Griffin."

I let his words sink in. I let the scenarios swirl through my mind as my heart rate soars with the fear coursing through my veins.

"Am I still classed as a traitor if I kill one of you in self-defence?"

His brows lift at my question before a frown tugs them back down. "That depends on why you need to defend yourself. If it's because you've been a traitor, then yes."

I nod, my eyes falling from his piercing glare to my feet as I try to get a handle on my emotions.

"Miss Fiera, if you're asking what would happen if things simply don't work out between you and Griffin, or if you realise at some point that you can't handle the life, or you don't love each other or fall out of love and end up hating each other, or perhaps *he* cheats on *you*, then you should know you are free to go as long as our business remains secret."

I don't know why he couldn't have just said that in the first place, but of course, he was making sure I understood that my death isn't off the table. If I want to avoid it, I need to leave now, or make sure I comply.

The thought of not getting to see Griffin again, getting to feel his touch, or taste his lips, or hear his gravelly voice that deepens with lust when he talks quietly in my ear, sends an unbelievable ache straight to my heart. Is he worth this risk? Is he worth potentially putting my life in danger?

I'm not one hundred percent convinced, but I know I need to at least try.

"I'm not ready to walk away from your son, Ewan. I need to see where it leads us. So I will take your warning seriously, but I'm not walking away. You should get used to seeing my face."

I give Griffin's dad my back as I leave the room without another word. When I step out into the passage, my eyes instantly fall on Griffin, who is leaning against the wall next to the door.

"Did you hear that?" I whisper, working like crazy to keep my emotions in check.

He pushes off the wall, his warm hand reaching up to cup my cheek. "Yes." He whispers back. "I'm so sorry he did that. Said those things. I will talk to him."

I shake my head. "No. It's between him and me."

Griffin frowns, his other hand coming up to cup my other cheek.

"No, little elf. He fucking tried to bribe you to leave me. It makes me wonder how many times he's done something like this to my siblings. Maybe it's why they never bring anyone home."

"Please don't say anything." I shake my head as much as I can while held between his hands. "I need to prove my strength to him so he will accept me. I can't do that if you fight my battles for me."

"You shouldn't have to, though." He presses his forehead to mine, and the lump in my throat returns, and with it, a flood of emotions.

"It is what it is, Griff." I take a step back from him, watching his face contort in hurt confusion. "I need a minute."

I spin on my heel, following the passage back to the bedroom we were in before as hot tears stream from my eyes. Clenching my jaw tight, my teeth feel like they may shatter as I bolt through the bedroom and lock myself in the bathroom.

Grabbing a towel, I shove it against my face and scream into it over and over, the muffled sound bouncing off the walls in the small space as I sink to the floor and cry.

I tried to hold strong when I was in the room with Mr Marx, but I'm not that strong. I can't just go and join Griffin's family up on deck and pretend that I didn't just learn a very raw truth about entering this family.

I don't like Ewan Marx. Not only is he a scary motherfucker, but his eyes are like dark pools of death. I'm fairly certain he is the spawn of the devil himself.

"Aggie." Griffin's quiet voice comes through the closed bathroom door right before he taps on it. "Open the door, little elf. Let me in."

His voice. The care it holds breaks me, and more tears burst free as I beg myself to pull my shit together. It doesn't work.

"I-I just ne-need a minute." I blubber quietly.

Everything we shared over the last ten days comes crashing in. It's been a whirlwind. One minute I was living my boring life, and the next, Griffin Marx barged his way in, posing as fucking Santa. He's tricked me, kept me in the dark, thrilled me, consumed me, sent me to highs I've never reached before, pissed me off, and made me fall for him in the process.

"Aggie, baby. Open the door, please. Let me in. I'm not going anywhere, so you can either cry alone in there or open this door and let me hold you. You don't need to be alone anymore."

I consider his words. I hate being alone. I've done it for so long because I had to, but do I really have to keep living that way?

The overwhelming need to be close to Griffin is what makes me reach up from where I'm sitting on the tiled floor, slumped against the wall. I click off the locking mechanism and a moment later the door opens from the other side.

I don't need to look up to find Griffin because he is already sitting on the floor on the other side of the door.

"Do you hate me?" He whispers, and hell, my heart cracks open at the look of fear on his face.

"No, of course not." I sob, swiping at my tears.

He shifts forward on the floor, breaching the threshold of the bathroom, and I climb onto his lap, straddling him as I sob into his neck.

"Shhh, little elf. I've got you."

"I'm sorry." I blubber. "I'm not good with confrontation. I can't just pretend my conversation with your dad wasn't terrifying."

"Fuck, Aggie. I don't expect you to act like he didn't just threaten you. I want to fucking kill him." His pained voice is enough to make me want to kill Ewan Marx myself.

"I just need to regroup. I'll be ok in a few minutes. Or hours." I try to giggle, but it makes me cry more.

"You were a total badass, you know. You probably don't realise that you just earned his respect. It's fucked up, I know, but he's looking out for his family, and you totally put him in his place. He won't dislike you for that. In fact, I bet it's had the opposite effect."

I don't really care if Ewan Marx likes me or not. He can suck my biggest dildo and choke on it for all I care.

"A sensible girl would jump off this boat now and swim for her life." I mutter and Griffin chuckles.

"Thank fuck you're not that sensible, then."

We both laugh then, the light feeling helping to dry up my tears.

As Griffin holds me to him, he brushes his fingers through my hair, rubs my back, and presses his lips to the top of my head, not able to hold himself back.

It feels amazing.

When I'm able to climb off the floor and freshen up my face with a cold splash of water, we go back up on deck to join Griffin's family. Griff hands me his sunnies, and I don't even question why he's giving them to me. I saw my red puffy eyes in the mirror. I'm thankful that I can hide them so we can avoid any questions, as well as hiding the aftermath of Ewan's little chat.

I don't miss the way Griffin glares at his dad for the remainder of the trip. He doesn't once let go of me, as if making his own silent statement to his dad.

I'm not sure if it's a good thing, or if me being here has just started a war.

CHAPTER TWENTY-ONE

PAYBACK

Agatha

The drive home is long, and my emotional exhaustion sends me to sleep for most of the trip. It's only when the car slows and the road under the tires gets bumpy that my eyes flutter open to take in my surroundings.

"Where are we?" I rasp with my sleepy voice.

"Home." Griffin responds and I turn my frown to him before glancing back out the window.

"This isn't my driveway." I sit up a little higher in the seat, noticing a structure up ahead.

"No, that's your house there." Griffin's voice is smug as he points out the window and my eyes widen as I see my house from the opposite side.

"I'm confused." I mutter, and he chuckles.

"I thought it was about time I showed you my house."

It takes me a moment to comprehend his words, but when I do, I remember his confession a couple of days ago, and my mouth drops open as I turn my glare to take in his shit-eating grin.

"I can't believe you've been right next door this whole time."

"Believe it." He chuckles, and I can't hold back. I punch his arm, hard.

"Ouch." He whimpers like a little bitch, his hand moving up to cover the spot on his arm that will most likely bruise.

"You fucking smug shit!" I hiss. "Not only are you my landlord, but you live right next door, in this," I point to his mansion made of concrete, timber and glass, "uppity mansion."

He barks another laugh, his face light with happiness.

"Correct."

I gape at him.

"Come on, little elf. Let me show you where I've been watching you from."

I shoot him daggers, but he just chuckles again, unfazed by my attempt at intimidation.

Griffin gets out of the car, rounding it to open my door like the sexy mafia gentleman he is. My eyes dart from his masterpiece mansion to my little Hamptons style rental, and I note that it's actually a little hard to see much through the scrub other than the light grey weatherboards of my house.

"I can't believe you were right next door the whole time." I mutter, still shocked.

"It made things easier for me." He admits, only chuckling when I shoot him another glare.

Leading me up the steps to an oversized glass and timber door, Griffin keys a pin code into the electronic panel and the door clicks open. I'm in awe as we step over the threshold, my eyes roaming over the slick modern design created by natural elements of stone and timber. It's not really a mansion in comparison to his dad's home, but it's oversized enough in comparison to the little house I rent next door.

The one thing I notice is the lack of anything personal. There are no pictures of family members on the walls. No little knick knacks that one gathers over the years. This house could be a designer display home with how it's presented. It's certainly nice but tells me nothing about the man I'm holding hands with, other than he has money.

"This is my personal office." Griffin opens a door to a large room which houses a large glass top desk and a sofa. "Here, this is where I watched you." He picks up a remote, and the wall panels opposite the sofa open up to reveal a wall of TV screens, and there on the screens is the inside of my house.

"Fucking hell." I murmur, dropping his hand to approach the screens, looking at each one to find different angles of my bathroom and bedroom, as well as the guest room where I service my clients, the living areas, and even the guest bathroom and the laundry.

Slowly, I turn to face Griffin as anger engulfs me.

"This... you..." I can't find words to describe how I'm feeling right now.

Like I know he was watching me. But somehow seeing it takes away the mystery, and inside my head is screaming *stalker. Peeping tom. Sicko.*

I shake my head, not able to form words, and I dart towards the door.

"Don't go." He begs, pain lacing his tone. I stop in the doorway and turn back to see the pain etched on his face.

"This..." I gesture to the screens, taking a moment to swallow. "Is a lot."

"I had to test you." He takes a step towards me, so I take one back, putting more space between us. "I needed to make sure you wouldn't be a threat to my family before I brought you in."

"I don't understand how that," I point to the wall of monitors, "was testing me for that."

"Aside from the sex stuff, which I'll admit was purely my own depravity, I needed to make sure you could be loyal. By mentioning that I saw your sex parties, I was testing you, Aggie. I needed to know if you were the type of person that would disregard your client's privacy once you knew it was at risk. I would have been concerned if you didn't cancel your sex party, because above all else, I need my woman to be loyal to me and my family." He steps forward, closing the distance, and cups my face. "Coming into the Marx fold is a huge commitment. This may have started with a game, but my intentions are serious, Aggie."

"A week, Griff. That's not enough time to know someone and decide they are worthy enough." I whisper, leaning into his touch because I can't help myself.

"Maybe. But I knew the moment I saw you that there was more to you. I knew you could match my energy. My drive for sex, even if it's a little messy or unsavoury. And I knew, deep in my gut, that you are the woman put on this earth to be by my side and make me a better man."

"Oh my god. Is this a proposal?" I balk, remembering his question earlier on the boat.

"Hell no. My proposal will be a grand gesture or something way more creative. Rest assured." He says in all seriousness, and I shake my head.

"You're crazy."

"Probably." He grins, his dimples making an appearance. "Be crazy with me."

"Maybe tomorrow." I sigh, taking a step back from his tempting touch. "Tonight, I want a shower and ten hours of sleep. You're exhausting Mr Marx."

"Stop calling me that. You're making my dick hard." He grumbles and I grin.

"Good to know." I smirk before it falls from my face. "But seriously. I need a night to myself."

Griffin nods. "Ok. I can do that."

"Can you turn those off?" I ask, and he smirks.

"Nope."

"Yes, you can." I snap.

"I can, but I'm not going to." He chuckles at my glare.

"It's not really having time to myself if you're watching me."

He sighs and presses a button on the remote and the wall panels start closing over the screens, blocking them from view.

"Here. You take the remote." He holds it out to me, and I take it. "Take the night, and I'll see you in the morning."

Handing me the remote means everything, and I almost want to give it back.

Almost.

After a long, deep kiss, Griffin walks me back to my house and we part ways for the night.

I wasn't lying when I said I needed the night to myself. Not only do I have some thinking to do, but I have some revenge to plan. As I eat a microwave meal for dinner, a plan starts to form, and I go through my normal routine, just in case Griffin can somehow still watch me on the cameras.

At about 4am, I creep out of bed and grab a can of dry shampoo. After seeing the monitors streaming a live feed into Griffin's office, I took note of the rough locations that the cameras must be in each room, so I take the can of dry shampoo and locate all the cameras, spraying them with the white spray to cover the lenses. After I finish, I slip on a pair of shoes, go to my garage and search through the boxes for my old padlocks and keys, and then sneak through the scrub to Griffin's house.

Payback is a bitch, and revenge is sweet.

I quickly turn off the main power switch in his meter box before securing the padlock, and I run like someone is chasing me, back to the safety of my little rental. Before I go inside, I put the second padlock on my meter box to ensure Griffin can't repay the favour, and then I lock myself inside.

I manage to get a couple more hours of sleep before the phone starts ringing just after 9am. A grin tugs at my lips before I even crack my eyes open. Revenge is sweet after all.

"Really, Aggie?" Griffin snaps when I answer the phone.

"Good morning to you, too," I say with a grin.

"Is this payback?" He snaps again and I bite the inside of my cheek to hold back my laugh.

"Maybe."

"And a lock, too? You know I can get bolt cutters from my garage and cut it off, right?"

"Ok." I'm smug, and I know he can hear it in my tone.

"Or maybe I'll just come over there and spank you until you tell me where the key is."

I giggle. "Well, Mr Marx. If you can catch me, you can have the key."

I hang up, and hurry into the bathroom, picking up the key which is now safely tied inside a condom, and I part my legs and slip it inside me, getting it into position.

I know my taunt will turn him on as much as it will frustrate him, but hopefully it will also help show him that I'm willing to test the waters a little more.

Hurrying out of my bathroom, I rush through my house to the back end and into the laundry, quietly closing the internal door just as his heavy feet pound up the steps at my front door.

My heart leaps in my chest with the thrill of what I'm doing, and I quickly and quietly open the back laundry door right before I hear the front door click open.

"Where are you, little elf?" Griffin's voice is a deep rasp, filled with determination.

I slip out through the back laundry door and close it as quietly as I can before I run. I dart past the clothesline and through the scrub towards Griffin's house as his heavy feet pound through my rental in search of me.

By the time my feet carry me past his car, his voice bellows from outside my rental.

"Agatha!"

The fierceness in his tone causes me to jump in fright and a squeal escapes me, giving away my location.

He chuckles loudly. "You'd better run fast, woman! I'm going to fucking punish you when I get my hands on you!"

I grin even as I squeak, in fear that he's going to catch me too soon.

Griffin's front door is up ahead, and I push my legs harder as I climb the steps two at a time but instead of trying the door, I dart along the path that leads to the waterfront and round the corner, the long rectangular pool coming into view.

I'm hoping to put the pool between me and Griffin, but I'm not fast enough, and strong arms wrap around my waist, catapulting us into the cold water with a splash. Griffin's grip on me doesn't ease up while we are under the water, and he pushes us to the surface, both of us gasping for air.

"When are you going to learn that I'll always catch you, little elf? You can't run from me." He nips at my ear as we wrestle, and before I know what's happening, he's turned me to face him, with my wrists pinned behind my back.

"But running from you is fun." I grin with satisfaction, and he growls, baring his teeth.

"Yes, it fucking is, especially the part where I catch you and punish you."

Using his other hand, he fists my hair and tugs my head back before slamming his lips into mine. His tongue forces my lips apart and he invades my mouth in the best way, my body igniting with heat even though I'm immersed in cold water. The moment I moan, he breaks the kiss.

"Where's the key?"

I smirk, my head still pulled back by his grip. "Somewhere safe."

"Do I have to drag you back to your house and punish you until you show me where you hid it?" He hisses and my smirk grows wider.

"No need to drag me back there. You can punish me right here." I urge, loving the feel of his heated body against mine and the cold silk of my nightgown clinging to my skin.

Griffin's face contorts into a grin as he studies my expression. "What aren't you telling me, little elf?"

I grin wickedly. "I have the key right now, Santa. You just need to find it."

His dark eyes drop from my face to my cleavage, and he chuckles. "Oh, you have been a naughty elf." He releases my wrists but not my hair as he wades through the water to the edge of the pool. "You are fucking perfect for me, little elf. I'm never letting you go."

Before I can respond, he releases my hair and lifts me out of the water onto the ledge of the pool, parting my legs as his eyes scan over my nightgown. It's clinging to me like a second skin, and he licks his lips as his hands join the action, cupping my breasts and rolling my pebbled nipples through the fabric.

"The key doesn't seem to be here." He rasps before tugging the fabric down and releasing my breast. It strains painfully as the air hits it, but a moment later, Griffin's hot mouth closes over it and I tip my head back, moaning.

I'm well aware that we are outside right now and anyone walking along the shore front or in boats on the lake nearby probably has a great view, but I don't care. I love the thought of being caught. I love the thought of someone stumbling upon us and not having the willpower to turn away. I love the idea that they will get turned on and perhaps pleasure themselves as they watch.

"Fuck, Aggie. These tits are the most perfect tits I've ever come across." His voice is a deep rumble as he pulls back, looking further down my body. "I want to eat every fucking inch of you."

I catch his dark eyes for a brief moment before a sinister smirk lifts his lips, and a moment later, he flips me roughly over. The movement jolts me, and I catch myself just before my face slams into the warm, paved ground.

"What are you doing?" I squeak as he reefs up my nightgown to bare my panty clad arse. Then, the thin fabric is torn from my flesh.

"I'm punishing you." He growls loudly before the sharp sting of his palm comes down hard on my arse cheek.

I squeal from the pain, and don't realise until it's too late that he has my legs spread wide, their lower half immersed in the cold water. Griffin is still in the pool, gripping my legs in place so I can't get up and run, where he continues his teasing assault on me.

I wait for his fingers to delve into my pussy in search of the key, but instead, he spreads my arse cheeks wide, opening my back passage to him.

"Is it in this tight little hole, little elf?" He asks, not giving me a moment to respond before he presses his face between my cheeks. The drag of his tongue is searing on my cold flesh as Griffin begins to eat me, rimming style.

I'd never cared that much for being rimmed before, but it's different with Griffin. Everything is different with Griffin. His skills combined with his scent and this addiction I seem to have for him just heightens everything he does to me.

I find myself relaxing and trying to use my muscles to open myself more to him, desperate to have him inside me, and he takes the lead, pushing his strong long tongue inside my puckered passage.

I cry out as the combination of stimulation and psychological arousal engulfs me, making me quiver with need.

"More." I cry out, desperate and starved, and Griffin doesn't disappoint.

Slowly, he sinks a digit inside my pussy, swirling it around before he pulls back and chuckles.

"I think I found the key, little elf." He slips in another digit, using them both to hunt down the object hidden deep inside me, and a moment later he eases it from my cunt. "There it is. Thank you for keeping it safe." He chuckles before placing it next to my head and bringing his palm down on my other arse cheek again. Hard.

I cry out, but it quickly falls silent as he sinks his finger inside my pussy again. I relax on the paved poolside, spreading my legs even more, a silent invitation to fill me. But he doesn't. Not in the way I think he's going to, anyway.

Withdrawing his finger, he parts my arse cheeks again and spits on my puckered rose before easing his finger, lubed with my pussy juice inside my back passage.

I moan and push back, desperate for more, and a moment later he slips two fingers from his other hand into my pussy.

"You like that, little elf? You like to be filled from both sides?" He rasps and I try to nod, but I think I fail.

"Yes." I pant, my pelvis rocking with the motion of his finger fucking.

"So fucking dirty." He growls. "And so fucking mine."

I lose any control I have at that point. His onslaught from both sides of my g-spot shoot me high quickly, and I convulse around his fingers as I explode.

"Yes." I cry out, the knowing feeling of wet heat squirts between my legs, before Griffin's hot mouth closes over my cunt, drinking down my spray.

Griffin

I've never had the urge to eat arse before, but there's something about my little elf that makes it really fucking hard for me not to want to do all the dirtiest things possible. And fuuuck, when I parted her cheeks and spat on her puckered pink rose, she pushed her hungry arse closer to me.

The way her body lit up was reward enough, and I knew this was going to be something I'll be doing again and again to please her.

Now, with my dick tenting my pants, I leap up out of the water and scoop Aggie up off the ground, still face down. A squeak flies from her, and she starts squirming, probably because this position isn't the best to be carried in, and I toss her face first onto the sun lounge.

"Your punishment isn't over yet, little elf." I hiss while freeing my dick and kneeling between her legs.

She tries to sit up to turn and face me, but I shove the back of her head, pushing her back to the cushioned lounge before giving her arse another hard slap.

"Griff!" Her voice is a combination of a gasp and a groan, and I grin, revelling in the pink hand mark on her pale skin.

"Stick your arse up and open wide for me." I demand, running my finger over her back passage to show what it is exactly that I want her to open for me. She moans, doing as I ask, raising her hips up, supported by her knees, while keeping her face pressed to the padded surface.

Reaching over to the table next to the lounge, I take the bottle of oil sitting there like it was meant to be, and I pour a generous amount over her rose before slathering my cock with it.

I release my own moan as I pump my dick a few times, loving the slippery feel of the oil, and then turn my attention back to my Goddess, spread wide on display for me.

"You like taking it in the arse, little elf?" I ask as I slide two fingers in, and instead of tensing, she relaxes, taking the invasion.

"Yes." She pants, already aroused.

"You want me to sink my dick in here?" I ask as I ease a third finger in, and the little minx pushes back so my fingers sink deep.

"Yes."

"Fuuuck. You are so fucking perfect, Aggie." I bite my lip as I try to hold back the monster in me that simply wants to slam into her and destroy her arse.

She whimpers with need, so I add a fourth digit, stretching her wide as I ease my fingers slowly in and out.

"Fill me up, Santa." She pants, and fuck, calling me Santa makes my dick jerk.

I ease my fingers out as I chuckle and inspect the open passage of her arse.

"Fuck, that's a beautiful sight." I hiss, struggling to hold myself back before I press the tip of my cock to her open passage. "You ready, little elf?"

"Yes." She cries with desperate need, and I grin.

"Atta girl."

I slowly surge forward and push my straining cock into the tight passage, holding my breath as I go, trying to remain in control.

"Yes." Aggie cries out, pushing back against me, taking me in faster and deeper. "Fuck my arse."

Fuuuck, I love this side of her. There's no embarrassment or shame. She knows what she wants, and she's not afraid to ask.

Not wanting to disappoint my little elf, I do as she begged, and I fuck her arse. Brutally.

Chapter Twenty-Two

Tease

Agatha

I'm not unfamiliar with strip clubs. I danced in one when I was nineteen, which led me to sex clubs. I've sat in strip clubs and paid the women for lap dances, and even a friction fuck once or twice. But I've never been to one with a partner before. And I especially haven't been to one with the owner of the establishment.

Yes, Griffin Marx owns a strip club. Or maybe it's more like his family owns it. Who knows?

The Red Room is in Redfield and is actually quite classy compared to a lot of the other establishments I've been to before. As you can guess, the main colour theme is red, and the waitresses walk around topless, wearing nothing but a red lace G-string.

After Griffin carried me inside his house from the pool, he fucked me so hard that I couldn't walk for an hour afterwards. He has skills that turn my legs into jelly. I'm not complaining. His punishment was worth the wait. I'd fallen asleep after that, cuddled into his side in his oversized bed that looks out over the lake.

At some point he'd gotten up and turned his power back on, and I was woken mid-afternoon by lunch in bed. Which then included Griffin as dessert.

Again, no complaints here.

It's easy to forget who he really is when it's just the two of us by the lake with no other worries in sight. Unfortunately, Griffin's phone had other ideas, and he had to go into work to deal with something.

I'd mentally prepared that it meant I'd be heading back to my little rental to pass the time until he finished, but Griffin insisted that I come with him, so here we are in the late afternoon walking around a strip club.

I get introduced to the bouncers and bar staff and a couple of the strippers before we take a seat in a booth to watch the girls dance. Well, I watch the girls dance. Griffin watches me watching the girls.

It's quiet in here, since happy hour doesn't start for another two hours, so some of the girls are using this time to practise their routines. I've always wondered what my life would have turned out like if I continued to be a stripper. The pay is good, and since I love being watched, I didn't mind the eyes on me. But, back when I did it, men didn't treat me well. They would call me a whore and thought I was there to be used. So I left. Granted, some may call me a whore for the tantra I offer now, but my clients treat me with respect.

Since I love attention and eyes on me, as well as taunting my Santa, I turn my eyes to him as a plan forms in my mind.

"What sort of resume does a girl need to have to become a stripper?" I ask Griffin, watching as a small smirk tugs his lips north.

"A well-endowed rack is always a good start, but not essential. Well-groomed and have a knack for flirting and be able to move their hips sensually. The rest they learn on the job."

"So, someone like me could dance up there then?" I ask, watching for how he will react, and he doesn't disappoint.

"Someone like *you* would own that stage, Aggie." He grins.

"Can I audition for you?" I smile and he tilts his head to the side as he studies me.

"You're serious? You want to strip on stage?"

"I'm serious about getting on that stage right now and stripping for you. But I'm not looking for a new job."

He runs his hand down over his face as he chuckles. "Have at it, little elf."

Standing, I move out of the booth and approach the DJ, who is just one of the other strippers, and she giggles at my song request before announcing me onto the stage.

"We have a surprise appearance from Santa's little helper, and she is dancing to Santa Baby."

The two guys sitting in the front give me a hoot as the bar girls cheer and some others clap as I step up onto the stage. The music starts playing and I sway my hips as I walk along the stage to the pole. Gripping it with one hand, I slowly strut around it, my eyes falling to the two men sitting at the foot of the stage.

One looks like he stepped out of an accounting firm to spend his hard-earned money on whores, and the other looks like he drives trucks for a living, his round belly and overgrown beard catching the peanuts that don't manage to make it inside his mouth.

I slowly drop, my knees parting wide as I do, my short sundress sure to be giving the men a little peekaboo.

As I stand again, my eyes move to the back of the room where Griffin is now standing outside the booth we were in. His eyes are dark with desire as he watches me, and I'm helpless to fight the way he makes me feel, my hand coming up to palm my tit while the other travels down between my legs.

Griffin stalks towards me then, his eyes only for me, and I take it further, as I start to pop the buttons free on my dress. As he steps in line with the other two men ogling me, I tug my dress open and let it fall to the stage, leaving me standing in only my red lace panties and bra that leaves little to the imagination.

My attention snags on the trucker guy as he starts rubbing over his hard bulge in his pants and Griffin notices, following my gaze.

At first, I think he's going to lose his temper, but instead, he waves over a girl, whispering something in her ear, and the next moment, she whispers in the trucker's ear, and he nods frantically before following her through the red curtain to the side of the room.

I turn my back on my audience, doing a sharp bend to flash my lace covered arse at them before I drop down in a bouncing squat.

When I turn back, Griffin is whispering to another girl, and she too moves to the second guy, offering him some sort of service, which he accepts and leaves with her through the curtains.

"I'm running out of audience, Mr Marx. Who will I flash these to?" My tone is laced with innocence as I unclasp my bra, letting it fall to the stage, releasing my tits.

"Everyone out!" Griffin yells, all remaining eyes going wide as they look at him.

They must think he's joking, but his words and tone the second time ensure they know he's not joking.

"If you are not out of here in thirty fucking seconds, you are all fired!" He bellows and everyone in the room bails fast.

I pout. "But Santa, who will see this?" I ask, turning my back on him before hooking my fingers in my panties and dragging them slowly down. I bend as I do it, exposing my arse and pussy, looking upside down through my legs at Griffin as I give my arse a little shake.

"Bring that pussy over here now." He hisses and I grin before hiding it, turning around to face my man and the now empty strip club.

"You mean *this* pussy?" I ask as I press my back to the pole and sink down, parting my knees to give him an intimate view.

"Yes."

"But Santa. I'm too horny to move," I say innocently, grazing my fingers down my front and in between my legs.

"Fuck, Aggie. Bring me that cunt!"

I whimper at his demand, his voice sending heat to my core.

"This cunt?" I pant, circling my clit.

"Fuck yes. I need to fuck you right now."

"Right now?" I say sweetly, so fucking turned on by the heated look in his eyes.

"Stop stalling and get the fuck over here." He demands, and I give in, desperate to have him yet again. I can't seem to get enough.

I drop forward onto all fours and crawl across the stage to him. The moment I'm in arm's reach, he tugs me the rest of the way, flipping me around so my arse lands on the stage and spreads my legs open wide.

“Can you suppress the urge to squirt?” he asks as he frees his hard cock, and I nod.

“Avoid my g-spot and we should be all good. It’s not foolproof, though.” I admit, and he shrugs.

“Good enough for me.”

Griffin doesn’t wait another second, sinking his dick inside me, causing my back to arch off the stage. “Fuuuck, you feel so good.”

It’s a compliment I love to hear, and I give myself over to him as he fucks me on the edge of the stage while I’m sure some of the staff are watching on from somewhere.

I don’t care though. Fucking Griffin Marx should be a public display each and every time.

Griffin slams into me over and over in punishing thrusts as he fucks me, building my pleasure deep inside. He uses his thumb to circle my clit, something he obviously knows will help me get over the line quicker, and before I know it, I’m clamping around his dick, squeezing it to send Griffin over the edge too as he fills me with his cum.

Griffin collapses forward to brace himself above me, and I swear I’ve never seen a more beautiful sight with him hovering over me.

“You’re hired.” He pants, grinning at me. “To be my private dancer.”

Giggling, I nod, happy with that arrangement before he slides out of me and grabs some napkins off the nearby table to clean himself up before cleaning me up too.

When I’ve redressed, Griffin calls his staff back in, and they don’t even bat an eyelid at knowing what just went down, and I only blush for a few minutes until my skin cools.

Griffin gives me a tour of the rest of the establishment then, showing me the private rooms and the lap dance lounge before leading me to his office. Once inside, he shuts the door and watches me as I assess everything.

His desk here is older and more worn out than the one at his house, but looks sturdy, so I make my way over and sit my arse on it as he takes a seat in front of me in his office chair.

"So, Mr Marx." I grin, spreading my legs, resting my feet on each arm of his seat. "Do you have a gun?"

"Yes." He grins, running his hands up and down my bare legs.

"How many?" I ask, shooting him a smile, and he chuckles.

"Many."

"Do you have one here now?" I ask, and he nods.

"Yes."

My brows shoot up. "Show me." I urge, and again, he chuckles before leaning to the side to open the second drawer down, revealing a tin with a keypad on it. I watch as he presses a pin into the keypad before the lid clicks open, and then he pulls out a black and silver gun.

I lean forward to touch it, but he holds it back out of my way.

"Uh-uh. Not for you, little elf."

I frown. "Shouldn't I have a gun if I'm to be part of your world?"

He eyes me for a few beats before responding. "Yes. But not today, and not *this* gun."

"Why not that gun?" I eye the gun in question curiously.

"I don't want your prints on this gun. It's ended too many lives already. When you hold a gun, it will be clean and guilt free."

My brows shoot up at his admission, and I nod. "Ok."

His shoulders relax at my agreement, and I study him for a moment.

"How many people have you killed?"

"You don't need to know that." He frowns and I frown back.

"Why?"

"Because." He grunts.

"Because why?" I pout, and he shrugs.

"Maybe I'm worried you'll think differently of me."

That surprises me. "I won't."

"You don't know that." He rasps, his eyes falling to the gun.

"Hey." I say quietly, slipping from the desk to straddle his lap. "I'm aware of what you do for a living, Griff."

"I wish you didn't know. I wish I could be the good person you deserve."

Not for the first time, the need to tell him about my past is on the tip of my tongue. I'm sure he'd understand, yet I can't bring myself to say the words.

"Griff. You *are* a good person. Just because you've had to do some bad things, you did them for the good of something else."

"Not always, little elf. I've had my share of fuck-ups as well."

Reaching up, I cup his stubbled jaw. "Haven't we all?" I offer him a warm, reassuring smile before pressing my lips to his.

Our kiss is slow and long, and I feel like a teenager again when kissing was such a big deal and thought about all the damn time. It seems to be a big deal again, thanks to this man, and even though my body heats with arousal, the flutters in my belly and chest are more powerful, overriding everything else.

We eventually part, and Griffin locks away his gun, never letting me touch it, which I respect. Then he has to go off and deal with some stripper issues while I watch all the action from his office through the mirrored viewing window.

When Griffin returns to me, he seems distracted, worry lines etched in his forehead. He takes a phone call and answers some emails before his brother, Oswald, comes in and takes over the shift for the night.

As we drive back to Redfield Lake, Griffin remains quiet and distracted, and it makes me uneasy.

"Is everything ok?" I ask, breaking the uncomfortable silence in the car.

Griffin shakes his head like he's trying to wake himself up or something, and then turns his dark gaze to me. "Yes. Of course."

I frown. "Liar."

Sighing, Griffin's grip on the steering wheel tightens before he glances back at me. "Sorry, Aggie. It's just boring work stuff."

"Did the strippers run out of lube or something?" I joke, and he smirks.

"I wish that was all it was."

"I may not know a lot about running a strip club, but I know stuff, Griffin. I can help if you need it. Or just listen if you need to vent."

A small smile tugs at his lips as his eyes dart to mine briefly. "In all seriousness, Aggie. Can I keep you? Please?"

There's pain laced in his tone that causes hot tears to irritate the backs of my eyes. There's also longing in his tone, too.

"Yes." I whisper loud enough for him to hear me, and his eyes dart back to mine.

"For real? You'll be my woman? You'll stick around and keep playing these games with me?"

"Yes. But no lies, ok? And we are exclusive. I have no intention of dating anyone else, and I expect the same in return."

"I only have eyes, heart and dick for you, my little elf."

I grin and he drops one hand from the steering wheel to take mine, resting it on his thigh as he drives.

I'd thought after the chat I had with his dad he knew I wasn't going anywhere, but he obviously needed it confirmed. For someone that does what he does and carries such an air of confidence, he's just shown me how insecure he can be.

And honestly, it makes him more human to me.

We return to my house, but we aren't there for long before Griffin's phone starts blowing up with messages and phone calls. I know straight away it has something to do with why he's been so distracted. He steps outside to take the calls, watching me through the windows every now and then as he talks or yells at someone, and when he returns inside, he looks frazzled.

"I'm sorry to do this, Aggie, but I have to go."

My brows shoot up as I turn from the salad I've just made us.

"What's going on?"

He shakes his head, stepping up to me, and clasps my head between his strong hands. "It's family business, I'm afraid. That's all I can tell you. I'll be back as soon as I can."

My eyes study his for answers, but it only leaves me with more questions. Leaning down, Griffin presses his lips to mine in a searing kiss that reminds me of how much he cares, and when he pulls back, he presses his forehead to mine, breathing the same air as me.

"I'm sorry."

They are the last words he says before he turns to leave me in my little rental, and I spend most of the night looking out at the moon's reflection on the lake as my little Christmas flower arrangement twinkles next to me.

For the first time in days, the familiar feeling of loneliness creeps in, and I have no idea how to deal with it.

Chapter Twenty-Three

Trepidation

Agatha

Griffin didn't come back last night. Or this morning. Or this afternoon. Now, as the sun starts to dip past the trees, I wonder if he's ever going to return at all.

Since he left last night, I've felt uneasy. I can't figure out why exactly, and I keep putting it down to feeling lonely.

I tried to call Griffin multiple times throughout the day, but he didn't pick up. I've sent him text messages, and his one worded response on occasion is the only inkling I have that he's still alive.

It's such a contrast to how things have been between us that it's really throwing me. Since I'm not all that familiar with relationships, I have no idea if this is normal. Like is that it? Is the honeymoon over already?

I worry I've done something wrong, but then I worry something else is going on with his family business, and maybe he's in danger.

I've tried to keep myself busy, spending the day catching up on mundane chores, and I forced myself into two yoga and meditation sessions, trying to keep myself from spiralling over something I'm not even sure is an issue.

Standing at the sink, I wash my dinner plate, having only eaten a few bites before giving up on eating. I have no appetite, too consumed with this unrelenting worry. My stomach is nothing but knots as I close my eyes and take in a steadying breath.

The sound of something moving on the front porch snaps my eyes open, and I spin quickly to face the entrance as a shadow moves past the frosted glass window.

Is that Griffin?

Movement out of the corner of my eye sends my heart into overdrive as I realise there's more than one person outside.

The moment I see black-clad men dart past the living room window holding guns, I slap my hand over my mouth to stifle my scream.

Loud thuds sound on the front door, and I drop to the floor behind the kitchen bench.

"Miss Fiera! My name is Barton. Mr Marx sent us here to protect you."

What? Barton? Protect me?

Loud thuds rattle the door again. "Miss Fiera, please come to the door so I can speak with you. We are here to help."

My limbs are trembling, and I try to make them work, only just managing to shuffle myself along the floor to reach up and grab my phone off the kitchen bench. As my heart thunders in my ears, I tap the screen and unlock the phone, open the contacts and press call on Griffin's number.

It fails.

Frowning as more bangs sound on the front door, I notice that my phone has no signal.

Shit.

"Miss Fiera. Please come to the front door. You don't have to answer it, but I'd rather not yell."

What the hell is going on?

"Miss Fiera!"

"What do you want!" I yell back, staying hidden behind the kitchen bench.

"I have Mr Marx on the phone. He'd like to speak to you."

Frowning, I lift myself up off the floor, my legs trembling, making the task harder than it needs to be. I suck in a deep breath and move towards the front entrance.

"Griffin is on the phone?" I call, my voice sounding strained.

"Yes, Miss Fiera. It's a secure phone which can't be blocked like yours is. I'm going to place it on the mat and step away from the door. Please check the doorbell camera to confirm it's safe for you to retrieve the phone."

What? My phone is being blocked?

I turn to the panel on the wall and tap the screen, lighting it up. Pressing the front door icon, the screen changes to show the other side of the front door, and a phone laying on the doormat as a black-clad man steps away from it.

What the hell is going on?

Slowly, I unlock the door and ease it open just enough to squat down and slip my hand through, quickly grabbing the phone before slamming the door shut and locking it again.

I quickly put the phone to my ear. "Griff?"

"Fuck, Aggie. Are you ok?"

A sob escapes me before I slap my hand over my mouth again, tears blurring my eyes.

"Aggie?"

"What's going on?" I whisper-yell, dropping my hand from my mouth to bat my tears away. "There are men here with guns. What the fuck is going on?"

"I'm sorry, Aggie. I'm in the city. I'm working on getting back to you, but I needed to make sure you had protection until I got there." Griffin sounds frantic, and instead of upsetting me, a calmness washes over me.

He doesn't need me freaking out right now. He needs me level-headed and calm so he doesn't have to worry and can focus on whatever it is that's going on.

"It's ok. Explain to me what's going on, and what you need me to do."

Griffin is quiet for a few beats before his deep, raspy voice comes through the line.

"Devon, my cousin, is on his way to you. Please let him in when he gets there. I need to know you are safe until I get there, little elf. I just need you safe."

"Safe from who?" I ask calmly, even though I'm spiralling inside my head.

"One of our enemies has been hitting some of our establishments today. We thought we had it handled until he sent through a picture of you. Are you wearing a yellow sundress?"

The blood freezes in my veins as I glance down at the yellow sundress I'm wearing.

"Yes," I whisper.

"Fuck." He hisses. "Stay inside. Let Devon in when he gets there, and do exactly what he says until I arrive. Do you understand me, Aggie? Now is one of those times that I need you to obey."

"Ok." I nod, even though he can't see me. "But I need you to do something for me, too."

"Anything." He rasps.

I suck in a shuddering breath, hoping my voice remains steady. "Be careful and come back to me safe and alive."

"Nothing on this earth will keep me from getting to you, little elf. That's a fact."

A slight grin tugs at my lips at hearing the determination in his tone.

"Good. I'll obey then."

"Atta girl." His tone is pleased, and I can just imagine his sexy smirk tugging up the corners of his mouth. "Keep the phone with you. I'll be there as soon as I can."

We say our goodbyes, and I find myself wanting to say something more. I'm not sure what. The term, I love you, doesn't seem like something I should be wanting to say yet. How can I love someone I've only known for a short time? It's impossible. Right?

Even though I fooled Griffin into thinking I was cool, calm and collected over the phone, I'm anything but. I'm freaking the fuck out because someone, an enemy of the Marx family, was here today, taking photos of me.

Who the fuck does that?

Besides Griffin, of course.

While he has a few stalker tendencies, I'm not scared of him. These other people, on the other hand, have me losing my mind.

I pace for what feels like hours, but I'm sure it's nowhere near as long, until a couple of cars pull up outside, and heavy feet thud on the deck of my rental.

Devon Marx is not like Griffin in any way but looks. Sure, they have the same shade of dark hair and brown eyes, but Devon Marx doesn't have a caring bone in his body.

To put it politely, he's an arrogant prick.

He lets himself in with a key, his eyes landing on me and giving me a once over before glancing around the living room.

"You the piece of arse?"

"Excuse me?" I hiss, and he waves me off.

"You're the girl, right? Agatha?" His dark eyes travel over me, making me squirm, and I automatically wrap my arms around myself.

"I am Agatha." I confirm in a blunt tone, and he nods.

"Mmm." His eyes travelling over my body, again.

"Dude, what are you looking at?" I hiss, feeling extremely uncomfortable with the way his eyes roam. I know Griff told me to do exactly what this guy says, but if he tells me to do anything remotely sexual, I'm going to get a knife from the block in the kitchen and sink it through his heart.

Devon chuckles. "Just trying to figure out what's got my cousin so whipped by you."

My brows hitch. "Arsehole much?"

"Always." He grins like it's a good thing. *Wanker.* "You're stunning, but that's not why he's so caught up with you. He can have any woman he wants. But he's infatuated with you. Why is that?"

"Maybe I've got a dick. Maybe you don't know everything about your cousin." I deadpan and Devon's dark brows lift before he throws his head back, laughing.

"You have wit. He'd definitely like that. It's not the reason why he's so wrapped up in you, though."

I sigh and shrug. "He once told me that I match his energy."

"How does that work? You're like the zen yoga lady and he's like an uptight hitman."

"She's the calm against my storm." Griffin's voice sounds behind us, and I spin to see him standing there, face a little bruised and suit looking a little ruffled.

My feet move before I realise and I launch myself at Griffin, wrapping my legs around his waist. He catches me easily, and his strong hands hold me close as he claims my lips, and a whimper escapes me even as I try to wind myself tighter around him.

Breaking our kiss, Griffin looks over my shoulder and barks an order to his arrogant cousin. "Make yourself scarce, Dev."

Chapter Twenty-Four

The Storm

Griffin

Sweat drips from our skin as we recover from the desperate claiming we just inflicted on each other. I fucked my little elf right there in front of the open living room windows on the kitchen bench of her rental. We didn't care who could have been watching. All we cared about was having each other as close as we could. It was rough, desperate and fast, but intense with all the emotions we both had.

To say I feel bad that Aggie has been dragged into my bullshit is an understatement. I can't fucking stop apologising to her. I don't think I've ever apologised so much in my life.

I knew Aggie would eventually get dragged into my business, but I hadn't thought it would be so fucking soon. It makes me crazed to think some fucker was so close that he was able to take photos of my beautiful little elf.

I help Aggie down off the bench, and she picks up her dress from the floor, slipping back into it, remaining very quiet. She's not looking at me. Almost like she can't bear it.

Fuck.

She hates me.

She's having second thoughts about sharing this life with me.

She's going to run.

Normally I would go into Alpha mode. I'd assert my dominance over her, forcing her to remember that she's mine. Tonight, however, I can't find that beast inside me.

I step into my pants, tugging them up and zipping them closed. Aggie still won't look at me as she secures the last button on her dress, her long golden waves acting as a shield to hide her face.

"Aggie?"

My voice is hoarse, yet quiet, but I know she hears me by the way her shoulders tense. Still, she doesn't look at me as her bare feet pad over the timber floors, making her way to the open glass doors as she looks out to the moon's shimmering reflection over the lake.

My heart thunders in my ears as I step up behind her, not sure what to do. Knowing she was in danger had nearly stopped my heart altogether. I've never in my life been so scared, and I've been involved in some scary fucking stuff over my years.

But this. Her. I can't lose her.

Reaching out, I place my hand gently on her shoulder, and she stiffens. I only leave it there a moment before I drop my arm, letting my emotions take over.

I sink to the floor, kneeling behind her, and she slowly turns around. Her caramel eyes are glassy with unshed tears, and her lower lip trembles every so often as she looks down at me.

"Aggie." I whisper, pain slicing through my chest in fear of what might happen here tonight. "Does this make you want to leave me?"

The pain in the centre of my chest is excruciating as I imagine her turning her back and walking away from me forever. It's so bad I worry I might be having a heart attack.

"Griff." Aggie sobs before dropping to her knees and throwing her arms around my neck. "I was so scared you weren't going to come back. I thought something was going to happen to you."

The pain in her voice breaks me. I can't remember the last time I fucking cried, and I chew the inside of my cheek to fight it off as much as I can, but a couple of tears escape, anyway.

"Fuck, Aggie." I hiss, squeezing her tight against me. "Does this mean you aren't going to leave me?"

Aggie pulls back, not caring that she's crying as she studies my face and sees my damp cheeks. "I'm never leaving you, Griffin. Ever."

My lips quirk up slightly. "We aren't immortal, little elf. We will be separated by death one day."

She shakes her head furiously. "Nope. When you die, I'm coming with you."

I frown. "You don't want to come with me, Aggie. I'll be going straight to hell for the sins I've committed."

"Then that's where I will be, too. Because I'm telling you right now, Griffin Marx, nothing, not even death or the devil himself, will keep us apart."

Fuck. If I'd been unsure of her feelings towards me, I'm not anymore. They are as real as mine are for her.

Cupping her face between my hands, I claim her lips. Her tears still fall, but she winds her arms around me so tightly, and I know she wants to climb under my skin, just as I want to do to her.

We kiss desperately for a long time, and I feel like I'm back in high school when a kiss was everything. It is now too. Aggie's lips, her tongue. The way they connect with mine is fucking everything.

Eventually, we come up for air. We remain kneeling on the hard timber floor, ignoring the discomfort to our knees, as we press our foreheads together, looking into each other's eyes.

This woman has claimed my very soul.

After we drag ourselves up and pull our emotions together, I suggest going to my house to spend the night as the security is better there. Aggie happily agrees, and my team and Devon flank us as we cross from her house to mine in the dark, their guns at the ready, prepared for the first hint of danger.

Once we locked ourselves in, I introduced Aggie to my bed, where we explored each other some more before passing out in each other's arms.

Agatha

Just before dawn, a loud crack in the air sends both of us bolting upright as commotion comes from outside. Then another loud crack makes me stiffen as I realise what the noise is.

It's gunfire.

“Stay here!” Griffin hisses, leaping from the bed. “Do not leave this house.”

“What? Where are you going?” I leap up too, scrambling to find some clothes to slip on.

“Stay the fuck here, Aggie. You hear me?” Griffin hisses again, and my eyes find his across the bed.

His brown pools are wild with panic, but then again, so are mine.

“You stay here, too!” I hiss back and his brows hitch.

“I can’t, little elf. This is what I do. Stay here. I’ll be back soon. Stay in this room and do not leave this house.”

Griffin tugs up his jeans and moves to a wall panel that opens somehow, to reveal a safe. After keying in a code, it clicks open, and he pulls out a gun, checking it’s loaded before glancing back at me.

“I’ll be back soon.”

Then he darts out of the bedroom.

My heart just about leaps out of my throat when I hear yelling and more gunfire. With worry for Griffin’s safety, I dart out of the bedroom I was ordered to stay in, and my legs carry me fast through Griffin’s fancy house in time to see him run out the front door.

Because this house is made of a lot of glass, when I step around the corner, I can see everything that’s going on outside.

There in the courtyard is a man on his knees surrounded by the black-clad men that came to my house last night, as well as Devon. Griffin approaches them, his gun raised at the man’s head as he speaks, the expression on his face just as scary and menacing as his dad’s.

My breath hitches in my throat as I witness my Santa change into a completely different person. His face, a mask of hatred and fury.

I can hear Griffin's snarling voice, yet I can't make out what he's saying. The man on his knees looks up at Griff with his own snarl, and I see his lips move, saying something to Griffin.

Then Griffin pulls the trigger.

Another thunderous crack vibrates through the air, and as if I were watching in slow motion, I see blood spray from the man's skull, showering the feet of the bystanders.

A gasp escapes me. My hands fly to my throat as a memory I've tried to keep buried slams into me.

I no longer see Griffin standing over the lifeless body of a man with the gun still in his hand. Instead, I see *me*. I have the gun, and I'm standing over a lifeless body, although I'm a much younger version of myself.

"Aggie!" My name is called frantically, but I can't seem to stop my memories from engulfing me as I walk backwards and run into something hard.

A wall.

"Aggie!"

The voice is closer, but I can't see anything but my teenage self.

"Aggie!" Strong hands grip my shoulders, giving me a shake, and my memory slips away as Griffin comes into view. "You weren't meant to see that. I told you to stay in the room."

I don't speak, my eyes trying to focus on his dark gaze as he scans my face.

"Aggie. Talk to me."

I shake my head, not able to find words. I need to tell him. I need to get this nightmare out of me once and for all, but I can't seem to make the words form.

"Aggie." Griffin shakes me a little, and I push him away.

He drops his hold on me, and I turn and run, bolting for the glass doors that lead out to the pool. The moment I have them open, I spring forward and leap into the cold water, releasing my pent-up scream as I sink to the bottom.

Griffin has been honest with me. He's brought me into his world and trusts me with the secrets of his family, yet I haven't told him about my past, or just how similar we are.

Movement in the water next to me is my only warning before Griffin's hands are on me, tugging me up to the surface. When we breach, I suck in the air my lungs are so desperate for, and Griffin hugs me to his chest.

"Fuck, Aggie. I'm sorry. I should have taken him somewhere else, so you didn't have to see that."

I shake my head, wishing he wouldn't blame himself. He has no idea this is about something else.

"It's not that." I say quietly before he eases back to look into my eyes.

"What is it?" he asks, and I shake my head as my bottom lip trembles. "Talk to me, little elf."

I go to open my mouth to speak, but before I can, Devon's voice reminds me that we aren't alone.

"We have his phone, Griff. He's definitely the one who took the pictures and sent us on a wild goose chase."

Griffin drags his gaze from mine to glare at his cousin. "Do we know why?"

"No. Still working on that." Devon responds and Griffin growls.

"Get it fucking done. I get the feeling he wasn't working alone."

"On it, you grumpy bastard." Devon chuckles before I hear his footsteps heading in the other direction.

When Griffin returns his dark eyes to mine, they soften, and he wades us through the cold water to the steps where we climb out of the pool. He doesn't say anything else as he leads me over to the side and wraps a towel around me. Then he leads me back through his house and up to his bedroom.

The moment we are in his oversized bathroom, I start tugging off the wet clothes and Griff flicks on the shower. Steam quickly fills the air before he takes my hand again and leads me into the large shower that could fit four standard sized showers in it.

Tugging me under the hot spray of water, Griffin's hands roam over my skin as he washes me, my body warming quickly from the water and his touch.

We go through the process of washing each other's hair in silence, and when we're done and I know I can't keep stalling, I finally open my mouth.

"I need to take you to Queensland."

His brows hitch. "Queensland? To meet your mum and sister?"

My brows shoot up this time. "You know where they are?"

A wide grin spreads across his face. "I did my homework on you, remember? I know where you used to live, little elf. I know who I have in my arms right now."

My heart sinks.

No, he doesn't.

"You told me once you knew my parents' and my sister's names. But do you know much about them?" I ask, and he nods.

"Yes. Your father Dougal went missing years ago. I haven't been able to find anything else on him, but your mum, Roma, has been in a good relationship for the last five years. Brett seems like a good guy."

My brows shoot up. "She's in a relationship? Brett who?"

Griff frowns. "Don't you know?"

I shake my head. "No. I haven't seen my mum since I left years ago. I wasn't even sure if she was alive."

Griffin's frown deepens. "If you're estranged from your mother, then why do you want me to meet her?"

I drop my gaze to his chest, not able to look into his eyes. "I don't want to take you there to meet my mum."

"Your sister Elizabeth, then?"

I shake my head. "No. I need to show you something." My eyes dart back up to his. "And after that, we'll know if you really *do* want to keep me."

He frowns. "What does that mean?"

I shake my head as shame fills me. "I can't say the words, Griff, so I need to show you."

Griffin studies my face for a few long, drawn-out moments. "Ok, then. Let's go to Queensland. We can leave soon. I'll arrange our private plane to take us."

"Private plane?" I ask, my mouth dropping open in surprise, and Griffin grins.

"There are a lot of perks to being with a Marx man, little elf. Private planes are one of them."

I nod, letting a small smile break free.

"Aggie..." Griffin's face morphs into concern. "I just shot someone in front of you. Are you sure you don't hate me?"

I shake my head. "No, I don't think I could ever hate you, Griff. I just hope you still feel the same way about me once you learn the truth."

Chapter Twenty-Five

Homecoming

Agatha

Within two hours, we are on a private plane, flying to Queensland. The plane is small, with a pilot and a hostess, and it's a surreal experience to fly in such privacy. When Griffin doesn't think I can see him, he looks at me with worry. I see it in the blurred reflection of the car and plane windows and the mirrors across the space.

Is he still worried about killing a man in front of me, or worried about what he is going to learn about me? I feel sick to my stomach with worry over the latter. I've never spoken a word about this to anyone and I'm terrified that not only will I lose Griffin over it, but I may lose my life over it. Either by death, or prison.

I have to go through with this, though. I've lived too many lonely Christmases to give up the chance that Griffin might be the only person on the planet that will understand.

I fucking hope he does.

"You wanna tell me about your mum and sister?"

Griffin's words drag my gaze from the fluffy white clouds below us, and I see him looking relaxed as he sips on his whiskey next to me.

"Do *you* want to tell me about my mum and sister? I get the feeling you know more about them than I do."

He smirks. "I didn't know you were estranged from them, so I guess I don't know everything."

Smiling, I nod before my face falls neutral. "Is my sister ok? She must be in her mid-twenties now."

Griffin offers me a warm smile. "As far as I can tell, she is. She's married, actually. Just had her first child."

"What?" My brows shoot up as pain laces my heart. "My little sister has a baby?"

"Yes. A daughter."

"Wow." I mutter, my eyes falling to my fidgeting hands in my lap.

Griffin reaches over and takes one of my hands, linking his fingers with mine. "She called her Marie."

My gaze darts to his as my emotions become overwhelming, and my eyes fill with tears. "Marie?"

"Yes." He nods, offering me a sympathetic smile. "That's your middle name, right?"

I nod as a hot tear escapes, and Griff reaches up to catch it after setting his whiskey aside.

"It probably doesn't mean anything." I speak quietly, trying to fight back more tears. "Marie is a popular name."

"Maybe." Griffin rasps. "Or maybe it means your sister named her daughter after you."

My eyes flash up to Griffin's again. I don't know what to say to that, but I don't need to. Griffin understands me more than I realise, his dark eyes softening, showing me how much he cares.

It's not long before the plane is landing in a small airstrip in Queensland's Glass House Mountains. As soon as we step off the plane, the familiarity of the humid air sends me back to my childhood, and despite the crap I had to deal with growing up, I sure miss the times that me and Lizzy ran free, sweat beading over our skin from the Queensland heat.

As we step off the plane, my eyes land on a couple of men waiting for us on the tarmac. They are both covered in tattoos. One has a long brown beard, and the other one has a three-day growth. I don't know who is who, but one is named Eddy, and the other is named Freddie. Weird, I know.

Freddie, or perhaps it's Eddy, hands Griff a set of keys after a brief greeting, and we head to a black Jeep parked nearby while the two men approach a motorbike.

Griffin ushers me into the passenger seat before rounding the car to get behind the wheel, and I watch the two gruff men in the side mirror as they squeeze onto the motorbike together.

"So, how do you know Freddie and Eddy?" I try not to giggle at their rhyming names as I click my seatbelt into place and Griffin starts up the engine.

"They are a part of the Maroochydore Southern Sadists chapter."

"Chapter? Southern Sadists? Is that like a motorbike gang or something?"

Griffin grins as he glances over at me before turning his eyes back to the road as we leave the airfield.

"Yep, it's an MC. They work closely with the Marx crew and the Angels."

"The Angels? Are they another motorbike gang?" I ask, and Griffin chuckles.

"No. The Angels are two sisters that basically run the underworld in this country. They were the ones that asked us to help remove certain names from the Vixen's Lodge Feast list."

My brows shoot up. "Really? I had no idea. Tyler and Shane sorted it out. I didn't ask them how they arranged it."

"Tyler? He's the underage girl's secret teacher lover, isn't he?"

I narrow my eyes at Griffin. "He *was* her teacher."

He chuckles again. "I get it. You're all friends and you're protecting him and the girl. I wasn't judging."

I don't say anything to that, instead I poke my tongue out at him, winning me a magnificent Griffin Marx smile with dimples.

Swoon!

"Where are we going now, little elf?" he asks, and I glance at the side mirror to see the motorbike still behind us.

"Are they staying with us?"

"Yep. Just some extra protection given recent events."

I frown, turning to glance back at Griffin. "I don't want anyone else knowing about this, Griff. Can they please go somewhere else?"

Griffin shoots me a concerned look. "That depends on where we are going."

I sigh. "Conondale National Park. We need to make a stop first at a hardware store."

His eyes shoot to me. "For?"

"A shovel."

Griffin is quiet for a beat, so I risk a glance at him to see his brows tugging down as he watches the road.

"Ok. So, no backup is required at the National Park then?"

"Not unless you want to fend off some birds," I say playfully.

Griffin chuckles before pressing 'call' on his phone and a moment later, loud road noise comes through the speakers.

"Yeah?" the gruff voice answers.

"Jump ahead of us and lead us to a hardware store."

"No worries, mate." Eddy or Freddie, I don't know which one it was, disconnects the call before the motorbike comes racing past us to take the lead.

We follow behind as Griffin accepts a call from Devon, so I relax back in the seat, watching the beautiful countryside pass by. Devon doesn't have much to report other than confirming there was definitely someone working with the guy Griffin killed, and Griff barks a few more orders before hanging up.

Driving through a small town, we pull in next to Freddie and Eddy out the front of a hardware store before we get out of the car for a stretch.

"I'll be right back." I call before leaving Griffin with his biker friends.

He frowns as I ditch him, but I need a minute to myself. This is all a lot. Griffin can be intense, which I do love, but I'm exhausted from pretending that I'm ok.

I'm not ok. None of this is ok. And I don't know if it will turn out ok, but all I can do is hope.

I locate the shovels, finding one that will cut through earth the easiest, and I pay with cash, keeping my head turned away from the security camera above the counter.

When I return out to the street, Griffin, Freddie and Eddy all fall quiet as they watch me approach. I don't miss the look one of the bikers gives the other at seeing the shovel in my hand, but I ignore it and move to the back of the car, stashing the shovel inside.

"Ok. You guys know the drill. Hang back on the main road and we will return to you when we are done."

"No worries." The long-bearded biker nods before turning to the bike.

We get back into the car and buckle up before following Freddie and Eddy out of town, heading west towards Conondale National Park. The closer we get, the more my stomach rolls as memories of a past I tried to forget assault me.

"Talk to me, Aggie. Tell me about where you grew up." Griffin insists, and for the first time ever, I actually feel like sharing this information.

"The town I grew up in is a couple of hours east, towards the coast. We lived in a run-down Queenslander home. My parents rented it. My dad could never afford a mortgage. Probably because he could never hold down a job. Growing up, things were... rough."

My eyes dart to Griffin, who shifts his eyes from the road to me and back again.

"How so?"

"You know the age-old tale. Things were tough, so my parents turned to drugs and alcohol, not caring that it made things harder. Especially for me and Lizzy. Mum was a lazy drunk, and dad was an abusive drunk. Not a good mix."

"Shit, Aggie. I'm sorry."

I shrug. "It is what it is."

"Are you going to tell me why we are driving into the thick forest of a national park with a shovel?"

I shake my head. "No. I'd rather just show you if that's ok?"

I catch his smile as he turns it to me. "I can handle that."

I hope he can. I'm counting on it, otherwise I don't know what I'll do.

I direct Griffin to the turnoff up ahead, and the two bikers slow down and pull over as we pull off the main road onto a dirt track.

"Just stay on this road and keep driving until the road runs out," I direct, and Griffin nods.

The deeper into the forest we get, the bumpier the dirt track is, and I have to latch onto the grip handle above my head to keep myself from getting thrown around too much.

When we eventually run out of road, we get out of the Jeep, and I take the shovel out of the back before turning to face Griffin.

"I hope you don't mind a bit of a walk." I try to offer Griff a smile, but it falls flat.

"Hey." He catches up to me as I start walking on the path, and takes my hand, stopping me. "I'm not sure what this is all about, but I want you to know we don't have to do this. I can see it's killing you inside, and I hate to see you in so much pain."

It is killing me inside, but I don't think I can move forward with him without doing this.

"It's fine. I need to do this." I gesture my head up the path. "Come on."

His lips thin as he studies my face, and I see the moment he gives in before he leans over and takes the shovel from my grip. "Fine, but I'm carrying this."

He keeps our hands linked as we walk, and the butterflies it gives me nearly scares the nausea away. When we get to the fork in the path, I take the left path and start counting my steps out loud.

"One, two, three, four..."

Griffin doesn't interrupt, which I'm glad for. If I lose count, I'd have to go back and start again. When we get to fifty-seven steps, I veer off the path, stepping through the two thick trunks and start counting my steps again. For every ten steps, I stick up a finger until I finally hit one hundred, and then I start again.

It's not an exact science, especially on the uneven forest floor and steep inclines, but it works well enough.

When we get to another hundred, I start again until we get to thirty-seven. Then I stop, glancing up ahead to find the boulder that looks so out of place on its own in the scrub. I step up to it and hold out my hand, not looking at Griffin, but waiting until he hands me the shovel. And then I start digging.

"Can I do that for you?" Griffin asks, sounding concerned.

"No." I mutter, wishing the damn ground was softer.

"Not to brag or anything, but I'm familiar with digging holes big enough to fit bodies in, so I think I can handle this."

A laugh escapes me, and I shake my head.

Here I am, digging up a ghost of my past, and Griffin is making me laugh. I'm sure he'll be feeling the opposite of amused when he finds out what I'm digging for.

I keep digging, all the while watching Griffin in my peripheral as he leans against the boulder. The hole gets deeper and wider as I go, while the sheen of sweat coating my skin helps to keep me cool in the humid heat.

Griffin offers to dig for me more times than I can count, but I shake my head and stay focused on my task, knowing it's only a matter of time now until I reach what I'm looking for.

The moment the shovel hits something harder than the rich soil I've been excavating, I freeze, and my heart just about leaps out of my throat. I suck in a deep breath and carefully dig smaller piles out until it comes into view.

"Fuck." Griffin hisses beside me, but I keep digging, my hands trembling as my eyes blur with tears. "Aggie, talk to me."

I keep digging until more bones appear, as well as a dirty glint of metal. I drop the shovel then, jumping down into the hole to pick up the heavy piece of metal before finally looking up at Griffin.

"Little elf. Who is that?"

I reach my hand up, hoping he'll take it, and he does, tugging me up out of the hole.

When I'm back standing next to Griffin, I look down into the hole and try to push the words out.

"That's my dad." I hold up the heavy object in my hand and start dusting off the dirt. "And this is the gun I used to kill him."

Chapter Twenty-Six

Destroying the Evidence

Griffin

Finally. Her real secret. I knew she'd been holding back on me. I knew there was something she was too scared to tell me. But I hadn't even considered this.

I knew her dad had disappeared. Her mum had filed a missing person's report and everything, but given their history, the local cops had declared that he just up and left her and probably skipped town. It happens all the time, so I stupidly believed what I'd read in the police files.

But this? I never would have guessed.

Aggie's expression as she looks at me tells me she's waiting for me to freak out. I drag my eyes away from her caramel pools and glance back down to the skull in the ground and then to the gun in her hand, before realising what I need to do.

Taking out my phone, I call Eddy, and he answers on the first ring.

"Marx?"

"We are going to need a drum. The contents will need an acid treatment and a meltdown." I bark and Eddy doesn't miss a beat.

"No worries. We will head back to the club and grab the truck. Be back as soon as we can." Then he hangs up.

Slipping my phone back into my pocket, I lift my eyes back to Aggie. "We'll get this sorted, little elf."

"What do you mean?" She frowns as I take the gun from her grip and inspect it.

"Freddie and Eddy will be here soon, and we will destroy any evidence, so this never comes back to you." I advise, my eyes lifting back to meet hers.

"Is that why you think I brought you here?" She hisses. "To destroy the evidence?"

I frown at her reaction before tilting my head to study her. "Is it *not* why we are here?" I know we aren't here because she wants to destroy the evidence, but I need her to admit that it's because she wanted to share this secret with me.

Her brows shoot up and she takes a step back from me, and I chew the inside of my cheek, trying to hold back my grin. Come on, little elf, tell me how it is.

"We are here because I needed to tell you that I killed someone. I killed my dad, Griffin. What you did to that man this morning was exactly what I did to my dad. My own flesh and blood." She spins and points to the forest floor at her side. "Right there is where he kneeled before I pressed the gun to his head and pulled the trigger."

Slowly, I nod, glad she admitted her dark secret to me by using her voice. "I'm assuming he must have done something bad to make you want to kill him."

"What if I say he didn't do anything? What if I tell you I'm nothing more than a crazy bitch?"

Huh, she's trying to test me. Trying to see if I'll flip on her. Silly little elf, she needs to learn I will always have her back.

My lips thin and I step towards her. "You're not a crazy bitch, Aggie. If you brought me here to admit something, then out with it so we can move on, because let me tell you right now, there's nothing you can say that will scare me away. Hell, even if there were thirty dead bodies in that hole, *care of you*, I still wouldn't walk away from you."

"I guess that would make you the crazy one, then." She mumbles, and I frown.

Closing the distance between us, I press my finger under her chin and lift her head.

"I'm crazy as fuck, little elf. But when I'm around you, I feel *less* crazy." I lean forward and press my lips to her forehead. "I guess what you witnessed this morning was a trigger for you?"

She nods. "Yes. In a way." She sighs, taking a moment before continuing. "I had flashbacks. That's what I was freaking out about."

"I'm assuming your dad hurt you? Or your mum or sister? Did he hit you? Or... touch you inappropriately?" I growl, the idea of it nearly sending me into a fit of rage, because if he did hurt her, I would go to hell right fucking now and kill him all over again.

"He used his fists on us." Aggie admits, nodding her head. "Mainly mum. Sometimes when he didn't pay the electricity bill because he used the money on drugs, he would chase us through the dark house at night, swinging his fist at anything that moved. We learned to be still after a while." She closes her eyes, squeezing them tight like she is trying to push away the memories. "I just couldn't take it anymore." Her eyes dart open and lock with mine. "Mum had been pregnant at the time. She had sobered up to have a clean pregnancy, but dad didn't stop indulging, and one night, he decided he didn't want her to have the baby anymore. So he beat her... her pregnant tummy, like it was a boxing bag." A sob escapes my little elf. "She was seven months pregnant."

"Fuck." I hiss, reaching for Aggie and pulling her to my chest. She curls into me, even while continuing her story.

"He ran off, and I got mum to the hospital. They had to induce her labour, and she had to deliver the baby. He was stillborn. My mum named him Cody." The sob that escapes her this time is guttural, and her knees nearly give way, so I hold her tighter, keeping her in my embrace. "A-after she delivered Cody, she cried with him in her arms until the nurses took him away. I left Lizzy at the hospital and got a taxi home to get mum some clothes and stuff, and that's when I found dad passed out on the backseat of our car with the door wide open." She shakes her head against my chest. "I went inside to his gun box. The idiot never kept it locked, and I grabbed the gun, went back out to the car, put the child lock on the back door and closed it before driving out here."

Aggie's shoulders grow strong then, and she steps back from me, sniffing and batting away her tears. She steps closer to the hole she dug and looks in.

"I tricked him when we got here. He was already so drunk and half asleep. I told him there was a little country bar out in the woods, and the idiot followed me. He started getting angry by the time we reached this boulder, and I knew this was it. This was the place he would die."

She darts her caramel gaze back up to me, and I'm sure she can see the empathy in my glassy eyes.

"I've never told a single person about this until now. Not even mum or Lizzy. I let them think he'd taken off and didn't return. What I didn't expect was for mum to be so heartbroken over it. He'd just killed her baby, for fuck's sake. It tore me up to see her in so much pain and she turned back to drugs so easily. So I left. I was wracked with guilt that I had ruined her life."

"Shit, Aggie. You didn't ruin her life." I step up to her, and she lifts her gaze to remain on mine. "If my research is right, then I think you made it better."

"I hope so." She sobs, and again, I pull her into my arms to embrace her.

"I'm so sorry about all of this, little elf. I totally understand if my world is too much for you. Just tell me now if you need to walk away." I hate saying the words, and even after last night's revelations, I know if I have to let her go for her own sanity, I will. I might suffer eternal heartache, but it will be worth it if she is happy.

Aggie pulls back from my chest, frowning up at me. "I just dragged you halfway across the country to dig up the remains of my dad and admit that I killed him, and you're asking me if *your* world is too much?"

"Yes."

"Is *my* world too much for you?" She asks, exasperated, and I quickly shake my head.

"Your past doesn't scare me, Aggie. The sex parties sound good to me... as long as I'm invited. And I'll gladly submit to you and let you tantra the fuck out of me any time you like. The question is, can *you* handle *my* family? *My* lifestyle? *My* ways?

Because this," I point to the open grave she dug, "is part of my world."

"Then I guess I'm already part of it." She states with honesty.

Once again, I drag her in for a hug, and she finally relaxes. She's not running from me, and I'm not running from her, and the skeletons in our closets have been revealed. Well, mostly hers. I have too fucking many.

Freddie and Eddy turn up about an hour later, not asking any questions when I order them to dig up the rest of the remains before they carry the bones of Aggie's dad and the gun out of the national park in a drum.

They load it into the small truck, and we follow behind as they drive to their MC club house in Caloundra. I keep Aggie by my side the whole time we are there. An MC club house is no place for any female that isn't a whore, but Aggie doesn't seem too concerned with the brutes drinking beer and manhandling women.

To make sure the job is done, we watch the gun get melted down to molten metal in a furnace and watch the bones fizzle as acid fills the drum to engulf them.

"The bones will dissolve in a couple of days." I mumble close to Aggie's ear as she watches on curiously, and she nods, not able to find her voice in that moment.

The events of the last twenty-four hours have been a lot for the both of us, so I wrap up business quickly, paying Freddie and Eddy for their time and assistance before I take my woman away from that place and back to the airstrip.

We both sleep most of the trip back on the plane, and by the time we finally get back to Redfield Lake, the clock ticks over to the next day.

I ask Aggie if she wants to stay at my house or if she needs some time alone.

She doesn't even need to consider her answer before responding.

"I never want to spend a night without you again."

Chapter Twenty-Seven

Party Favours

Agatha

Thank God for rich men and private jets or we would have spent the entire night travelling home. Instead, by 1am, we were snuggling up together in Griffin's bed, where we both slept soundly until late Monday morning.

"Should I cancel tonight?" I ask Griffin as he sets down a plate of poached eggs, toast, and bacon in front of me.

"What's tonight?"

"Monday night." I grin, waiting for him to understand.

He eyes me for a moment before taking his seat and a grin spreads his kissable lips.

"Ahh. Sex party night." He nods. "Do you want to cancel?"

"Well, I'm pretty tired... but." I bite my lip and he shoots me a devilish smirk.

"But?"

"I feel bad for cancelling last week." I say as I pierce my egg with my fork and rich yolky goodness oozes out. "Some of my guests really need these parties."

"Then don't cancel." Griffin mutters around a piece of bacon.

I take a few minutes, considering the situation as I eat the food Griffin cooked me. He's a great cook, which is just another thing that works in his favour.

"Are you going to come?" I ask, after taking a sip of my orange juice.

I can see he's fighting off a grin as he considers how to answer that. Then he peers up at me. "Do you want me to come?"

I shrug. "I don't know how I feel about it." I say before taking a bite of my toast. "Well, I kind of know." My voice is muffled with the food in my mouth.

"Please explain." Griffin chuckles at me as I try to swallow.

I take a big gulp of my juice again, letting it wash the toast down, and then I turn my focus to Griff as I tell him this truth. "The thought of you touching another woman is kinda making me want to commit murder. Again."

Throwing his head back, Griffin's laughter fills the room, its deep baritone sounding light and carefree before he's able to form words. "I like that you feel jealous. How about if I just watch? Is that allowed?"

My brows shoot to my hairline. "You wanna come to the sex party and not join in?"

"Well, my little elf. There *will* be a point that I'll want to join in, which is when *you* will service *me*."

"You want to fuck me in front of people?" I ask, needing to confirm.

"Fuck yes. I practically fucked you in front of people at the Red Room. I guarantee some of those dirty fuckers were hiding somewhere to watch. I also fucked you out by the pool. I'm sure we gave a show to some lucky arsehole passing by. And then there were my brothers."

"I get it." I smirk. "You're into exhibitionism." I state, more than ask.

"Maybe." He grins and I grin back.

"I'd say yes."

He places his fork on the table and leans back in his chair. "Is that a problem?"

"No." I shake my head. "Not at all."

"Good. It's settled then." He shifts forward again to continue eating.

"Wait. Won't you get jealous if I fuck someone else?"

"Fucking oath, I will." He says with a fierceness that sends a chill up my spine.

"You can't kill my guests, Griff."

He rolls his eyes. "Well, that's boring."

I giggle. "It's a rule."

"I do like rules. Especially when they are in my favour." He grins. "Perhaps we can have some rules of our own."

"Like?"

"How about every time I hate having to watch you fuck someone else, you earn yourself a punishment that I can claim at any time after the party?"

My skin heats while a flush reddens my cheeks and Griffin chuckles.

"Shit, Griff. Ok. Let's make that a rule."

A low growl sounds in his chest and he drags my chair closer to him before nipping at my lips. "Such a dirty little elf."

He claims my lips then. It's a brutally searing kiss with tongues dancing, desperate for more. I can taste the bacon he just ate, and I'm sure he can taste my breakfast too, which makes the kiss all the more hotter.

When we break apart, he bites my lip before turning back to his food, and I'm left with wet hot heat pooling between my thighs.

"We need a safe word." Griffin states like he's not at all burning up from the kiss we just shared. "Because if I feel like I'm about to kill some fucker because I can't handle seeing him or her touch you, then things are going to go south really fucking fast."

He has a point. "You don't want to use the universal safe word?"

"Which is?"

"Cactus."

He shakes his head. "Nope. We need one for just the two of us."

"Ok. How about Christmas? It's just for the party, right?" I pick up my bacon and dip it in the yolk before taking a bite and close my eyes. Mmmm, soooo gooood.

"Yes. Just for the party." There's amusement in his tone, so I snap my eyes open to see Griffin smirking at me. "You make eating bacon look explicit."

I grin. "It's a talent."

He chuckles, relaxing back in his chair to watch me eat.

This feels good. Sharing breakfast. Fun banter. A girl could get used to this.

We spend the day preparing for the party. Griffin disconnects most of my cameras in my rental, leaving the ones in my bedroom connected, but switched off. Since it's New Year's Eve tomorrow, a lot of my guests are away, but ten accept the invitation, and by the time the sun is setting, my house has the familiar sounds of sex and foreplay filling the air.

Griffin isn't here yet. He said he'd give me some time to greet my guests. I'm actually nervous about having him here. I've never shared something like this with a lover before.

Since Griffin and I have been playing Christmas games, I've found myself more partial to my red lingerie, but tonight, I'm wearing white.

There's just something dirty about wearing the colour of purity and innocence in such a sensual way. I love the way it makes my skin seem more sun kissed than it really is. I love the way my dark nipples stand out behind the stark lace, and the shadow of my slit hints teasingly.

The mask I have on is floral, which covers my hair like a hat, and comes down to cover my face, stopping just above my lips. There are cut outs for my eyes and breathing holes, of course, plus a slit in the crown where my ponytail is set free. My heels are a similar floral pattern, making it look like the whole outfit goes together, and I can't wait for Griffin to see it.

"Thanks for throwing the party, Moxie." Sheriff, AKA Ben, smiles past his black leather mask as I walk by him and his secret lover Shane, also known as Tradie at these parties, but to me, Shane will always be police officer Shane Kent. We have become good friends outside the parties we attend, and Shane and Ben are probably the only people I've gotten relatively close to, aside from Griffin.

I shoot them a wink, and they quickly turn back to each other, kissing like they haven't seen each other in months. A lot of guests at these types of parties don't tend to kiss, but we all secretly know these two guys are in love with each other, and we let them share the time together without interrupting them.

As I walk through my rental, which now resembles a porn scene, I don't find myself as excited to participate as usual. I'm anxious. Nervous. What if I join in on some action and Griffin changes his mind about me? I don't need this sort of thing in my life as much as I thought I did a couple of weeks ago.

Back then, I needed it because I was lonely, and I didn't know how to have a relationship with someone without them freaking out about my desires.

Now, my desires are consumed by a dark-haired, dark-eyed bad boy, and nothing else seems to compare.

"Moxie. Come over here and let me taste your honey."

The familiar voice of Butterfly draws my attention to see her getting pounded from behind by Grizzly on my couch. Butterfly pats the couch in front of her as she smiles past her pink leather mask.

"Lay down here and let me make you feel good."

My shoulders relax, and I smile at Butterfly as I approach. She's one of the dirtiest girls I've ever come across. She's into some stuff that just seems vile to me, but she knows which parties she can and can't step over some extremely thick lines with. Some of the parties she attends have no boundaries at all. I'd be terrified to step foot in one of those clubs.

"How are you, Butterfly?" I ask as I slip my panties off and lower myself to the couch, shuffling my arse closer to her face as I spread my legs wide. I hook one leg over the back of the couch and drop the other over the edge to the floor as Butterfly flashes her teeth at me.

"I've been dreaming of your cunt, Moxie. That's how I've been." She smiles before turning her head over her shoulder to address Grizzly. "Change to my arse, Grizz. I wanna feel you tear my arse to shreds."

Grizzly growls, something he's known for. He doesn't say much, but the scary fucker can growl like a bear chasing its prey. Hence, his nickname.

When Butterfly stiffens, I know Grizzly is doing what she asked, and she turns back to me as she licks her lips. "I'm thirsty, Mox. Make sure you give me a drink at the end."

I grin. She knows I'm a squirter.

The moment she lowers her face between my legs and I feel the hot press of her tongue through my folds is the moment that Griffin appears behind Grizzly and Butterfly.

A gasp escapes me, partially from the sensations building between my legs, and partially because I feel like I've just been caught doing something wrong.

Griffin is wearing nothing but a black leather mask, and he steps up beside us as he strokes his hard length, a slight smirk tugging at the corner of his mouth. Seeing him standing there with his eyes dark with lust while he fists his dick has to be one of the hottest things I've ever seen. The only thing that would make it better is if I could see his face.

Grizzly studies Griffin as he pounds into Butterfly's arse, so I decide to introduce them.

"Grizzly, this is Mafia."

I can tell by his slight grin that Griffin wasn't expecting me to call him that. We hadn't discussed what his club name would be, but I think it's fitting.

Butterfly pops her head up from her task between my legs and runs her eyes over my man.

"Why hello good sir. Would you like me to replace your hand with mine while I have a snack?"

I'm about to tell her to back off, but Griffin answers first.

"No, thank you. I'm only here to watch for now."

"Mmmm, you can watch Grizzly destroy my arse any time you like, Mr Delicious." Butterfly bites her lip as she ogles my man, and I release my own growl, fisting her hair and dragging her attention back to me.

"I thought you were thirsty?"

She grins. "Oooh, dominating Moxie is hot. Fuck yes, I'm thirsty."

She doesn't say anything else before diving back in.

I throw my head back, moaning as Butterfly presses my legs wider and starts fucking me with her long-pierced tongue. I'm helpless to hold back.

A strong hand fists in my hair, and my eyes fly open to connect with the dark pools of my Santa.

"Fuck her face." He rumbles, and I glance down to Butterfly's green eyes looking up past the mound of my sex. I start thrusting my hips up, and she shoves her face firmer into my parted legs like she is trying to climb inside me.

"Fuck." I rasp as I do exactly what Griffin asked me to.

His fist tightens in my hair as he leans down to whisper in my ear. "That's a good little elf."

His encouragement eggs me on, and I let my walls down, becoming Moxie and taking what I need. The whole scene has me ready to explode and as Butterfly grinds her nose against my clit, I know I'm not far off.

"Open." Griffin rasps tugging tighter on my hair, and my eyes meet his as I open my mouth before he moves closer, pistoning his straining cock in the palm of his hand.

"Fuuuck." He groans before the first spurt of cum hits my tongue, and that's the moment I soar.

I cry out, even as my mouth fills with Griffin's cum, and Butterfly gets exactly what she wanted as I spray right into her mouth. That's the moment she comes, too, which milks Grizzly of his orgasm, leaving all four of us panting.

As we come down from our highs, Grizzly slips from Butterfly's arse, and she sits up from between my legs.

"Well, that was fun." She smirks as she wipes her glistening chin before her eyes land on someone across the other side of the room. Unabashed, she leaps up off the couch and strolls towards the kitchen where there's some food play happening.

Grizzly frowns and follows her and not for the first time, I think he has a thing for her.

"Are those two a thing?" Griffin asks, helping me stand as I shrug.

"Not that I know of, but it sure looks like Grizzly is interested."

"Yep. It sure does." Griffin grins as he watches Grizzly drop to his knees to start eating Butterfly's pussy while she sucks whipped cream off someone else's dick.

"So... Did you get jealous?" I ask Griffin as he turns his smirk to me.

"A little. Not enough that would warrant a punishment, though."

"Hmmm." I tap my finger to my chin. "I wonder what it would take." I start walking, looking for a new play partner, and Griff chuckles behind me.

"You're asking for trouble, little elf."

I shrug. "Maybe I am."

Stepping into the guest room, I see Rodeo standing over the Pepper twins as they perform a little scissor twin-cest action on each other. Those two girls should be making porn videos. They are a taboo attraction that most don't have the will to shy away from. With the typical beach babe blonde hair, blue eyes, and tanned skin, they put on a good show for whoever is around.

"Hey Rodeo. You want me to help you with that?" I ask, gaining his attention as he runs his hand up and down the length of his cock.

"Fuck yes, Moxie. It's been a while since I felt your lips wrapped around my dick."

A low growl comes from behind me, and I turn to see Griffin's eyes focused on Rodeo.

"Are you using the safe word yet, Mafia?" I ask quietly, and his eyes flick to mine as his jaw ticks. Then he shakes his head.

My heart races at his response as my brows shoot up in surprise.

Is he really going to watch me suck another guy's dick?

Part of me wants to back out, but I know if he wants me to stop, he will speak up. Griffin will be honest and use the safe word if he feels it necessary, so I turn back to Rodeo and step over the Pepper twins to kneel.

Rodeo has a long dick, but it's not as thick as some. It also has a weird bend to it, which honestly is perfect for hitting the A-spot deep inside. Not so great when you're trying to give him head, but I never back down from a challenge, and I've done this before. I know what he likes.

As I reach up and wrap my hand around his dick, I see movement in my peripheral, and turn my head to see Griffin placing a chair close by so he has a good view of the show I'm about to give.

I stare at him for a few long moments as I start pumping Rodeo's cock, feeling a little off about touching another man this way, and I wait, giving Griff another chance to use the safe word. He doesn't, so I glance up at Rodeo, who is looking longingly at his dick, not me, and I flick my tongue out to have a taste.

"Fuck yes, Mox. You have the best tongue."

I strain my ears to listen for a hiss, or growl, or some sort of protest from Griffin, but I don't catch anything, so with a tinge of disappointment, I part my lips and ease Rodeo inside.

That's the moment when I do hear a low growl, and my heart does a little flip. Yes! He doesn't like seeing me do this.

Since no safe word is spoken, I push forward, working my tongue and lips over Rodeo's shaft, giving him the head job he's been longing for.

As the Pepper twins start moaning louder and coming undone on each other's cunts, Rodeo grabs my head, taking control as he starts thrusting into my mouth. I gag over and over, and one look up at him shows his eyes darting between where his dick disappears into my mouth, and whatever the Pepper twins are doing behind me.

Meanwhile, I'm repulsed. Mostly at myself.

This is not Griffin's dick. I don't want this!

I know Rodeo's not far off from losing his load, and I know without a doubt that I don't want to taste it. I have before. It's never been rank or anything, but it's not Griffin's, and I just don't want it.

I give his thigh a pinch, and he releases my head so I can pull back. He frowns, his lips parting to probably ask me what's wrong, but I shuffle to the side a bit while wanking his dick and direct it towards the twins, and the whole time I fight off the urge to hurl.

I think about sucking on one of his nuts, but the thought *does* make me gag this time, so I use my free hand, cupping and gently tugging on his right nut. He quickly forgets to care about his dick not choking me, and he thrusts in sync with my hand before a yell leaves him and he shoots cum over the twins below.

I release his nut and my hold of his cock before turning back to Griffin. He snarls at me and holds up a finger, indicating that I've earnt a punishment.

I grin, because a punishment from him is really a *fun*ishment, which I'm totally down for. It also confirms that he didn't like seeing that, which pleases me, because I didn't like doing that.

"You ready to use the safe word?" I tease, yet really wish he'd use it, but he shakes his head before gesturing to the Pepper twins.

"Join them." He rasps, and I grin.

Cheeky fucker is just playing with me now.

I turn to the twins to see Pepper one licking Rodeo's cum off Pepper two's back, and I crawl up to join them.

Like moths to a flame, they engulf me, sandwiching me between them as one peels back the lace of my bra and nibbles on my tits, while the other reaches around from behind to palm my pussy. I let my head fall back on Pepper two's shoulder as I turn my gaze to Griffin who has his dick in his hand once again. I gyrate and writhe between the twins, feeling my pleasure build.

Pepper one drops to the floor and tugs me down with her until we are humping each other's thighs. I kiss her neck and down to her perky little tits, giving them a squeeze before I suck her nipple into my mouth. She lets out an exaggerated moan and Pepper two kneels behind me and tugs my arse up so I'm no longer humping her twin sister's thigh, only to slide her long thin fingers inside my dripping pussy.

I moan around Pepper one's nipple, pushing back to bury Pepper two's fingers deeper.

"Here, let me." Rodeo's voice comes from behind me, and I feel a stream of lube rush down between my arse cheeks.

My heart starts to race, but not with anticipation. I don't want this to happen.

Even as I think it, Rodeo nudges his dick at the entrance of my back passage, and the deep rumble of Griffin's voice fills the room.

"Christmas!"

I freeze, knowing he just used the safe word, but the others don't know we have our own safe word, and given the position I'm in, I'm not really in control of what Rodeo is about to do.

"Cactus!" I yell a little louder than I needed to, and Rodeo and the Pepper twins freeze before they pull back to look at me.

I sit up, my eyes finding Griffin's immediately as he glares at Rodeo, who is none-the-wiser.

"You want to stop Mox?" Rodeo asks, and I nod.

"Yes, sorry. I'm not feeling very well." I stand quickly, avoiding their shocked gazes as I hurry from the room, and I know by the sound of heavy feet behind me on the timber floors that Griffin is following.

I dart into my bedroom, and a moment later the door closes behind me, the click of the lock loud in the space.

I'm about to turn to face Griffin, but his hands push me roughly face first to the bed, and he presses into my back.

"I can't fucking do it. I can't watch another man stick his dick in here." He slams his dick into my dripping pussy, and I cry out. "Or here." He slides his fingers through the lube before easing two inside my arse. "These are mine!"

Chapter Twenty-Eight

Mine

Griffin

I slam into my little elf brutally as my fingers stretch her puckered rose, and I watch as she clenches the sheets to hold herself in place from the force of my assault.

"Your arse is mine, and no one else's." I rasp in her ear, pressing my chest to her back.

"Yes." She pants quickly, like she already knew this.

"Before I take your arse again." I hiss, nipping at her ear. "I'm going to punish you."

There is so much darkness and menace in my tone that I almost scare myself.

My little elf isn't scared of me, though. I may be a monster to some people, but not to her.

Slipping my fingers from her arse, I ease my cock out of her hot cunt and grip her legs tight before dragging her to the end of the bed. Then I give her arse cheek a stinging slap.

She yelps at the shock of it, and I lean down and hiss in her ear.

"Stay the fuck there. Do not move."

She does as I demand, her bare arse over the end of the bed while her top half is face down on the mattress.

I move quickly to her wardrobe, grabbing the supplies I need, and return to her a minute later to tie her wrists together with a scarf.

I like to dominate, and Aggie knew that from the moment she received the invitation to join me for the game of subbing for Santa. I wasn't entirely sure she would enjoy it, but she fucking does. My dominance makes her drip with need.

After securing her wrists, I tie the satin cord of her dressing gown around the scarf, holding her wrists together before tugging it up to the head of her bed and tying it there so she can't move away.

"Let the punishment begin." I rumble before sliding my fingers through her exposed folds and sink three in.

Instantly her body ignites, her back arching which causes her arse to raise up with need as I finger fuck her, quickly building her pleasure.

Unfortunately for my little elf, seeing her take another man's cock in her mouth has flipped a switch in me, and I'm not ready to let her enjoy this. After all, this is a punishment.

So, before she reaches her climax, I stop.

"Griff!" She hisses, and I chuckle.

"You don't get off that easily, little elf." I graze my fingers up her spine and into her thick waves before dragging them back down between her folds, to start again.

I do this over and over, relishing in the way my little elf writhes on the bed before me, desperate to come.

"Griffin, please." She begs, probably for the hundredth time. "Just fuck me already."

I growl and slap her arse hard before circling my fingers over her clit, quickly building her up again.

"You don't get to come until I say so, little elf." I hiss, trying to ignore the way my dick is weeping to dive back inside her.

I can sense her orgasm rushing at her again, ready to finally send her over, but just when it nearly hits, I stop.

That's when she breaks.

Her sobs start to fill the room, and as if a bucket of ice is thrown on me, I snap the fuck out of my haze.

"Shit." I hiss, leaning down over Aggie to see her face.

Tears stream from her eyes, falling to the sheet under her, and my heart sinks.

"Fuck, Aggie. I'm sorry. I got carried away."

I shift up, making quick work of the tie and scarf, releasing her, and her exhausted body slumps to the floor.

"Shit, Aggie. What can I do?" I beg, falling to the floor next to her, desperate to make things better.

"Fuck me." She whispers on a sob, and I reach over, cupping her face as I press my forehead to hers.

"Are you sure you want me to do that? You're exhausted. And I really don't fucking deserve it." I swipe my thumb over her cheek, trying to wipe away her tears.

"You said I was yours. You said my arse belongs to no one else but you." She sucks in a shuddering breath. "So, claim it already. Make me yours in every way possible."

"Fuck. I don't deserve you."

"Yes, you do, Griff. We deserve each other."

I lean in to kiss her, but she stops me, pressing her fingers to my lips and pushes me back. Confused, I frown, but a moment later, she drops her head into my lap and sucks my cock deep into her mouth.

"Fuuuck." I hiss, my hand coming to rest on the top of her head. "What are you doing, little elf?"

She doesn't answer me, instead, deep throating me, making herself gag a few times. I fight the urge to thrust my hips. She doesn't deserve my brutality tonight. Not when I've already pushed her too far.

After a minute, Aggie slowly eases my cock from her mouth with a pop, and looks back up to me, her caramel eyes wide with excitement, and something that looks a hell of a lot like love.

"I didn't want to kiss you after the last thing I had in my mouth was another man's cock." She admits, as she straddles me. "And I need you to know. I didn't enjoy any of that." She gestures to her bedroom door with her thumb and shakes her head. "I don't want any other man touching me, Griffin. I love being watched, but I won't take another cock that isn't yours."

Fuck. I didn't realise how much I needed to hear her say that. It was torture watching her with another man. The women, well, that part was fun, but not another man.

"Good." I give a single nod. "Because if any other man so much as looks at you, I'll fucking kill him."

Her eyes widen right before I slam my lips into hers. She clings to me instantly, our emotions taking over, and we kiss so fiercely that I'm scared I'm going to break her. Our tongues clash and our teeth knock, and I swear it probably looks like we are trying to eat each other's faces.

I eventually break the kiss, trailing down her neck as my hands come behind her to unclasp her bra. The moment her tits spill free, I have one filling my palm and the other in my mouth as I worship my queen.

When my hand slides between her legs, I release her nipple to pull back and stare into her eyes.

"You're so wet, little elf. Is that all for me?"

She nods. "Always, only you."

A grin spreads my lips wide, and I stand, lifting Aggie up with me. I peck her lips one last time before lowering her legs to the floor and showing her that my monster is still here with us in the room.

"On the bed on all fours."

A mischievous grin turns up her lips, and she crawls onto the centre of the bed, on all fours, as I commanded. Coming up behind her, I gently run my hand up her spine before I press her shoulders down. "Head down. Arse up."

She does as she's told, lowering down onto her elbows as she sticks her arse up in the air. I part her legs wider before grabbing the lube next to the bed and pour it over her puckered rose. Just like with the oil next to the pool, I slather my cock with the lube and give it a few pumps before nudging Aggie's arse with my tip.

"You want me to work you wider with my fingers first, little elf?"

She shakes her head. "No. Just go slow."

I growl like the animal I am. "Of course."

Tortuously slow, I ease my dick inside my little elf's arse, and by the time I'm fully seated, we are both burning up with need.

"Are you ready for me to fuck you now, Aggie?" I ask, my voice sounding strained as I try to keep my composure.

"Yes." She begs. "Please."

So, I do. No longer taking time to be slow and careful, I thrust into her arse in a way that I can only explain as claiming.

It doesn't take long for Aggie to come hard. Twice. Her body reacting to me like I own her soul.

As she contracts around me the second time, I hiss and still as my balls tighten and a wave of ecstasy rushes over me. My cock jerks as it pumps ropes of hot cum into her arse, and when I'm done, we both collapse to the mattress in a sweaty heap, our panting breaths filling the room.

After a beat, we roll to face each other, a tangle of arms and legs as we hug impossibly close. I know I'll never get enough of this woman. She was put on this earth for me.

"Aggie?"

"Yes?" She whispers, taking in the sure expression I'm wearing.

"I fucking love you."

Chapter Twenty-Nine

Games, Guns & Gunk

Agatha

The ocean is flat today, which is a good thing because '*The Audrey*' has been turned into a party boat to say goodbye to the year and hello to the new one.

At first, I was reluctant to spend this celebration with Ewan Marx, but then I remembered I need to prove to him that I belong in this family, so I agreed and packed an overnight bag for the trip.

There are five crew on today, plus ten of us. The two underage teens have spent a lot of the day pouting about having to be on the boat with their parents for New Year's Eve instead of seeing the new year in with their friends. Along with me, Griffin, Ewan and his wife, Selena, the other Marx family members on board are Oswald, Cassandra, Kendrick and Bernadette. Meanwhile, some of the other Marx adults are together clubbing at one of their clubs in the city.

The last day of the year is a beautiful sunny day with not a breath of wind. We've sailed, we've swum, we've drunk, and we've eaten, and not once did Ewan make me feel like I didn't belong.

As the sun goes down, the music turns up and the drinks start flowing even faster.

Everett and Ethan have been pinching beers from the coolers, thinking they are being sneaky since they aren't legally old enough to drink yet. But I've seen Ewan notice on more than one occasion, and instead of scolding his young sons, he turns a blind eye to the mischief the teens are getting into.

"Here, little elf." Griffin whispers, gaining my attention, and my eyes fall to the piece of paper he is handing me. "Give me five minutes and then begin." He rasps in my ear, and I grin and frown at the same time, confused, before he chuckles and presses his lips to my forehead. I'm about to ask him what's going on, but he saunters away, leaving the main deck.

With a grin spreading my lips wide, I give in to my curiosity and glance at the paper, unfolding it.

Tonight, we are playing
Subbing for Santa
– New Year's Edition!

The rules of the game are simple.
If Santa issues an order,
you must obey.
If not, you will be punished.

Your first order is to go to the
bathroom on the deck below and
find the gift I've hidden.

I bite the inside of my cheek as I try to hide my reaction to the note. My cheeks are on fire though, so if anyone is paying me attention, they will probably notice.

I excuse myself, going down the steep stairs to the deck below and lock myself inside the toilet. There aren't many hiding places in here, but I open the compartment under the sink and find a wrapped gift.

Smiling, I tear into the paper quickly to reveal a small jewellery box. I open the lid, and inside is a bracelet with a single charm hanging off it. It's an elf.

My laugh is loud in the small space, and I quickly remove it from the box and fasten it to my wrist, taking a moment to admire it. Not able to wipe the smile off my face, I glance back at the box and notice a piece of paper tucked into the lid, so I pull it free and unfold it.

Put the bracelet on, and
find the key above the
mirror.
If you can find what
it opens,
you can have what's inside.

I grin. This feels more like a treasure hunt than obeying an order, but it's fun, and I love the effort Griffin has put into it.

Looking up at the mirror, I reach up and run my hand along the frame until I find a small key. Bingo! I catch my huge grin in the reflection of the mirror, but a second later, the light goes out. Turning to the switch, I try it a few times before giving up and opening the door. I'm expecting the cabin beyond to still be lit, but I'm met with darkness and only a hint of moonlight streaming in through some of the windows.

Then I grin. Griffin isn't going to make this easy for me. He knows how I feel about the dark after admitting that my dad used to hunt us down when we had no electricity, so I'm not sure what sort of angle Griffin is playing here, but that's ok. He's not the only one that knows how to hand out punishments. I'll make him pay for this.

Knowing I now have to find whatever it is that this key opens in the dark, I steel my nerves and begin my search. Stumbling through the main cabin, I feel my way around, trying to find anything that needs a key to open it. The only thing I find is some sort of ornamental box on display, but it's unlocked, and there's nothing inside.

A thud sounds from the passage at the other end of the room, and I spin, thinking someone is there.

"Griffin?"

Nothing. Just silence.

That's strange.

I decide to head that way, since maybe it's Griffin giving me a clue for the direction I need to head in. I open the door to the kitchen cabin, only to find it empty and dark, too. I still for a moment, realising that it's kind of strange for the kitchen to be vacant since one or two of the staff should be in here preparing the food that's been left unattended on the benchtops.

For all I know, Griffin could have orchestrated this whole bloody thing. He probably asked them to make themselves scarce so he can fuck me in here. I grin, yet I still feel nervous about the darkness and lack of people around.

"Griffin. This isn't funny." I call, only to be met with silence.

Another thud snaps my head to the left. It wasn't as loud as the one before, and it sounded like it came from below deck.

An uneasy feeling settles over me, and my palms begin to sweat.

Slowly, I creep out of the kitchen cabin and down the passage to the stairs that go below deck. It's so dark down there, but my phone is down there, and if I can find it, I can use the torch light on it.

Deciding that's the best option right now, I blindly step down until my foot meets the step and then repeat the process again and again as I enter the lower level. It really is dark down here, more so than on the level above. I'm not familiar enough with this boat to know my way around in the dark, which is so thick that I won't know if I'm about to run into something until I hit it.

Fuck this.

I'm about to turn back and head up the stairs when I hear another noise.

"Griffin?" I whisper-yell, hoping if he's pulling a prank on me, he knows he's likely to lose his balls over this.

Silence.

It's then that I realise the music isn't playing up on the top deck either, and there are absolutely no sounds of the laughter I left behind.

Something's not right.

My legs start to shake as the rush of my blood starts to overtake my hearing. I need to go back to the top deck and see what's going on. There must be a power outage across the entire boat, so this game with Griffin will have to wait until after that's sorted out.

The moment I turn, a crackling sound fills the space before a voice comes through the intercom speakers.

"Agatha Fiera. Where are you?"

What the hell? Whose voice is that?

"You are needed on the top deck. Don't make me come looking for you."

My heart pounds in my chest as I try to calm it enough to think straight.

"If you want to see your boyfriend alive, you will get your pretty little arse back to the top deck, now!"

I stop breathing.

The reason I don't recognise the voice is because it's not Griffin's or one of his family. It's someone else. I doubt one of the staff would speak that way, so it can't be one of them either.

It was only a few days ago that someone was targeting Marx establishments and sent Griffin a picture of me that I didn't know had been taken. Griffin killed that man. I saw it with my own eyes, but Griffin had said he had a feeling that guy wasn't working alone. This has to be the other guy.

Panic washes over me as I try to figure out what to do.

"You have one minute. If you're not here by then, I'll start spraying the deck with Marx brains. I think I'll start with the baby of the family. Ethan."

A sob leaps out of my throat as I slap my hand over my mouth. Hot tears pool in my eyes, and I try to blink them away, not wanting them to distort my vision.

"Fifty seconds!"

I turn and stumble back up the stairs, passing Ewan's office before I skid to a stop and push the door open. I need a gun.

There has to be a gun in here. What Mafia boss wouldn't have a fucking gun in his desk, right?

I scurry inside, moving around the desk to tug the drawers open.

"Forty seconds." The voice chuckles, and a whimper escapes me as I tug another draw open.

Yes. A gun safe.

I lift it out, hoping like hell that Ewan is like my dad and doesn't lock his gun up. I nearly yell out a cheer when the lid lifts open, and under the moonlight coming through the office window, I see not one, but two handguns.

"Thirty seconds."

I quickly check that they are loaded and slip one down the back of my denim shorts before I run out of the office, gripping the other one in my hand.

"Twenty seconds. Tick tock, Agatha."

I bolt onto the back deck and hurriedly climb the steep stairs, making it on top just as the voice yells.

"TEN FUCKING SECONDS!"

"I'm here!" I yell, darting forward with the gun raised at the lanky man who I realise was one of the boat crew.

The entire Marx family, and the remaining four staff, are on their knees in a line facing the man, their hands tied behind their backs, with gags stopping them from speaking. My eyes find Griffin's, which are wide with fear as he glances frantically between me and the man.

The man in question chuckles, his bony features picked up under the moonlight.

"Well, well. Just in the nick of time. What are you going to do with that? Shoot me? You're a civilian, Agatha. You wouldn't even know how to shoot a gun."

"Wanna test that theory?" I hiss, pretty happy with how brave my tone is right now.

Again, he chuckles before pointing the gun in his hand towards Griffin's head.

"The real question is. Do you? Because if you miss, you're gonna have to say goodbye to lover boy here."

"What the fuck do you want?" I snap, not sure what else to do but stall this crazy fucker.

"Revenge. I thought that was obvious. Now, either you put that gun down, or say goodbye to this arsehole." When the man shoves the barrel of the gun hard against Griffin's forehead, I cave and drop the gun.

"Ok. Stop!" I cry, my tears searing as they stream down my cheeks.

"Come here." He hisses, and I slowly walk towards him with my hands up in the air, my legs trembling as my eyes glance at each one of the captives.

The moment I'm close enough, he fists my hair, tugging me to my knees, and he holds me in place.

"She is a pretty one, isn't she?" The guy chuckles sadistically. "Maybe I'll fuck her first before I kill her. It's not exactly the way you killed my sister," he glances at Griffin, "but it will feel good making you suffer."

Griffin starts to struggle against his bonds, and his voice is a muffled yell that's incomprehensible. It just makes this crazy fucker laugh even more.

When the man turns back to face me with menace written all over his face, I reach back to the gun shoved in the back of my shorts and whip it out as fast as I can, pressing it under his chin before he comprehends what has happened. His eyes widen a split second before I pull the trigger and the crack of the gun is loud, echoing out into the vast ocean surrounding us as blood, skull and brain matter rain down on me.

The cries, whimpers and muffled yells of the captives shake me out of my daze after I watch the body slump to the floor with a thud.

I scramble up, dropping the gun before rushing over to Griffin and removing his gag.

"Aggie. Fuck, honey. Cut me loose."

I'm sobbing, I realise as my body starts to convulse with shock, and it takes me way too long to figure out how to cut him free of the zip ties.

"There's a knife over on the bench." Griffin instructs, and I go to stand, but my legs collapse under me, sending me crashing to the floor.

"Aggie. Baby. It's ok. We are all ok. Just slow your breathing."

I try to do as Griffin says, willing my body to comply, and after a few attempts, it starts to work. I crawl over to the bench and pull myself up to stand, finding the knife before stumbling back to Griffin.

I cut the zip ties around his ankles and wrists, and the moment he's free, he pulls me in his arms.

"It's ok." He squeezes me close. "You're ok."

I nod, still crying as I pull back, and we both pull apart before Griffin takes the knife off me and starts to cut his family free.

As soon as Ethan and Everett are free, they slam into me, throwing their arms around me despite the fact that I'm covered in blood and brain matter.

We collapse to the floor together before more family members, and even crew, show their appreciation. It's only when Ewan approaches that everyone moves away from me, and I glance up at the man who has the power to keep me alive or end my life.

"Agatha. We are in your debt. I'm so sorry that you had to do that, but I am eternally grateful. Thank you."

I give Ewan a nod, because I don't really know what to say, and the next thing I know, Oswald has turned the power back on, and Griffin is leading me downstairs to shower.

The moment I see my reflection in the bathroom mirror, I lose all the contents of my stomach. I retch over the toilet while Griffin tries to soothe me, and once I'm done, he removes my clothes.

"Keep your eyes closed. I'll tell you when it's ok to open them." His words are laced with pain. I can tell he feels bad that I had to kill a man to save him and his family. I want to tell him I would have done it even if I didn't know them, but I can't form words right now. So, I let Griffin lead me to the shower as I keep my eyes closed, and he spends an hour washing the gunk out of my hair.

Griffin

I thought she was going to die. I didn't care that my end was about to be delivered. All I cared about was Aggie and keeping her safe, yet I didn't. Me and my family were overpowered by a single fucking psychopath. I'm not sure how that happened, but I can tell you right fucking now, heads will roll!

My younger brothers have had little training, something my dad has fallen light handed on over the years, but all it did was make us weak when the arsehole posing as one of the crew held a gun to their heads.

None of us were prepared. We had no weapons on the top deck, falling complacent that we were fucking safe. And just like that, we weren't. The threat to kill Ethan and Everett had stunned us in place, and Selena's cries were the only thing we could hear as she begged the man to spare their lives.

"Sure, mummy Marx. I'll spare them if you tie the others up."

So, she did, taking the zip ties the man tossed at her and secured our arms behind our backs followed by our ankles. He had watched her carefully, making her pull the ties impossibly tight so we couldn't break them.

He knew what he was doing.

Then he made her do the same to her youngest sons, before he finished the job, pushing her to her knees and binding her wrists and ankles, too.

The way he tormented my woman over the speaker made me crazed. I wanted to kill the motherfucker. Tear him apart, piece by piece, so he wished for death to come quickly.

But my little elf not only turned up before the end of his countdown, but she turned up with two guns.

And fuck, the look in the stupid fuck's eyes when she pressed the second gun under his jaw was priceless. I was worried she wouldn't be able to pull the trigger, but she didn't even hesitate in sending him to hell to save me. To save my family.

There's no doubt in my mind that I've met my future wife. Let's just hope that when I ask, Aggie says yes.

Chapter Thirty

Fireworks

Agatha

Two hours ago, I killed a man. He's not the first man I killed, and I realise, if I stay in this life with Griffin, he may not be the last.

As fireworks shoot high in the sky around different parts of the bay, we watch from afar in silence, as we all try to comprehend what just happened here tonight.

Griffin has been quiet, only speaking in hushed tones with his parents and siblings a few times, but staying by my side for the most part. The body of the man I killed is nowhere in sight, and the deck floor has been cleaned so you can't even tell anything happened.

I'm not entirely sure where the body went. I have a feeling it went in the ocean, but I do know that I don't care. Just as long as it's gone, and I don't have to look at it again.

Apparently, the guy's name was Russell Elk, and he was seeking revenge after Griffin killed his older sister. She had been a piece of shit who lured young girls in to groom them before having them sex trafficked. In my eyes, she deserved to die. People like that shouldn't be allowed to live.

"I'm so sorry things turned out like this. It's not how I wanted to see in the new year with you."

I turn in Griffin's arms, putting my back to the fireworks.

"How did you picture it going?"

His eyes dip to mine, his skin lighting up with reds and greens from the glow of the fireworks.

"Well, I had hoped that by the time the fireworks were starting, we'd be about to finish our game."

"Shit. Our game. I must have dropped the key."

He smiles, but it doesn't reach his eyes. "I have a spare."

"You should finish your game." Selena says as she steps up to the railing next to us. "We could use a little fun and celebration right now."

Griffin turns his frown at Selena, while I frown at his chest, trying to figure out what Selena means. Why would our game be a cause for celebration?

"I don't think sending her on a scavenger hunt now is a good idea." Griffin sighs and Ewan comes to stand on the other side of his wife, putting his arm around her waist.

"Why not give her the gifts she was meant to find?"

My frown deepens as Griffin looks at his dad before he glances back down at me.

"I don't know. I don't want the two things tied together on the same day."

"It's Wednesday now." Bernadette comes to stand on our other side. "And a new year. Why not start it off with something good?"

"But, what if..." Griffin frowns at his older sister, not completing the sentence, and I'm left to wonder what the hell they are all talking about.

"I think you'd be surprised, Griff. She loves you. She didn't need to save us to show me that." Ewan comments, and I'm left reeling.

"Care to clue me in?" I ask, and Griffin turns his gaze back to me, studying my face.

He reaches up to graze his fingers over my cheek before stepping back and releasing me.

"I'll be right back."

As Griffin rushes off below deck, I glance at his family, who are no longer wearing sadness or trauma, but are instead, smiling.

"Come on. Let's sit down." Bernadette takes my hand, leading me to the oversized outdoor lounge, and everyone joins us.

The air sparks with an excitement I'm not privy to, and I eye each of the Marx family here with me, trying to pick up on what's going on. When Griffin returns with a box, his family members shift around in anticipation, leaving me even more stumped.

Taking a seat next to me, Griffin places the box on the table and turns to me.

"So, you found the bracelet and elf charm, and the key." He holds up a key. "You were looking for what it opens." He holds up a small timber box and hands me the key. "Open it."

Smiling, I take the key and insert it in the keyhole, turning it all the way around until it clicks. Then I lift the lid to find another charm. Reaching in, I pull it out, and a laugh bubbles up as I see what it is.

"Santa." I giggle, and everyone around us joins in.

"Here, let me put the charm on for you." Cassandra offers, holding her hand out, and Griffin unclasps the bracelet from around my wrist before he passes it to his sister.

"What else is in the box?" Griffin asks, and I grin, looking inside to find another note.

With shaky hands, I unfold the note, my eyes reading over it before they flash back up to Griffin.

Go to the bedroom
and open my drawer.
When you find the latex,
you'll have all the
access you want.
You can come when
you please.

I frown through my smirk, not sure I understand, and Griffin passes me a box of condoms. Everyone starts laughing, but Griffin's eyes don't leave mine as I eye the box curiously before opening it to find a condom, slightly ballooned, with a key inside and a note.

I throw my head back laughing this time, hoping like hell that his family doesn't ask what the significance of the key in a condom is. That's not really a story I want to share with anyone but Griff. Sucking my lips in to calm my giddiness, I tug the ballooned condom free and look up to Griff.

"What's the key for?"

"Take it out and have a look." He smiles, gesturing to my hands.

Grinning, I untie the greasy latex and slip the key free, turning it over to see something engraved in it. I hold it up closer, squinting to see the fine message.

My brows shoot high as I look from the key to Griffin.

"Your house?"

"Yes." He nods, and I giggle as the clue for this gift begins to make sense. He's telling me I can go to his house whenever I please.

Heat bursts inside my chest as my emotions start to play havoc with me. No one has ever given me a key to their home before.

Taking a moment to inhale the ocean air, I steady my emotions and shoot Griffin a smile before opening the new note.

Now that you have
the key to my house,
and you already know you
have my heart,
it's time to decide if you
can handle answering
one more question.

Think long and hard
about this, because if you
meet me up on the
top deck at the
strike of midnight,
I'll ask it, and this time,
you can't run.

Tears begin to blur my eyes as I comprehend what the note means, and I glance up at Griffin as he slides off the couch and onto one knee.

Gasps and faint giggles sound around us, and even the telltale sniff of someone crying, but I don't take my eyes off Griffin. Not even for a second.

"Would you have come to the top deck at the strike of midnight, Aggie?"

My bottom lip trembles as I study this man's face, so consumed with love for me as he asks me the tough question I would have run from a few days earlier.

"Yes." I whisper as a tear rolls down my cheek.

Griffin reaches up and wipes it away, his fingers a gentle caress on my searing skin.

"I know we only just met. I know this is totally crazy, but I don't see the point in delaying it just because society says it's too soon. If I have to have a one week engagement or five-year engagement with you, I don't care, as long as you wear my ring and stand by my side. I'm in love with you. No one has ever set fire to my soul like you do Agatha Marie Fiera. Marry me. Be mine and let me be yours."

He shifts and pulls out a small box from the bigger box on the table, easing the lid open to reveal a ring with a large diamond set on a gold band.

A sob escapes me as I nod my head, my eyes darting from the ring to Griffin's face. "Yes."

His face lights up. "Yes?"

I nod again. "Yes. Yes. Yes."

I leap forward, wrapping my arms around his neck, and we nearly tumble backwards as Griffin struggles to keep us upright. When he pulls back, his eyes are alight with excitement and love, and he claims my lips right there in front of his family.

Cheers ring out around us, and as the Marx family begin to celebrate, I break our kiss and press my forehead to Griffin's.

"I love you, Griffin Marx."

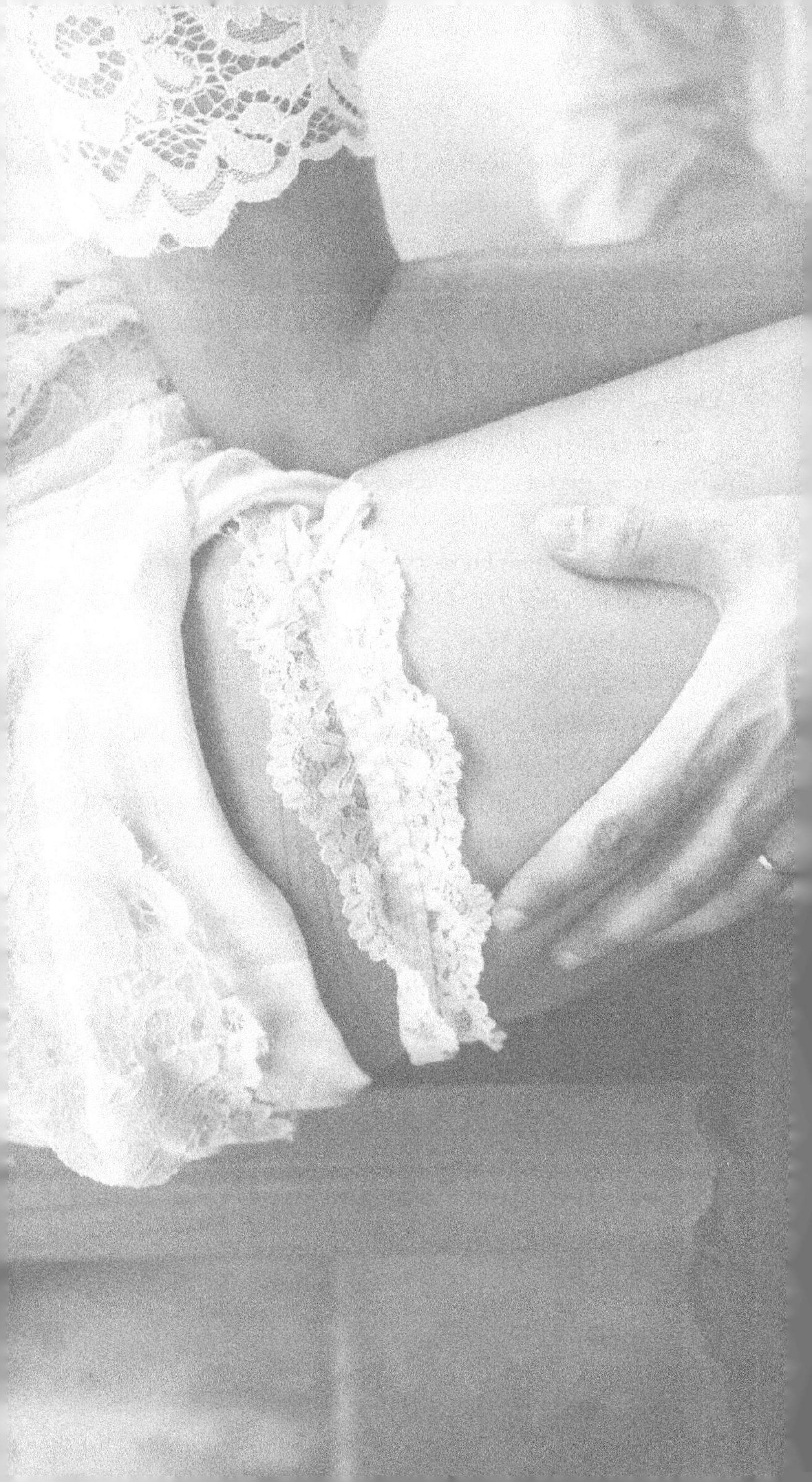

Chapter Thirty-One

Atta Girl

Agatha

Nerves race through me as I stare at myself in the mirror, taking in my caramel brown eyes that are framed with dark lashes, a little thicker than they usually are. I look beautiful, made up like this. My skin is flawless, and my hair is a waterfall of golden blonde curls that cascade down my mostly bare back.

"He's going to shit a brick." Ben laughs as he comes up behind me.

"Either that or cum in his pants in front of everyone." Shane laughs, standing next to his secret lover.

"Stop it." I laugh, turning away from the mirror to face my friends. "You think he'll like it?"

"Girl, if he doesn't like it, then he needs a lobotomy." Ben chuckles and Shane nods in agreement.

"Oh. I almost forgot." Shane pulls out a gift-wrapped box. "He asked me to give you this."

My grin spreads across my face as I accept the gift, excited to see what's inside.

"Meet you outside in five minutes." Ben calls as they turn and leave me in my bedroom.

I open the gift quickly, wondering what on earth Griffin could have gotten me. The moment I see it, a laugh bursts free, and I throw my head back, nearly dislodging my veil. My fiancé, and soon to be husband, gave me an insertable remote vibrator, similar to the one we used when I was subbing for Santa.

Like always with Griffin's gifts, there's a note, so I unfold it.

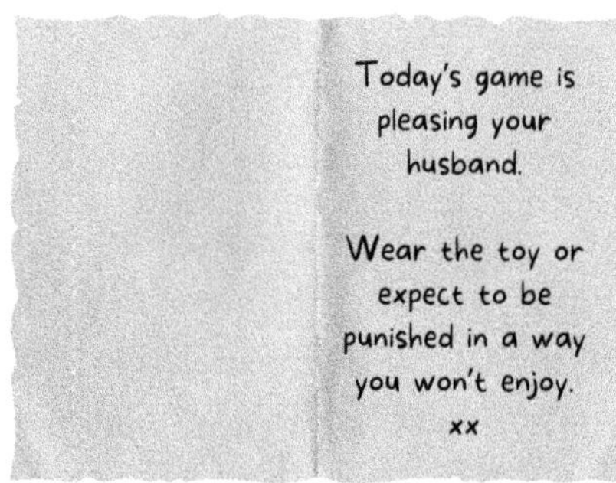
Today's game is pleasing your husband.

Wear the toy or expect to be punished in a way you won't enjoy.

xx

I laugh again, dropping the note and taking the toy from its box.

"The things I do for you, Griffin Marx." I say to myself as I hitch my ivory dress up and spread my legs. I use a little lube, being careful to avoid spilling any on my dress, and I slide the toy inside, putting it in place.

A knock on my door sends me into a scurry to pull my dress back down, and I stand up to take one last look at myself in the mirror, feeling a little emotional since I never thought I'd get to be a bride or wife.

Leaving my house, Shane and Ben walk me down to the Redfield Lake waterfront where the Marx women have spent the last few days decorating for our big day. When Gracie sees me coming, she tells everyone to take their seats and a moment later the hauntingly beautiful sound of cellos starts to play.

Griffin and I have remained living here at Redfield Lake over the last year. I've been living with him but have kept the rental to run my business and parties out of.

Things with his family business have been tense. There has been a lot happening in the area, and the Marx family have made themselves known to the locals to the extent that there have been some gang wars and murders between their competitors in certain trades.

Despite this, Griffin and I have done nothing but grow closer, and as I prepare to walk down the aisle towards the man of my dreams, I know without a doubt that there is no one on this earth that would even compare to him. He is my everything.

There are familiar faces in the crowd, three of which are sitting on my side of the aisle. I never thought I'd have many people sitting on my side, especially not my mum, sister, and niece. But after some encouragement, Griffin convinced me to reconnect with my mum and sister a few months back, and aside from letting Griffin into my life, it was one of the best decisions I ever made.

The majority of the guests are Marx family and crew, including Fallon, who still glares at me every chance she gets. She blames me for the demotion her dad punished her with, and while I've tried to not think too much about her anger towards me, I was relieved when she and Griffin finally started talking again a couple of months ago.

After Shane and Ben take their seats, turning back to offer me beaming smiles, I suck in a deep breath and prepare for my walk down the red carpet, strewn with rose petals.

I had considered having someone give me away, but since the only man I have ever belonged to is waiting for me at the altar, I knew the only person that needed to be walking the carpet today is me.

As I close the distance between me and Griffin, the moment I see the tears of happiness in my mum's eyes, my own start to heat as they glass over. I quickly drag my gaze from her, turning my focus to the man I no longer run from, but towards.

Well, except when we do primal play. Then I run!

As I get closer, I realise Griff's eyes are red with his own unshed tears, and I nearly lose it and ugly cry right then and there.

Thankfully, the gentle buzz deep inside me sends my tears packing, and I try to hide the little jerk my body attempts to make as the intensity increases.

"You look stunning." Griff whispers as I step up to him, and I give him a strained smile. "Are you wearing it?"

"Yes." I whisper through gritted teeth, and his grin widens.

"Atta girl."

"Turn it off." I hiss quietly and he sucks in his lips, trying not to laugh, before slipping his hand in his pocket.

I relax a moment later, when the vibrations stop just in time for the celebrant to start the service.

Griffin and I go through the motions, saying our vows and signing the papers, posing for photos, and taking time to thank everyone individually for coming.

We take some time to get some photos done around the area while our guests eat canapés and drink champagne. Griffin plays around with the remote all day, gently edging me, and by the time the moon is high in the sky, and the last guests have left, I'm nearly standing in a puddle.

I start to tidy up some of the mess left behind, knowing that my husband—I really fucking love saying that—is watching my every move.

"Come here, wife." Griffin demands as he sits on a chair by the pool, his tux jacket nowhere to be seen, and his top buttons open on his shirt with the sleeves rolled up, displaying his delicious forearms and the intricate tattoos.

I grin slowly, putting down the glasses I was picking up, and make my way over to him.

"Yes, husband?" I ask, smiling down at him as he eyes me. Then he starts to undo his pants before releasing his straining cock.

"Oh my, Mr Marx. Where did that come from?" I ask, giggling.

"I've had this fucker all day. That dress is not only stunning, but fucking teasing. Why do you think I've been edging you all day? Because every time I look at you, you edge me, woman."

I laugh, shooting him a playful grin.

"Pull up your dress." He demands, and my grin turns into a smirk as I slowly scrunch the fabric up higher and higher.

"The fuck?" he hisses, gripping his dick even tighter. "When did you take your panties off?"

"I never had them on to begin with." I smirk and he growls, his fist stilling mid pump.

"You mean to say you've been bare all fucking day?"

"Yes, husband." I widen my stance, giving him a better view. "All. Fucking. Day."

"Bring that juicy pussy over here right fucking now."

I love it when Griffin gets like this. Demanding and dominant, and impatient.

I do as my husband commands, climbing onto his lap to straddle him as I ease down on his cock. He moans loudly as I take him inside, but then he freezes and looks at me accusingly.

"Where's the toy?"

"Turn it on and see if you can find it." I smirk and his eyes narrow before he pulls the remote from his pocket and turns it on.

His eyes widen, and his mouth drops open as his hips jerk in reaction.

"Fuck, little elf. Is that?"

"In my arse?" I lean forward and nip at his lips. "Yes."

"Fuuuck." He turns the vibrations up, and I moan as the combination of being filled with his cock and stimulated through the wall of my back passage consumes me.

I'm helpless not to gyrate, need slamming into me as I chase the orgasm that's been sitting on the sidelines all day. Griffin loses any control he has too, and I love that we are both getting something out of this sex toy.

He starts to piston inside me punishingly, and I grip his shoulders, holding on for the ride as my first orgasm slams into me.

Griffin speeds up, sweat beading on his forehead as he hammers inside me over and over, and I take the remote from his grip, turning it up to the highest setting.

The yell that leaps from Griffin's mouth is unlike anything I've heard him make, and as he erupts inside me, I convulse around his cock for the second time.

My orgasm sends me senseless, and in my flurry, I drop the remote. Griffin abruptly lifts me off him as his sensitivity becomes too much, and I leap off his lap in a most un-lady-like fashion, bending over to find the little tag that is protruding from my arse as the vibrator continues its assault.

I squeal, and Griffin starts to laugh as I jump around, trying to get a grip on the tag.

"Stop laughing!" I squeal, but it just makes Griffin laugh even more.

My fingers finally grip the tag, and I tug so hard that the damn thing goes flying into the pool.

"Holy shit." Griffin tries to smother his laugh but fails. "I'm sorry, honey. I can't help it."

He's still fucking laughing.

I stomp towards him and point a stern finger in his face.

"You laugh now, but just wait until I stick it up your arse, Griffin Marx!"

His face pales.

I fall onto his lap laughing, and he wraps his arms around me, burying his face in my neck, holding me close.

"I fucking love you Mrs Marx." He rasps, nipping at my ear, and I turn to press my lips to his.

"I fucking love you too, Mr Marx."

The

End!

IF YOU ENJOYED SUBBING FOR SANTA

Please leave a review

AMAZON: Subbing For Santa: A Dark Christmas Romance
https://books2read.com/SubbingForSanta

GOODREADS: Subbing for Santa by Sarah J.D. | Goodreads
https://www.goodreads.com/book/show/63077168

Stay Connected

To stay connected and be in the know about future works for updates!
that may include some of the side characters from my books, join my reader's group:
Sarah JD's Vicious Kittens – a Sarah JD Readers Group
https://www.facebook.com/groups/sarahjaneduncanreadersgroup

Visit Sarah JD at
https://sarahjaneduncan.com

Stay Updated

Join my VIP Readers list and receive monthly newsletters jam packed with updates about your favourite Fox Pines characters!

SIGN UP HERE!

https://sarahjaneduncan.com/newsletter/

SARAH JD'S BOOKS

THE HEAVY HEARTS SERIES

https://books2read.com/HeavyHeartsBook1/
https://books2read.com/HeavyHeartsBook2/
https://books2read.com/HeavyHeartsBook3/
or
https://sarahjaneduncan.com/my-books/heavy-hearts-series/

THE INSATIABLE SERIES

https://books2read.com/KittenBookOne
https://books2read.com/Kitten2
https://books2read.com/KittenBookThree
or
https://sarahjaneduncan.com/my-books/the-insatiable-series/

BREAKING THE SILENCE DUET

SILENT HUSH – BOOK 1
https://books2read.com/BTSbook1
SAVAGE SCREAM – BOOK 2
https://books2read.com/BTSbook2

UPCOMING BOOKS

https://books2read.com/LilysAshSSbook2

About Sarah JD

Sarah JD, also known as Sarah Jane Duncan is a dark romance author, living in the beautiful Gippsland region in Victoria, Australia, with her high-school-sweetheart-turned-hubby and three grown children.

When she's not busy writing, Sarah can be found sewing dance costumes for her daughter or helping her hubby in their family business.

Sarah writes about females who have to fight against the odds to find their power, find their voice, and find their truth. The heroines in Sarah's stories possess the strength that only comes when you have to fight for your life!

www.ingramcontent.com/pod-product-compliance
Ingram Content Group UK Ltd.
Pitfield, Milton Keynes, MK11 3LW, UK
UKHW021350241224
3859UKWH00051B/477